THE DEED IS DUNN

THE DUNN FAMILY SERIES
BOOK 4

RICKY BLACK

CHAPTER ONE
OCTOBER 2021

DEVON THOMAS GLANCED around the Meanwood car park, rubbing his hands together. The air was thick with the acrid scent of burning rubber and petrol fumes from the nearby traffic. He leant against his ride, a black Mercedes Benz CLS with tinted rims. Glancing at the men who'd accompanied him, he shook his head.

'What the hell is taking so long?' he grumbled. Every nearby noise spooked him. The car park was practically empty, but he could hear nearby voices and traffic. It was nighttime, but the car park was dimly lit by flickering yellow bulbs that cast long shadows across the ground.

Despite his nervousness, Devon knew this way made the most sense. It was like something from a television show; hiding in plain sight.

Not that anyone would care about what he was doing, anyway.

Devon had been a member of the Dunn organisation for years, watching it grow into a powerhouse. There had been blips in the past year, but they'd still managed to survive.

Now, he wasn't so sure.

Though they'd recently eliminated a troublesome enemy and restored order in the streets, people were under no illusions about how long it would last. They'd won a battle, but a rot seemed to have spread within the crew, with clear battle lines being drawn. Devon didn't know the cause, but something needed to be done. He was one of Mitch Dunn's favourites, but he wasn't sure that was enough anymore.

Devon's men looked at him, assessing his gear. He was a high-ranking member of the organisation, and he dressed like it. His Benz had been bought with cash, and his designer clothing and jewellery were top-notch. Despite the gear, he looked haggard, with bags under his eyes and tension in his face that suggested he hadn't been sleeping well.

They didn't question it, though. They were there to provide backup and to ensure everything went smoothly.

Devon straightened when an Audi Q5 rumbled into the car park, music booming from the speakers. Devon cursed. Despite his dress sense, there were some levels even he didn't lower himself to. Playing loud rap music in public was a surefire way to get yourself noticed by the police.

The car pulled up next to theirs, and the window wound down.

'Let's get to it,' the driver said, grinning, revealing several gold teeth. 'I'm in a hurry. Got things to do.'

'Turn the fucking music down,' Devon hissed. 'Are you trying to get us noticed?'

The man rolled his eyes, then did as he was told. His driver kept his eyes straight ahead, his jaw tense.

Motioning to his man, Devon waited as he stepped forward, a large black sports bag in hand. At the same time, the man in the Audi dropped his own bag out of the car window onto the floor.

Before they could make the exchange, a shot rang out. One of Devon's men went for his gun, but he was too slow, and a bullet slammed into his leg. He dropped with a scream of pain.

The man in the Audi drove away, tires screeching as he zoomed from the car park.

'Don't move,' a voice growled, as two men stepped forward. Devon hadn't seen where they'd come from, but there were several cars in the car park they could have hidden in. He fought to control his fear. This was an off-the-books drug deal. He'd done it before and had skimmed profits off the top, overcharging dealers who couldn't get a steady supply anywhere else.

Now, he would need to talk his way out of this mess.

The men were both large, dressed in all black, and had their guns trained on the trio. Devon glanced at his guards, one on the floor moaning, and the other standing frozen, still holding the bag.

'Drop that bag,' one of the men said in a deep voice. The guard hesitated, and the man aimed his gun at his leg. 'I'm not gonna ask again.'

The guard dropped the bag.

'Right, take your mate off the floor and piss off. Do it quick enough, and we won't kill you,' the man said.

The guard did as ordered and lifted the bleeding guard off the floor, supporting him as they hobbled from the car park.

'What the fuck is this?' Devon asked, regaining some of his demeanour. 'Do you know who I am? What team I belong to? You take this shit, and there's a clock on your lives, I promise you that.'

'Really?' one of the voices sounded gleeful. He removed his mask, and Devon's stomach lurched when he realised who he was dealing with.

'Nat . . . what are you doing, man? We're on the same team.'

The smile slipped from Natty's face.

'That's what we're gonna find out. Get in the car. I haven't driven a Merc in a while.'

———

NATTY CHECKED his phone as Stefon secured Devon in a chair in the safe house. They'd stored the money and drugs. They hadn't come for them, but taking them would still be advantageous.

Natty was after something more important than money, and Devon was the man to help him get there. They'd worked together briefly in the past, but Mitch trusted him, and with the team currently in disarray, Mitch didn't have many people he trusted nowadays.

Natty glanced at his phone, straying to his call log, his face darkening when he looked at the calls he'd made to Lorraine over the past two weeks. Other than a few text messages to say she was okay, he hadn't heard from her.

'Yo, you good?' Stefon was looking at Natty, eyes narrowing. Stefon had returned to Leeds a few months earlier. With things cooling off in Leicester, he was keen to catch up with his cousin and re-establish himself. The pair clashed at first, but had reached a common ground, with Spence and Stefon both pledging themselves to Natty's mission.

They'd known they couldn't trust the majority of the organisation, and had set up multiple safe houses, this one in Harehills. It had a cramped cellar, where they were now. It was devoid of anything but the plastic flooring they'd prepared earlier. The walls were sound-proofed too, which cost a significant amount of money.

Natty smirked when he realised that the money they'd taken would more than cover the cost.

'I'm fine, Stef,' he finally said to his cousin. 'Let's see what this dickhead knows.'

'Nat . . . I dunno what you've got yourself into, but you know how this goes. If you touch me, there's gonna be a reckoning. People are gonna hunt you down. Let me go, and I promise I'll keep this quiet,' Devon said.

'How long have you been dipping on the side?' Natty asked. Stefon stepped back, watching from the corner as Natty stood over Devon.

'I haven't been dipping. I do my job. I set up my own deals, but so what? We all do that. I still check in more than most of the other lieutenants. You know that.'

'Are you saying you're kicking up your full share? I know about the deals you've been doing. We've been watching you. The numbers you're selling, and the prices you're selling for . . . you should be kicking back a lot more.'

'Am I not supposed to eat too?' Devon snapped. 'I'm risking it all out there in the streets. I deserve to get my cut.'

'What does my uncle think about that?'

Devon fell silent. Everyone knew Mitch's policy on skimming, and while people had received small punishments for daring to do so in the past, Devon was smart enough to know that he'd be made an example of. He'd squirrelled away thousands, and now it was all about to come undone.

'Mitch sent you then?'

'Don't worry about that for now. We'll get back to it,' Natty said. 'I wanna know what you know about my uncle.'

'What do you mean?'

'You're on the inside. My uncle likes you, so I need to know what he's planning and where he's staying. I know he's not at his house, and he isn't at any of the team safehouses, so where's he holed up?'

'You must be nuts,' Devon said. 'What the fuck is this? A loyalty test? I'm not gonna give anything up for you to go back to your uncle and tell him how disloyal I was. Like I said, let me go, and we can squash this shit.'

'I know you've seen him. You were bragging to your people. You've had dinner with him. You were even giddy about a bottle of liquor he gave you, like some fucking woman.' Natty smirked. 'I want to know where that spot is, and how many people are watching it.'

'Why do you want to know that?'

'Because I do.'

'You're planning summat, aren't you?' Devon said. Shaking his head, Natty pulled the trigger, the loud bang sounding around the room, followed by Devon's shriek of pain as the bullet lodged into his foot.

'You shot me!'

'Very observant,' Natty said dryly. 'Now, are you gonna tell me what I want to know, or do I need to go upstairs and get my tools?'

'You should have left them down here,' Stefon said, sniggering. 'Makes more sense than trailing up the stairs.'

'It's good exercise. It's important to stay fit,' Natty replied, and the pair sniggered as Devon shot them both incredulous looks.

'You two are crazy. Mitch will shut you lot down in an instant.'

Natty shrugged. 'Mitch is a two-faced piece of shit. You're not his friend, and he couldn't protect you. Your only way out is to deal with me. Are you gonna talk, or do I need to get those tools?'

Devon searched Natty's face for any weakness, but found none. He'd heard talk about how the heir apparent had stepped up his game in recent months. He was a killer, and Devon could see in his eyes that he wouldn't hesitate to maim him if he didn't cooperate.

'I don't know much . . .' he hung his head.

'Tell me what you *do* know then.'

Devon spilled his guts. He spoke about two safe houses that Mitch appeared to favour, both on the opposite sides of Leeds, with a fifty/fifty chance he could be at either one. There was also a new safe house he'd had commissioned a month ago, but Devon wasn't sure where it was.

It was the last piece of information that proved the most telling.

'Say that again?' Natty demanded. Devon wet his lips before repeating what he'd said.

'Mitch is favouring Morgan. He's been in the background, but he's got his own team. Off the books. I don't know what their mission is, but they don't answer to anyone. Not even you.'

Natty mulled that one over. Morgan had indeed been in the background. He oversaw a lot of financial matters, and Natty knew he'd worked alongside Mitch in some legitimate housing ventures, as well as overseeing a booming loansharking business.

Natty hadn't had many dealings with him, focusing more on the drug's side. With what Devon said, he wondered if Morgan was going to be his replacement, or if he'd been given another task.

'So, Morgan's the guy I need to see,' he mused. 'Okay. I can do that.' He sighed. 'Well, thanks for being so helpful, Devon, mate. I wish I could let you go, but you're a snake, and I can't trust you. Peace out.'

'Wait—' Devon started, before a bullet lodged into his head, snapping it back. Natty fired another shot, to be sure, staring at the man's dead body.

'Right then.' Stefon yawned. 'How are we gonna get to Morgan?'

———

'ARE WE READY?'

Zayan nodded at his partner Ghazan. They climbed from their car, heading to the house on the corner of the quiet street, their steps assured.

The front of the house was unremarkable, blending in with the other terraced houses that lined the street. The yellowish streetlights cast a dull glow over the neighbourhood, illuminating the pavement and the occasional parked car.

A small garden flanked the entrance, shielded from the street by a wrought-iron gate. The grass was patchy, and the bushes, unkempt and wild, threw long shadows across the doorway. A few windows on the upper floor glowed, their light painting a warm hue onto the curtains. However, the front door of the house was dark, giving no indication of the chaos that was about to unfold.

The camera above the front door was the only indication that the house was under surveillance.

It didn't matter to the pair. They had planned for it. Like all spots, it had a weak point and, right now, was undermanned. The pair had their orders and knew what was expected of them.

It took Ghazan a short time to break into the spot. As the pair barged into the house, the wooden floorboards groaned and complained under their weight. They burst into the first room, gunning down the man there. It was over in a flash, the light leaving the man's eyes before he could blink. The pair went from room to room, cutting down anyone they saw.

In the final room, a man stood in their way, his hand shaking as he held a Glock. The room was dimly lit, with only a single bulb for light. The walls were painted a dark blue, devoid of any decorations, and the air was thick with the smell of cigarette smoke and fear. The room was tense, with the only sounds being the soft creaks of the wooden floor-boards, and the steady breathing of the trio.

Piles of cash lay scattered across the large wooden table in the centre of the room.

'Stay back, before I shoot,' the man warned, taking a step to the side, as if attempting to block the money from the men.

Ghazan smiled.

'You get one of us, the other will shoot you in the leg, then the stomach. By the time we finish, you'll be begging for death.'

'The alternative,' Zayan said, 'is that you lower the gun, and we'll let you live.'

'You must be on crack,' the man spat. 'You killed everyone else.'

'We did,' Zayan said. 'Someone needed to be alive to pass on the message, though.'

The man lowered the gun, falling to his knees, and slowly placing it on the floor, keeping his eyes on the pair the whole time. He flinched, expecting to be shot. When he wasn't, he cautiously got back to his feet, surveying the pair. They wore nothing to cover their faces. They were both dressed in casual black gear, latex gloves and carried high-powered automatic weapons. He didn't know who they were repre-senting, but they were clearly serious.

'What's the message?' he asked, taking a deep breath.

'Speak to your boss. Inform him that he will pay for his mistakes, and that none of his people are safe. Now, you're going to lead us to the stash. Move.'

The man swallowed, but did as he was told, his stomach lurching as he saw the bodies of his comrades spread all over the spot. Some were on their backs, while others still held weapons they hadn't got the chance to shoot. The senseless violence broke his resolve. Before today, Blade had defined himself as a tough guy. He'd fired shots, had fights and generally played the crime game to the fullest, but right now, he felt like a baby. He wanted nothing more than to close his eyes and forget all of this, but he couldn't.

It took a few minutes to gather all of the money. When they had, they situated it in piles, pouring lighter fluid onto it. Ghazan flicked his lighter towards the pile, which instantly went up. Smiling, the pair led Blade from the house. It wouldn't take long for the house to go up. They'd made a lot of noise, but neither man cared. They were practised in doing these things, and had been told the job needed to be messy.

'Do you remember the message?' Zayan asked Blade, who nodded.

'I'll get word to Mitch.'

'You do that. Next time, we won't be so merciful. I suggest you get running. The police are probably on their way.'

Blade gave the pair a panicked look, then turned and took off, stumbling down the street. Zayan and Ghazan walked back to their car, and drove away, leaving the steadily burning house in their wake.

CHAPTER TWO

MORGAN BROODED at one of his Armley houses, sitting on a black leather sofa. He had a selection of spots in the area, rotating between them when needed. The interior was tidy, yet spartan, with worn floorboards and a scant selection of furniture reflecting utility over comfort. Along with the sofa, several old wooden chairs and a scratched coffee table dominated the living area, while heavy, dark curtains hid the room from prying eyes.

The faint aroma of antiseptic mixed with old cigarette smoke lingered in the air. The sounds of pain coming from the back room had grown easy to ignore after a while.

Morgan glanced at the other man in the room. He was brawny, though right now, he appeared chastened. Morgan kept up the look for a few more seconds. He was in his forties and wore glasses, his body starting to soften, despite his attempts to maintain a steady workout regime.

The door to the back room opened, a harassed-looking man around Morgan's age stepping out, closing the door behind him. Despite their similar ages, the man looked older, with deep bags around his eyes and a heavily lined forehead. His watery blue eyes met Morgan, who waited for him to speak.

'The bleeding has stopped. He's going to need physical therapy, and he's got a long recovery ahead of him. The bullet destroyed a significant portion of his kneecap. Whoever shot him knew what they were doing.'

Morgan tutted.

'Anything else?'

'He'll likely need a proper facility. He's over the worst of it, but there's too much risk to keep treating him here,' the doctor said.

'Fine. Get who you need to get, and make it happen. I'll have your money sent to the usual account.'

The doctor nodded, leaving a short while later. Morgan shot the big man another look, motioning for him to follow. Stepping out into the back garden, Morgan took a moment, observing the scene in silence.

'Tell me again what happened.'

'We were doing the deal. Shaun and his people showed up. Then the dudes came out nowhere, threatened us, and shot Mike in the leg.'

'Do you think Shaun was in on it?'

The guard shook his head. He'd seen a lot in his time working for the Dunns, but the shooting had definitely startled him. There was something foreboding about the robbers, and he felt lucky to be alive.

The way Morgan kept looking at him, he wondered how long he would stay that way.

'Nah. The robbers waited for him to drop the money before making their move. I don't think he'd have given it up, or put himself at risk.'

Morgan shook his head. This was going to cause a mess. Mitch would want an update on the situation. On top of that, Morgan was out thousands of pounds. He had authorised Devon's moves in exchange for a hefty cut. It was harmless, as long as Mitch didn't find out.

Now, it would shine a light and prevent other similar moves. Morgan would need to hang back, and do his best to find out who'd robbed and killed Devon.

'You didn't recognise the robbers?'

'Nah. They were masked up, but they seemed like big guys, and they had deep voices.'

Morgan took a moment before speaking.

'We're gonna talk again. For now, you're off duty. Make sure you stay close by. Got it?'

'Got it, Morgan. I will.' The guard stammered, his lip quivering. Morgan's phone rang. He signalled for the guard to leave before answering.

'What?'

'We got hit.'

Morgan's shoulders deflated. Someone was moving against the Dunns in a major way. 'When?'

'Less than an hour ago. Blade turned up at one of our spots. He looks like he's seen the devil. Some Asians shot up one of the stash spots. Killed everyone, burnt the money, but let him go.'

With his free hand, Morgan rubbed his forehead. After Roman's murder, he figured they were done with the drama, but he'd apparently been fooling himself.

'Keep Blade at the spot. Text me which one, and I'll be there soon.' Morgan hung up, glancing at his phone. He would reach out to Mitch.

———

'MORGAN, HUH?'

Natty, Spence, and Stefon sat around a small wooden kitchen table in another safe house. The faded red-bricked terraced house was situated on the outskirts of the Hood. The windows were covered with metal bars for added security, and the front door was reinforced steel, painted black.

They'd made little progress in the two weeks leading up to Devon's ambush. Mitch was in the wind, and the orders he'd delivered were designed to keep people separated. He and Natty had shared a terse conversation on the phone, and little was said.

Despite still leading the drug side of the organisation, Natty's power had been under scrutiny as of late, and his uncle had made several organisational changes, such as having Natty report directly to Clarke — before the older man's injury.

Now, Natty wondered what Mitch was telling Morgan.

'You ever hear his name when you were in charge?' he finally replied to Spence, who shook his head.

'Your unc kept me away from a lot of things when I was running it. I mostly focused on the Hood.'

'Why are we taking Devon so seriously? He might have been talking shit to avoid being killed,' Stefon said.

Natty shook his head. 'I don't see it. Devon figured we might keep him alive if he told us enough stuff. We're gonna need to dig into Morgan. If he can get us a clear shot on my unc, it's worth the risk.' Natty stared at his phone. He had a few notifications and missed calls he needed to return, but none from Lorraine.

Natty had tried giving her space. She was hurt over Natty's association with Lisa. Natty had been forced to kill in front of her. She had seen his street side, and there was no going back. He didn't know what to do about it. He missed her and Jaden. The family they'd built. They were his peace, his shield against the streets.

His mind traced through the past couple of months; the things that had happened, and the people he'd killed. Roman, his growing rival, and a corrupt police detective, Brown. Both had been wiped out because they were in the way, and they were detrimental to his plans.

Now, Natty knew what he needed to do next, but at the same time, he recognised it wouldn't be easy.

'Nat?'

Natty blinked, glancing at the pair, who were looking at him with raised eyebrows.

'Sorry, man. I blanked out. What's up?'

'I'm just saying, we need to get some help,' Spence repeated.

'Spence is right,' Stefon added. 'The three of us can't do this shit alone. There must be people in the organisation we can reach out to.'

'That's risky,' Natty said, getting his head back in the game. 'That's how Rudy messed up. He reached out to the wrong people when he was attempting his takeover, and it got him killed.'

'So, reach out to the right people,' Stefon said. 'We can at least rap to some. If they don't go along with it, we'll kill them.'

'We need to be discreet,' Natty pointed out. 'Devon was necessary to sell the story, but everybody we drop increases exposure. We need to cut the head off the snake as smoothly as we can.'

Stefon stretched, sliding to his feet.

'Fine. I'm gonna get my head down, anyway. I'm working later.' Nodding to both men, Stefon headed upstairs.

'What's going on?' Spence asked.

'You know what's going on,' Natty said, not even attempting to downplay it.

'Has she spoken to you yet?'

Natty shook his head. 'I did some wild shit that night, fam. Me and Lisa took out a lot of people. Getting past that shit isn't gonna be easy. With everything going on, It's probably safer to keep away, but at the same time, I need her, Spence.'

Spence nodded. He was pleased that Natty was in touch with his feelings. The old Natty would have denied his emotions and grown angry if Spence pressed. They both had their issues with females to deal with.

Spence had wanted to reach out to Rosie after she broke up with him, but he couldn't see it working out. He'd messed up by letting Anika back into his life. Even though he'd resolved that, it cost him his relationship, and he strongly believed there was no going back.

'Speak to her at least,' he finally said. 'She asked for space, but keep trying to speak to her anyway. She didn't say it was over. Maybe she no longer thinks you're shagging Lisa.'

Natty chuckled.

'I hope not. I don't think it was fully about that, anyway. I'm gonna kick back and watch a film or summat for now. I need to switch off for a while.'

Spence patted Natty's shoulder, nodding.

'Rest up, bro. We've got a long journey ahead of us.'

CHAPTER THREE

LORRAINE RICHARDS SIPPED her cup of tea, legs folded beneath her on the plush, floral-patterned sofa in her mum's living room, as she glanced at her phone. Every time she saw text messages or missed calls from Natty, it hurt a little more. Lorraine loved Natty, and hated the fact things were strained between them.

It felt like ever since she and Natty had become a couple, they'd fought tooth and nail to keep their relationship. They seemed to take turns falling out with each other, allowing outside forces to affect them.

Lorraine closed her eyes, still remembering the helplessness she'd felt at the house, as armed men had tried to kill her. Natty and his colleague, Lisa, had protected her. Lorraine had accepted nothing was going on between them, but they were equals. They had fought in sync and eliminated the men.

And that stuck with her more than anything.

Natty, the man she loved, wasn't just a killer. He was efficient, and deadly. He moved like he'd had training, and it was hard to reconcile that with the person she'd known since they were kids.

Lorraine's emotions were all over the place. She was angry, erratic, and she felt helpless.

And she was pregnant.

She'd told Rosie and her mum, but hadn't told Jaden yet.

She hadn't told Natty either. She wanted to, but had no idea how to bring it up.

Lorraine sighed, placing her cup on the coffee table and closing her eyes. She was still trying to make sense of it all. Lorraine felt in her heart she was reaching out for something, but wasn't sure what.

'Are you okay?'

Lorraine opened her eyes and looked up. Her mum stood in the doorway, watching her.

'I'm fine, mum.'

'Have you been sick again?'

Lorraine shook her head.

'I'm okay. I'm just thinking.'

Her mum came and sat next to her on the sofa.

'About Natty, I'm guessing.'

Lorraine didn't say anything. Her mum sighed.

'You know you can't avoid him forever, don't you . . .?'

'If you need Jaden and me to move out, then—'

'Shush, Lo. You know full well that's not what I'm saying. If it's not safe for you to be at home, then I want you and my grandson here with me. The focus is on you and Natty, and the impact that's having on Jaden.'

'What do you mean?'

'You know what I mean. He's confused. He's been through a lot, with everything that happened to his father, and now whatever is going on with you and Natty.'

A wave of sadness spread through Lorraine. The last thing she wanted was for her son to be affected. She knew how close Natty and Jaden were. It was one of the things she loved most about him. From the time Jaden was born, even before they became a couple, he was always there for them, always taking time to care for Jaden.

It was hard matching that against the cold, ruthless gangster side of him she'd now seen.

'I know, mum. I'm trying to work it all out myself.'

Her mum nodded. 'I'm not saying it will be easy, but the first step might be actually speaking to Natty, and taking it from there. I'm not asking you to tell me everything that's going on because I know Natty is no angel, but just think about it.'

Lorraine smiled. 'I will, mum.'

'Good. I'll let you have the living room. I have some work to do before I switch off for the night. Turn the heating off before you go to bed, please.' Her mum kissed Lorraine on the cheek and left the room.

Lorraine sighed. Her mum made sense, but it wasn't that easy. She stared at the call log again, her finger hovering over the *call* button, before she shook her head. Locking her phone, she focused on the television.

———

THE FOLLOWING MORNING, Natty left the Chapeltown safe house and drove to his home in Chapel Allerton. After sweeping through the house and checking nothing was amiss, he drove to Lorraine's mum's place, taking his time, ensuring he wasn't being followed. Ever since Roman's people had got the drop on him, he'd been extra vigilant.

Despite the fact Roman was dead and his crew scattered, Natty remained on his guard.

As always, the street was quiet when he arrived. He liked the fact Lorraine's mum had left the Hood behind, as he'd done, and had settled in a semi-detached house on the outskirts of Headingley.

Nodding at a man walking by with his dog, Natty approached the house, knocked on the door, and then faced the street, keeping an eye out for anything suspicious. He smiled broadly when he saw Lorraine, frozen in the doorway.

Natty immediately noticed how drawn she looked, her eyes heavy and her face drained. Yet she was as stunning as ever. He had always been attracted to Lorraine, but she had only grown more beautiful over the years, and was ageing like wine, with her long dark hair, currently in a ponytail, and her smooth brown skin and alluring features. His heart pounded as he stared, swallowing down a lump in his throat.

'Hey,' he said, when it became clear Lorraine wasn't going to speak.

'Hey, Natty.' Lorraine folded her arms. She glanced behind her, before shutting the door.

'How are you? Do you need anything?'

'I'm fine,' she replied, her expression unchanged, though her voice sounded fatigued, as if just speaking to him was a struggle. A growing sliver of concern spread throughout his body as they stood there, with Natty suddenly worried that there was no going back; that she wouldn't forgive him.

'If you need anything, day or night, I'm just a call away,' he said quickly.

'I know.'

'How's Jaden?'

Lorraine's face tensed, her eyes darkening for a moment. 'He's fine. He misses you.'

'I miss him too. I miss both of you, Lo. We need to deal with this.'

Lorraine sighed. 'I don't know how to do that yet, Natty. That's why I asked you to give me space.'

'I've given you space,' said Natty. 'I know that everything that happened was fucked up. I can own that. Fact is, I still need you, babe. And you need me too.'

'You really think it's that easy?' Lorraine frowned. Natty shook his head.

'I know it won't be that easy, but we still need to try. I know how fucked up things were before, but I took care of that. You have nothing to worry about.'

'Can you really guarantee that?' Lorraine's eyes met Natty's, her gaze searching.

He paused.

'I would never let anyone, or anything hurt you.'

'*You* hurt me, Natty.'

'I wasn't doing anything with Lisa. I promise,' Natty said, speaking quickly, needing her to listen. 'I know how it looked, but I would never do you like that.'

'No, you'd just make out like I was an idiot. I knew something was up with the pair of you, and what did I find? You two on a sofa, seconds away from kissing.'

'It wasn't like that,' Natty said.

'What was it like then?' Lorraine pressed. 'Why were you sitting so close to another woman, in a house by yourselves?'

Natty hesitated, and Lorraine shook her head.

'It doesn't really matter, anyway. Honestly, I made peace with that part. Those men, though . . . the things you did. It's like there's another side to you I don't recognise.' Lorraine sighed. 'I have things I need to focus on, Natty, including my son. Whatever you've got going on, I don't want to be a part of it.'

Natty was losing the conversation, and he knew it. He took a step towards her, holding her hand, gratified when she didn't pull away.

'I just want you, Lo. I don't wanna do this with you, fighting every two minutes, then one of us pulling away. Whatever's going on, I want to work through it.'

Lorraine stared into Natty's eyes, and his heart lifted as he hoped she was relenting. Then, her eyes hardened, and he knew it wouldn't be so easy.

'I don't have time for this, Natty. Please, just leave me alone for now.' Lorraine went back inside, shutting and locking the door.

Natty stared at the closed door, his thoughts racing. He'd thought he was making progress, but maybe showing up unannounced was a misstep. What Natty knew for sure was how much he needed Lorraine's presence, her spiritual guidance. But for now, all he could do was wonder what the next move should be.

With a sigh, Natty headed back to his car to regroup, missing Lorraine watching him through the window, a forlorn expression on her face.

———

AFTER RUNNING A FEW ERRANDS, Natty ended up at Amanda's gambling spot. As always, he was accosted and greeted by several people when he entered. He made small talk with the people he recognised, then made his way to the bar, ordering drinks for everyone. When the cheers died down, he sipped his brandy and coke as Amanda bustled over.

'You look terrible,' she said.

'Thanks,' Natty sarcastically replied. 'It's your warm and kind words that set you apart from other hostesses.'

'That's good to know,' said Amanda. There was a loud bang behind them, followed by yells, but neither moved, recognising the sounds of an intense game of dominoes. 'Have you messed up?'

Natty nodded, not bothering to deny it.

Amanda made herself a drink, then shouted for someone to cover her. She led Natty over to a table in the corner of the room. Natty was surprised it was vacant, but assumed it wasn't an accident. In this establishment, Amanda's word was law, and no one was going to challenge her.

'Tell me.'

'Me and Lorraine are on the outs,' Natty said, not holding back.

'What did you do?'

'She saw me with a woman, and she got the wrong end of the stick.' Natty wasn't going to give her the full story, but that was enough. Amanda's eyes narrowed.

'Please don't tell me you were that stupid.'

'I wasn't, Mandy. Give me some credit.'

'I do,' she scoffed. 'You're good with women. It's been a while, but I still remember all those silly little girls that would come in here looking for you, and those few times when the boyfriends would come, wanting revenge.'

'I'm not like that anymore.'

Amanda's eyes softened. 'You know . . . I believe you. I watched you when you brought Lorraine in that time. You were content.'

'What are you talking about?' Natty frowned.

'I've known you since you were little. Seen you evolve over the years, but you were comfortable in your own skin. You weren't performing, trying to be the big man. Not only that, you had your eye on Lorraine the whole time. Even when she was speaking with me, you were staring, and you had a look of love on your face that I'd never seen from you. I never thought I would ever see it.'

'So, what am I supposed to do?' Natty asked, skating by everything else she'd said. He wanted to unpack it, but it wasn't the time.

'I'm assuming you've said sorry?'

'Course I have.'

'Don't say it like that. You're a stubborn git when you want to be. If you've apologised and pled your case, the only thing you can do is wait,' Amanda said.

'What if waiting just makes things worse?'

'That's a chance you might just have to take, Natty. Whatever has gone on, whether you're telling me the truth or not, you hurt her. That's going to take a while for her to come to terms with. Just wait, and just be there if she needs you.'

Natty hung his head. It sounded like good advice, but he wasn't sure he could go along with it. In his mind, the longer they were away from one another, the more likely it seemed they would drift further apart.

He mulled over the situation, wondering if he could tell her it was safe to go home. The problem had been eliminated. Mitch was on the horizon, but Natty didn't think his uncle would kill a woman and her son.

Deciding to give it some more thought, he looked up, noting that Amanda had been quietly assessing him the whole time, her empty drink by her side.

'You've got it bad.' She shook her head.

'Get me another drink, and leave it,' Natty said, glaring at her. When she raised an eyebrow, his face softened. '. . . please.'

CHAPTER FOUR

AS HE'D DONE for the past few weeks, Mitch mulled over what to do about his nephew. He'd yet to return home after the attempt on his life, continuing to switch between different safe houses. His current locale was a luxury apartment in Shadwell. He had an armed guard in another room, along with men parked around the complex, also armed, just in case.

Tia's words had got to him, and Mitch inwardly cursed his dead brother's widow. She had revealed the long-held truth about his role in the murder of Nathaniel's father.

Mitch hadn't pulled the trigger on his brother, but he'd ordered it done, because it was necessary.

He needed to make Nathaniel understand that, but Tia's words lingered. Nathaniel was proud to be a Dunn, and had worshipped his father. Mitch wasn't sure he could talk him around, but he needed to try.

There was more going on than Nathaniel realised, and Mitch needed everyone focused on the main threat. The recent attacks were a sign of this.

Devon's murder had surprised him. He'd received the news that he'd been shot, and his body dumped for all to see. He'd been seen in and around Meanwood, before seemingly vanishing. The police had yet to begin an investigation, but they would soon enough.

Mitch had sent Morgan to interrogate members of Devon's crew, learning about the attempted deal that had been interrupted by two gunmen, though they'd been unable to give a description of the pair.

Despite his side dealings, Mitch had liked Devon. He was an ambitious lieutenant who was easily swayed by money and power. His death was a message, one Mitch needed to unpack.

The destruction of one of his stash houses was another message, though the enemy this time was clear. Blade had contacted his men. Clearly terrified, he'd told them the story of an Asian duo who massacred the men at the spot, burnt the money, and ordered Blade to pass on the message.

Jakkar was making his move, and he was working through this pair to do it.

Pouring himself a glass of red wine, Mitch sipped it slowly, allowing his thoughts to percolate. What he needed right now was intel. At first, he'd believed that the Asians were responsible for Devon's murder, but quickly changed his mind. Clearly, they wanted to be seen, and for the message to be loud. It didn't make sense to cover their faces when attacking Devon, but to show them when attacking his stash spot. That meant he had two different sets of trouble at present, and he needed to crush them both.

Nathaniel was at fault, he mused. He'd taken too long to eliminate Roman, and that had made the Dunns as a whole look weak to the streets.

Mitch sighed, holding his glass. If he didn't get things in line, his problems would mount. He needed capable people around him. There were plenty of men he could call on, but few solid leaders. Only Morgan. Clarke was still recovering from a serious injury. Lisa, Clarke's protégé, was impetuous, and too quick to deviate from her given mission.

Again, Mitch's thoughts returned to his nephew. He had cultivated Nathaniel for this reason: to be his eyes and ears on the streets, but now he wasn't sure if he could trust him. He didn't know how long Nathaniel had known about the circumstances behind his father's murder, or what he planned to do with the intel. Lately, they'd had few meetings and other than Nathaniel chafing under a few of his commands, they'd had little contact.

Was it all connected?

Mitch took another sip. Since killing Roman, Nathaniel's reputation had increased in the streets. Rather than basking in the kudos, Nathaniel had mostly kept to himself, overseeing the organisation, and reporting into Mitch's people as agreed. Meeting with him could be risky if he was holding a grudge, but it would also give Mitch the opportunity to gain the measure of his nephew, and see where his head was at.

In order of priority, Jakkar was the bigger problem. Mitch had poked the bear by having several of Jakkar's biggest sellers murdered, and he needed to escalate his plan to remove Jakkar completely. To do that, Nathaniel and his ever-increasing status could only benefit him.

There was a way to succeed here, he was sure of it. He just needed to work out precisely what it was.

———

'WHEN ARE you going to tell him?'

Rosie and Lorraine sat in a coffee shop. It was the afternoon after Natty had come to see her, and she'd spent the time since thinking about their conversation. It had been hard to stop herself from diving into his arms and letting him hold her. She craved the strength and power Natty exhibited, but she was inwardly at war, and didn't know how to get past it.

'I don't know,' she said. 'I know I need to tell him, and I considered doing it yesterday, but I couldn't.' She sighed.

'You know that he'd be happy, don't you?'

Lorraine glanced at Rosie. 'You can't say that. Neither of us have ever heard Natty mention kids.'

'Maybe not, but he loves you, and he loves Jaden. Do you really think he's going to see having a child with you as a negative?'

Lorraine wet her lips, holding her oversized coffee mug without drinking it. She hadn't been drinking as much coffee lately, as she worried it would affect the baby.

'Natty has a lot going on with his current business. I'm a burden, and there are issues of trust,' she pointed out.

'I'm not one to speak with about trust. I'm still trying to come to terms with Spence's actions. Let me ask you, though . . . do you really think Natty would have cheated with that woman?'

Lorraine squeezed her eyes closed, as images of the pair curled up on the sofa flitted to her brain. She took another deep breath, determined not to let them overcome her.

'No. It's more about how they looked, how they flowed together. She was on his level, and I'm not.'

'That's meaningless,' Rosie pointed out. 'He loves you. You love him. You're going to have a child together. That's the concern. That puts you on an unreachable level in Natty's mind.'

'What about my mind?' Lorraine retorted sharply. She shook her head. 'I'm sorry. I don't want to take it out on you.'

Rosie shot her a small smile. 'Do it if you need to, Lo. I can take it, and you need an outlet. What is it that you want?'

Lorraine sipped her drink. 'I want to stop feeling helpless. I don't want to feel like a liability anymore, needing to be rescued. Somewhere down the line, I've lost myself, and I don't know how to regain that feeling of strength that I felt defined me.' She again looked at her friend, noting the sadness in Rosie's eyes. 'Let's talk about you, Ro. What's going on?'

Rosie shrugged. 'I'm just keeping my head down and focusing on work. That's all I can do at the moment. I'm still figuring my long-term plan.'

'Is there any room for Spence in that long-term plan?'

'Spence and me are over, Lo. There's no going back from that.'

'I know we spoke about it a few weeks ago,' Lorraine started, choosing her words carefully, 'but do you really think that's still applicable?'

'What do you mean by that?' Rosie's eyes narrowed.

'Spence is a good man. He's trapped in the same game as Natty, and I don't know . . . I get the impression they need us, to stay whole. Keep their souls.'

'What if we can't help them?' Rosie's voice was barely above a whisper. Lorraine rubbed her hands together, having placed her mug on the table.

'I'm not sure, Ro. I'm not really sure about any of this. I just . . .' she hesitated. 'I just want to be okay. I want us all to be okay.'

Rosie reached out and squeezed Lorraine's hand, her eyes softening.

'One way or another, we will be. I guess we both have some thinking to do.'

The pair laughed, then changed the subject to more casual matters. Lorraine appreciated it. They made conversation and spoke about Poppy and their other friends, made plans for future events, and generally did everything to distract themselves from the mounting thoughts and issues surrounding the men in their lives.

As Lorraine headed back to her mum's after leaving Rosie, she mused that it had almost worked.

———

NATTY DROVE to Paula's house, happy for the distraction. He had a lot of balls in the air at present, but the fact he'd gained no joy in his dealings with Lorraine was hard to deal with. He wasn't sure what he needed to say to make things happen, but giving her time wasn't the best option. She was angry about Lisa, and he understood it, but wanted to move past it.

For now, he was focusing on business. Stefon was keeping an eye on the safe houses Devon had given up, but so far, Mitch hadn't been seen. The most important aspect was keeping things going as smoothly as possible.

People in the crew were worried about an attack that had been carried out, with lots of speculation on the Asians behind it. Natty, on the other hand, knew they were Jakkar's men.

After two weeks of relative peace after Roman's murder, something else had now cropped up, and he would be required to deal with it.

Paula smiled tightly when she saw Natty. After a brief hug, she led him through to the living room, where Clarke was sprawled out on the sofa, reading a book. On the coffee table next to him was an empty cup, along with a small bowl containing a few blueberries. Clarke glanced up when he saw Natty, giving him a smile.

'Nice to see you, Nat,' he said.

'You too,' Natty replied. Paula left them to it, and Natty took a seat on a chair.

'What's that you're reading?'

'*The Godfather*,' said Clarke, closing the book and placing it on the table. 'Good book. I prefer the films, though.'

Natty nodded. He hadn't seen the films in years, but enjoyed the trilogy.

'Sorry I haven't been by,' he said.

'You don't have to apologise, Nat. I imagine it's bedlam out there right now.'

'Even after Roman, other bits are cropping up,' said Natty. 'Seems mad we had so many years of relative peace.'

Clarke nodded. 'That's how it is sometimes.' He coughed, grimacing as his whole body shook. 'When people think you've been exposed, they'll go for you. They're gonna look for weaknesses and see what they can find.'

'I know. I'm on top of everything as much as I can be, but it's not easy. Forget that for now, though. What can I do for you? Is there anything you need?'

'I'm good,' said Clarke. 'I don't like being laid up like this, but I'm trying to make the most of it. Jamal did some fucking damage with those bullets, but if it wasn't for your boy Spence, I'd be a goner. I can deal with a bit of pain if the alternative is death.'

'Maybe it's a sign you need to hang it up for good,' said Natty. He was half-joking, but Clarke didn't even crack a smile.

'Paula is on my case, saying the same. It's not the first time I've taken a bullet, but I only got winged before. This was obviously a lot more serious, but it is what it is, Nat. It's the game. I know the risks just as much as you do.'

Natty didn't respond. Clarke sighed.

'Do you want a drink? We need to get into some serious stuff.'

'I'm fine,' Natty said.

'Okay. What's going on with your uncle?'

Natty paused, his eyes narrowing ever so slightly, as if weighing his next words. 'In what sense?'

'He came to see me shortly after the shooting, and he had a lot to say about you. You believe he ordered Ty's murder?'

Natty fought to keep his expression neutral, whilst his insides churned. It had to come out eventually, but it still shocked him to learn what his uncle knew. He would need to speak to the others and potentially accelerate any plans to go after Mitch, before his uncle went on the attack.

Suddenly, Morgan being brought into Mitch's inner circle made more sense. With his uncle now aware of what Natty knew, it appeared he had begun insulating himself from his nephew, breaking the dependency he'd once held for Natty.

'What else did he say?'

Clarke shook his head. 'You have to give to receive, Nat. You know that.'

Natty rubbed his cheek as he surveyed Clarke, before responding.

'You've spoken to me numerous times about loyalty. You're loyal to my uncle. You're loyal in general. Anyone who knows you knows that. But, if the man you're loyal to had his brother killed, how can you justify that?'

'He said it's not true,' Clarke replied.

'Do you believe him?'

'I take it you don't?'

'For fuck's sake,' Natty snapped. 'Why can't you just answer the question straight up?'

Clarke's expression darkened, his eyes narrowing.

'Careful. Just because I'm laid up, doesn't mean you can talk to me like that.'

'Sorry,' Natty said. 'I don't mean any disrespect, but I want you to think about whatever it is you want to say to me, before you say it.'

Slowly, Clarke sat up.

'Come on,' he said. 'I need some water, so we may as well walk and talk.'

They headed to the kitchen. Natty leant against the wall as Clarke fetched a bottle of water from the fridge, uncapped it, and took a deep swig.

'Are you sure I can't get you one?'

'I'm fine,' said Natty. 'You know that I could have got that for you, rather than you moving?'

'I'm not dead. I can do things for myself,' said Clarke. 'Bad enough I've got doctors telling me to rest all the time, and bloody Paula pouncing on me every time I breathe too loudly.' Clarke glanced towards the kitchen door, as if worried he'd see her standing there. Despite their recent conversation, Natty chuckled.

'I might tell her that you moved, just to be a dickhead.'

Both men laughed. As the laughter faded, Clarke's expression became serious.

'What's going on, Nat?'

'I'm hoping you can tell me. Did my uncle tell you the circumstances of how I learned what I did?'

'He said your mum told you.' Clarke took another sip of water, then sat down at the kitchen table.

'She did. If you're asking me if I believe what she said, then the answer's yes. She has no reason to lie. My uncle does.'

'What exactly did she tell you?' Clarke asked. Natty gave him an overview of their conversation. Clarke sat silently, allowing him to finish.

'Are you sure that she's not trying to destabilise Mitch, based on what you did to Rudy?'

'Yes, I am. I'm not saying that her reasons for telling me are benevolent. I grew up with her, and I'm sure she's got her own agenda, but there's no doubt in my mind that Mitch had my dad killed.' Natty was taking a big risk with the conversation, but he needed to understand precisely where Clarke stood.

Clarke sighed.

'Knowing that . . . what do you do next?'

'I live with it. The same way that I've been doing since I found out.'

'Just like that?' Clarke's eyes searched Natty's. 'I know how much you love your dad. I can't see you just swallowing that and moving on.'

'I don't have a choice,' said Natty. 'Let me return it back to you now. Once again, you talk about loyalty. You're loyal to the Dunns. My dad was a Dunn. He helped build the team. Can you honestly stay loyal to a man who had him killed . . . or who might have had him killed?'

'I can't answer that, Nat.' Clarke looked pained. Natty nodded.

'This is why I kept it to myself. Just think about that loyalty of yours, and who deserves it. Look after yourself, boss.' Natty went to leave.

'You and your cousin . . . how are you doing?'

Natty paused, facing Clarke again.

'We're fine.'

'He's the one who told Mitch that you and your mum weren't talking. Was he loyal to you when he did that?'

For a split second, a flicker of surprise crossed Natty's face. He hesitated, recomposing himself.

'Who even knows?' he replied. 'Loyalty isn't always what it's cracked up to be. Sometimes the people you're loyal to, disappoint you. Get some rest, Clarke.'

Natty left. There was another conversation with Stefon in his future, he mused as he said goodbye to Paula, then headed to his car and drove off.

CHAPTER FIVE

STEFON STRETCHED and leaned back on the sofa, letting out a deep sigh. He was at the spot he had been gifted upon returning to Leeds, a two-bedroomed townhouse property on Newton Garth, off Chapeltown Road. It could only be accessed via an integral garage on the ground floor, something Stefon felt added a nice layer of security. Upstairs, an open-plan lounge seamlessly melded with the dining and kitchen area. The sofa was light grey, the white coffee table and nearby television stand keeping up the light theme of the location.

Stefon tended to travel light, and hadn't spent much time at the house. Like most of them, today had been long. He'd spent almost four hours looking over both spots that Devon had given them, but had seen little movement in either area. On top of that, he'd overseen his drug spots, done drop-offs, and kept things moving for the team.

Someone needed to.

The past two weeks had been fraught with planning, sitting around and strategising, and Stefon wanted more action. In a battle of numbers, Mitch had them beaten. His name inspired fear in the rank and file, and Stefon felt they needed to keep knocking pieces off the board, along with getting their name out. Privately, he doubted their actions would remain secret. If they had more power and allies, they would be harder to take out.

Still, he respected Natty and Spence. He'd had his doubts when he'd come back to Leeds, but they'd proved themselves by killing Roman and his people.

Stefon sat up, considering cooking something to eat. When his phone rang, he abandoned the idea, snatching it off the coffee table and answering.

'Yo.'

'It's me,' Natty said. 'I'm outside. Let me in.'

'On it.'

Stefon frowned. He hadn't expected to see Natty, and he didn't sound happy. As he traipsed down the stairs and through the garage to unlock the door, he wondered what else could have transpired.

Natty was well-dressed as always, in a black bomber jacket, black trousers and boots. The pair touched fists, and walked upstairs. Natty sat on the sofa, and Stefon took a seat nearby.

'Everything good?' Stefon asked. Natty had an irritated look on his tired face. Stefon knew how hard his cousin was working. Since he'd returned to Leeds, it felt like Natty had been flat-out. One conflict followed another, and Natty had his own battles he was dealing with. On top of that, he was on the outs with his girlfriend, something Stefon knew Natty was hurting over.

'I went to see Clarke,' said Natty, his voice tight. 'Mitch told him he's worried about me, because I got it into my head that he had my dad killed.'

'How the hell did he learn that?' Stefon asked, baffled.

'He learned it because of you,' Natty said, glaring at Stefon.

'I never told him that. What are you on about?'

'You went to see him about my mum. He went to see her, and she told him.' Natty hung his head, taking a deep breath. Stefon got it. He'd messed up in a major way, and the fact they were still talking rather than throwing punches was a sign of how much their relationship had improved.

'I'm sorry, Nat. That wasn't my intention. Your mum got under my skin, and I went to see your unc to see if he could smooth things out between you. If I'd known what was gonna happen, I'd have kept my mouth shut.'

Closing his eyes, Natty rubbed his shoulder, then nodded.

'Stef, you were operating with the information you had. I get that. If I'd been a bit more forthcoming with what was going on at the time, it wouldn't have happened. It's out there now, and the fact my uncle hasn't tried to have me killed is probably a sign that there's a lot more going on.'

Stefon nodded now. 'I get that. I'm still sorry. What else did Clarke say?'

'Not much. You've been around him enough to know how he gets. He's loyal to a fault. I tried to find out whether he's loyal to Mitch, or to the Dunns as a whole.'

'Clarke's never gonna go against Mitch,' said Stefon. 'I know you like the guy, and I know he's done a lot for you, but it might be worth taking him out. Especially while he's laid up recovering.'

Natty shook his head. 'That's not an option, Stef. Nothing's gonna happen to Clarke.'

'I know you respect him, but we're talking about a war here. Even if Clarke can't run around shooting people right now, people know what he's about, and it'll make them more likely to pick Mitch's side over ours,' Stefon said.

'I know what you're saying, but that's final. Nothing happens to Clarke.'

'Even if he has a gun to your head?'

Natty again closed his eyes and leaned back. Stefon could almost feel the tiredness emanating from him.

'Self-defence is different. Clarke is still making his mind up about things. He doesn't know what's going on with Mitch and us, and I didn't give him any indication I was making a move.'

'They know you, Nat,' Stefon pointed out. 'You fucking worship your dad. There's no way they're gonna accept you're okay with it.'

'We're making a lot of assumptions,' Natty said, eyes still closed. 'Let's keep doing what we're doing, and wait until we know more.'

Both men sat in silence for a few minutes. Stefon clenched his fist under the table, a visible tremor running through it as he fought to control his frustration. He'd put his cousin in a precarious situation, potentially even blowing the element of surprise. The weight of it settled on him, and he shook his head slightly, annoyed with himself.

With his frustration growing, he considered whether going to the gym would help blow off some steam. He hadn't trained with Spence in weeks, debating contacting him so they could get into it. Before he could do anything, Natty sat forward, eyes open, his expression alert.

'We might have something,' he said.

'What the hell are you talking about?' Stefon asked.

'Mitch likes you. You told him about me and my mum. He might think we're still on the outs.'

'So? What are you getting at?'

'I'm saying that there might be an opportunity for you to use that relationship to your advantage,' Natty started, a growing smile appearing on his face.

———

SPENCE SAT in the kitchen at one of the Dunn spots in the heart of the Hood. He'd been there for a few hours, gauging the workers. Everyone was nervous and trying to hide it, believing the spot could be next to be attacked.

He'd had a busy day, arranging a drug delivery, then coordinating with various crew chiefs, ensuring everyone got their allocated share. There had been an issue with a rough team in Harehills that wanted more product than anticipated, but Spence had personally smoothed it over.

'Spence, are you busy, boss?'

'Course not.' Spence looked up from the kitchen table at Dennis, an older man who ran the spot. He was a short man with sloping shoulders and a fleshy face. 'What's going on?'

Dennis took a deep breath, looking as tired as Spence felt.

'Who's after us?' Dennis held up a hand when he saw Spence about to respond. 'I don't want to overstep the mark, but people are worried. It's been one thing after another for a while now, and everyone's jumpy.'

Spence appreciated the straight talk. He'd discussed it with Natty multiple times, and they'd agreed to operate as normally as possible to remove any suspicion. Dennis was a good man, but Spence couldn't give him the answers he wanted.

Instead, he would focus on providing reassurance.

'It's all in hand, Den. I won't tell you not to worry, because we're all playing the game, but Natty is on top of everything — that I can promise.'

'Still . . . a lot's happened, Spence. You've gotta admit that,' Dennis said.

'I know. We're at the top, though. These things happen, but we always win. I'm always around if anyone needs anything, but reach out to Stefon too, if something goes down.'

Dennis smiled.

'Thanks, Spence. I appreciate you stopping by. When you or Natty are around, it makes people feel secure. Same with Natty's cousin. I'm done for the night, anyway. I'll see you around.'

Spence left the spot a short while after Dennis, deep in thought. He'd never seen himself as one of the tough guys who could reassure people with his presence, but lately, he'd been through some battles of his own, taking several lives and defending his team. He was still coming to terms with everything, but it was a work in progress.

Spence drove to his house. The safe houses they'd picked out were available, but Spence preferred his own space, feeling they should only be used for business, or in extreme circumstances.

As he pulled up and headed inside, the fatigue flooding his body seemed to grow stronger. Going to the kitchen, he found a bottle of brandy he'd opened with Natty a while back, pouring himself a glass. Sipping it and closing his eyes, Spence leaned against the worktop, taking deep breaths.

Along with everything else, his sleep had been up and down. Often at night, he would close his eyes and still see Jamal's body hitting the ground, a leaden, uncontrollable anxiety encompassing him every time it happened. Despite Natty saying it got easier, he still had some work to do.

Opening his eyes, Spence finished his drink, leaving the cup on the counter and grabbing his phone. Rosie flitted to his mind. He wondered what she was doing. Staring at the screen, he considered calling her, but thought better of it. As he was about to lock the phone and put it down, an idea occurred to him.

Navigating his contacts, he found who he was looking for and hit *call.*

'Spence?' Lorraine asked, once she'd answered. Spence nearly hung up, feeling foolish.

'Hey, Lo. Sorry for disturbing you.'

'You're not disturbing me, Spence. Is everything okay? Is it Natty?'

'Natty's fine. I'm sorry for worrying you, I just wanted to see how you were doing.'

Lorraine paused for a moment, before responding.

'I can't pretend that isn't a little random, but I'm doing okay. The last few months have been up and down, and I'm trying to work my way through it, bit by bit.'

'I can relate,' said Spence truthfully. 'Lately, it feels like everything has been upside down. Is Jaden okay?'

'Yeah. He's a bit girl-crazy at the moment, which is a lot for me to deal with, but it's kinda cute at the same time.'

Spence laughed. Natty had told him about Jaden coming to him for relationship advice, and the situation still tickled him now.

'You have to start sometime, I guess.'

'I just wish he'd left it a bit longer. Still, he's happy, and that's the most important thing.'

'I'm really pleased for you both,' said Spence. The laughter had shifted, and now he felt a little awkward. It was good speaking to Lorraine, but he was also now wondering what he'd hoped to achieve by doing so. Pushing on, he spoke again. 'Is Rosie doing okay?'

Lorraine chuckled.

'I figured we'd get around to speaking about her.' The mirth left her voice. 'How do you think she's doing, Spence? You hurt her. She loved you, and you threw it all away.'

Spence didn't respond. He deserved every word Lorraine was throwing at him. At the time, speaking to his ex, Anika, had seemed like a good idea, and a way of venting, but looking back, it had been foolish.

'I know,' he finally said.

'Why did you do it? I don't know all the details, but Anika crushed you. She stamped on your heart and ran away, and Rosie picked it up. She helped you.'

'I know she did. With everything that was happening around me, I didn't know what to do. I felt like I couldn't vent to my friends, because they wouldn't understand. At the same time, I couldn't confide in Rosie, because I knew she would overreact.'

'You can't say that.'

'I can, because she did. I'm not even saying she's wrong for doing so. I'm just trying to answer your question. It's twisted, but part of me liked the idea that Anika was all messed up after abandoning me, and I liked that she wanted me back, even if I never wanted her in return. It was a dangerous, silly game, but that's the truth.'

'You never did anything with Anika then?'

'No. I wasn't even tempted to. It wasn't about that, Lo. I promise. Doesn't mean a thing now, because Rosie has made it clear she's done with me, but it's the truth.'

Lorraine sighed.

'I believe you, Spence. Really, I do. You have to consider things from Rosie's side, though. She's been messed around by guys before. I mean, Kyle . . . he put her through the wringer, and I never thought she'd be normal again after that. You were supposed to be a breath of fresh air for her.'

Spence absorbed Lorraine's words, appreciating that she was giving it to him straight. A fresh round of guilt surged within him, and he closed his eyes for a moment.

'Spence?'

'Sorry,' he said. 'I agree with what you're saying, and the thought that I'm now seen as one of those guys who has messed her around is tearing me apart, but ultimately, the situation with Anika had little to do with Rosie. I wasn't trying to hurt her, or go behind her back. I think I just wanted closure, and I got carried away in speaking to someone who I felt understood me and the world I come from.'

'I get that,' Lorraine replied, her voice softer. 'It's not easy, and I struggle with it every day, wondering what could go wrong. Even with your phone call . . . I thought you were giving me some bad news.'

Spence understood that. Lorraine wasn't in the streets with them, but she was smart enough to understand what she could and couldn't say on the phone.

'I'd give you bad news in person, Lo. I hope I never have to. I'm glad I spoke to you, though. Nothing's gonna change, but it was nice to get it out.'

'You can call me anytime, Spence. You're not with my girl anymore, but you're still part of my life.' Lorraine hesitated. ' . . . how's he doing?'

'I figured we'd get around to speaking about him,' Spence said, the smile on his face clear in his voice. Lorraine chuckled again.

'I didn't know you'd got a parrot, Spence. What have you called him?'

'*Natty Junior.*'

Lorraine cackled down the phone, Spence's smile widening. When the moment passed, the smile vanished, and Spence continued.

'He misses you like crazy. Jaden too. I think you already know that, though.'

'I do . . .' Lorraine's voice trailed off. 'I need to go, Spence. I'm sorry,' she said shakily.

'Take care of yourself, Lo,' said Spence, hanging up. Stretching, he glanced around the kitchen, feeling better. It had been nice expressing himself. As he poured himself another drink, he wondered if he had done so earlier, whether he could have saved his relationship with Rosie.

CHAPTER SIX

IN A SMALL, shabby house in Harehills, Zayan and Ghazan sat in the kitchen, eating in silence. Despite the overall look of the house, the kitchen was well laid out, with plenty of wooden fixtures and fittings. The walls were bubbled from condensation in several corners, but the floorboards were in good condition. It didn't matter to the pair.

They were staying temporarily, and had been given their pick of houses by Jakkar. In terms of opulence, neither needed much, and it hadn't taken much thought before they chose the house. Other than somewhere to eat and sleep, it had one other feature that they needed; one they were already making use of.

When they finished eating, both men shared a look, then stood. Almost in sync, they left the room, Ghazan walking in front. Moving a rug in the spare room, they opened the trap door below and entered, heading down the ladder.

The room beneath was more spacious than any of the upstairs rooms but was barren, other than a simple metal chair situated directly in the centre. Tied to the chair was a whimpering, shivering man with a grimy gag in his mouth. Despite the fact he was unharmed, his pale green eyes held a haunted look, his shoulders slumped. He had dark brown hair and a shaggy beard, with skinny arms and a large stomach.

Zayan hovered by the ladder, sipping a bottle of water he'd carried with him. He wore a neutral expression as Ghazan stepped closer to the man.

'Hello, Conrad. Apologies for keeping you waiting. You know how it is.'

They'd left him in the chair for half a day, having picked him up with little trouble. They hadn't said a word, tying him to the chair straight away and gagging him to prevent his screams. It wouldn't have made much difference. The room was soundproofed, the one concession they'd insisted on for any spot they stayed in.

Conrad Hall was a well-known facilitator. He was largely neutral, but had worked closely with several organisations in the past, enabling easy dealings and communications with gangs and crews that wouldn't normally do business. Conrad kept to himself for the most part, using his anonymity and neutrality as shields against retaliation.

For the first time, this had failed him.

Pulling the gag free of Conrad's mouth, Ghazan smiled at him.

'Everything okay?'

Conrad's shoulders straightened, and he glared at Ghazan, the pallor of defeat that had shrouded him seeming to disappear.

'If you know my name, then you know who I am, and you know the people I'm connected to. I don't have any money on me. I don't have access to any money, so just let me go, and that's the end of it. You have my word.'

Ghazan grinned, wondering if this was the best Conrad could muster. Despite his circumstances, he evidently thought that they could be bargained with. He looked forward to proving such an assertion wrong.

'You're right. We know your name, and we know exactly who you're involved with. That's why we're here.'

He'd stumped him, Ghazan could see it, and it only made his smile widen. Frowning, Conrad's eyes flickered from Ghazan to Zayan, who hadn't moved from his position.

'We want information on the Dunns. Mitch in particular,' said Ghazan.

Conrad wet his lips, eyes still darting between the pair. Finally, he shook his head.

'I don't know anything. I can't help you.'

Nodding, Ghazan's smile seemed fixed on his face, his eyes glittering.

'Are you thirsty?'

Warily, Conrad nodded.

'Yeah.'

Ghazan glanced at Zayan, who scowled, but headed up the ladder. Satisfied, Ghazan turned back to Conrad.

'Shouldn't take him long. Enough time for us to speak openly. Your reputation precedes you, Conrad. The fact you're here with us is the fault of one person. Mitch Dunn, a man you've done extensive business with in the past, reached too close to the sun. Due to this, he's earned the displeasure of people above him. Right now, that puts you in a terrible position.'

'Who do you work for?' Conrad asked, his voice hoarse. Ghazan shook his head.

'If I tell you that, your chance of surviving this lowers drastically. Do you still want to know?'

Before Conrad could reply, they heard Zayan returning. He descended into the room, unscrewing the bottle. Ghazan tilted Conrad's head back, allowing him to have a drink, before moving the bottle away.

'So,' said Ghazan. 'How are we going to do this?'

A few drops of the drink had missed Conrad's mouth, dribbling down his chin towards his pallid chest.

'You've got me all wrong,' said Conrad, his voice sounding better after getting some water. 'My connections . . . they're just for show. I've heard of Mitch. You can't live in Leeds and not have heard of him, but I barely know him.'

Ghazan sighed, looking genuinely sad.

'I hoped it wouldn't come to this,' he said in a soft voice. 'Go and get it,' he said to Zayan, who disappeared through the trap door once more. Ghazan noted the panicked look on Conrad's face, and the intense bobbing of his Adam's apple. Zayan returned, and when

Conrad saw what he held, he jerked back in his chair, eyes wide with terror.

'You know what it is then,' said Ghazan, referring to the electric shock device Zayan held. It was black and fairly small, but when Zayan turned it on, and it made a sharp buzzing noise, Conrad again jerked back, shaking his head frantically.

'Please,' he gasped. 'I don't know anything.'

'This is your last chance.' Ghazan's voice hardened. After Conrad again shook his head, he motioned to Zayan, who stepped forward gleefully.

'No!' Conrad screamed, but it was to no avail. Zayan pressed the device to Conrad's thigh, savouring his screams as he writhed in agony, his body spasming. After a few seconds, he released the device.

'Again,' said Ghazan. Zayan tilted his head, enjoying the anticipation, before again striking Conrad, this time on his side. Despite his best efforts, Conrad couldn't escape the pain.

Zayan shocked him twice more, and Conrad lost control of his bladder, urinating all over himself and the rough concrete floor. Neither man seemed fazed, Ghazan giving him a dead-eyed stare, while Zayan's expression remained gleeful.

'Mercy . . . please. I'll tell you what you want to know,' Conrad gasped hoarsely. He sobbed, shoulders shaking as he cried.

'We're waiting, Mr Hall.'

'Look . . . I don't know of any safe— wait!' He shrieked, as Zayan prepared to shock him again. 'I'm not part of the crew. I don't know where their safe houses are, but I can probably point you in the direction of people that do. I've known Mitch for a long time. I can give you information on distributors and moneymen that Mitch uses. I can give you stash spots where they keep money and drugs, but those get moved around often.' Again looking at both men, Conrad seemed even more terrified by their silence, his lips trembling, visible burns on his body from the torture. 'I can give you pressure points and people to focus on. Just please . . . no more.'

'We want Mitch. Can you get him in place for us?' Ghazan asked.

'No.' Conrad took several deep breaths. 'He's cautious. He doesn't deal with me like that, but he keeps me close, and I'm respected within the crew. If you want Mitch, you should start with someone who reports directly to him. Honestly, your best shot is Natty Deeds, his nephew,' Conrad croaked.

'We know of Natty Deeds,' Ghazan said. Natty had a stellar reputation, and he was on the chopping block regardless. If Conrad made it easier to get hold of him, he would play along.

'Natty is popular. He's done a lot of good for the crew, from what I've heard, but he and Mitch aren't getting along. I've heard things have been strained between them for a while.'

Ghazan and Zayan shared a look. Despite knowing of Natty, they hadn't heard anything to suggest there was tension within the organisation.

'How do you know this?'

'I talk to people in the team. It pays for me to stay well-informed. Natty took too long to do something, and Mitch was irritated about it. It's been a few weeks, but things are still the same.'

Ghazan nodded, and Zayan flicked off the device.

'Tell us more, Conrad, and hold nothing back. We want everything that you know.'

CHAPTER SEVEN

DAYS after his conversation with Stefon, Natty remained deep in thought. Though he hadn't held it against his cousin, the feeling that his hand had been tipped to Mitch gnawed at him, turning the situation dangerous. Yet, he would play it out. Retreating wasn't an option. If there was one thing Natty was sure of, it was that his reputation preceded him.

Despite the fact he'd calmed down, he was still seen as a man with a temper who would lash out when he was frustrated. When he'd spoken with Clarke, Natty had the impression that Clarke was expecting him to retaliate against Mitch.

It surprised him that Clarke hadn't connected the dots about him being behind the attempt on Mitch's life a few months back, but that meant little.

Clarke was cagey. The fact he hadn't said anything, didn't mean he wasn't thinking it.

Strangely, Natty had welcomed the added complications. It had kept him from thinking about Lorraine as much. He felt he had more direction and purpose, and despite the conflicting thoughts, he felt sharper.

Natty had made several calls and paid visits to people within their team. Not the higher ranking members, as they answered directly to Mitch, but the rank and file dealers and middlemen were fair game, and Natty knew they had influence over others.

He'd floated Morgan's name around, but being in Armley, he may as well have been in another universe. The people based in Chapeltown weren't checking for him, and though one of his confidants had stated that Devon and Morgan were close, Natty hadn't gained any further confirmation.

Climbing to his feet, Natty left the living room of the safe house and headed upstairs, the wooden steps creaking beneath his bulk. He'd lost a little weight since he'd started taking his training more seriously, but the safe house was old and had been picked with a purpose. Every sound seemed magnified, and he hoped that meant he would hear anyone attempting to make a move on him. As he was approaching the top step, his phone rang. He didn't recognise the number.

'Yeah?' He answered.

'Natty?'

'Who wants to know?' Natty didn't recognise the voice any more than he did the number.

'Otis. You know who I am?'

Natty thought for a moment, realising he did. Otis was one of Clarke's men.

'Yeah. What's up?'

'Your unc needs a conversation.'

Natty paused at the top of the stairs, his mind alight. Mitch was reaching out to speak to him, and he wasn't sure if that was a good thing.

'When?'

'Two days' time. I'll pick you up. I'll let you know what time later.'

'That's fine.'

Natty hung up. A moment of anxiety spiked within, but he quashed it. Overthinking things wouldn't help. It was inevitable he'd have to speak to his uncle eventually. When it happened, he would need to ensure he was on top of his game.

Selecting Spence's number, he called his friend.

'Nat, what's up?'

'If you were here, we could be having a face-to-face conversation.'

'Awww, are you lonely, Nathaniel?' Spence mocked.

'Prick.' Natty smirked at the phone. 'We need to talk, anyway. That and a change of scenery.'

'What are you thinking?' Spence asked.

'That's up to you, bro. 'I could do with a drink, so we can hit a club in town, or we can go to Amanda's, maybe play a game of dominoes.'

Despite himself, Spence chuckled.

'Fair enough. I'll get ready and have a think. Link up in an hour?'

'Sounds good.'

———

'I'M SURPRISED AT YOUR CHOICE.'

Spence and Natty climbed out of the Uber near Greek Street, immediately walking to find an establishment.

'I didn't fancy being in the hood,' said Spence. He'd heeded Natty's words and dressed up, wearing a navy designer sweater, black ripped jeans and a pair of Jordan 4s Natty had never seen him wear before. There was a tasteful watch on his wrist. It was a nice piece, but you'd have to look hard to know it was a Rolex.

'No complaints here,' said Natty. 'C'mon, anyway. Step up the pace. We've got drinking to do.'

The entrance of the club Natty picked was alight, and already swarming with sharply dressed patrons queuing outside, the line to enter extending along the pavement. Two bouncers were on crowd control, checking IDs and managing the people.

Natty's shoulders straightened as he approached, moving past the queue to the bouncers. They took one glance at Natty and stepped aside, allowing both he and Spence to enter, as the murmuring crowd grew louder, no doubt wondering who they were.

Upon entering, the pair were greeted by dim, atmospheric bright lighting, a *Mariah Carey* song that Natty remembered from his childhood playing in the background. He hadn't been to this club in a while, but the layout remained familiar. It had a spacious dance floor, surrounded by comfortable lounge seating at the heart of the club. A large LED screen served as a backdrop for the raised DJ booth, showcasing visuals that seemed to sync with the music.

The pair made their way through the energetic crowds toward the long, well-stocked bar running along one side of the club. It was staffed by four bartenders and lit by elegant pendant lights, creating an inviting ambience.

As Natty ordered drinks, Spence took in the surroundings. Being around a lot of people wasn't usually his thing, but he was already feeling looser than he had in a while.

Natty was already in his element, making small talk with the female bartender, who was giggling and playing with her hair. Spence rolled his eyes as he took his drink, sipping the Disaronno and surveying the scene. The club had a VIP section elevated above the main floor.

From their vantage point, he noted it had plush booths and bottle service. He couldn't see who was up there, but there were security guards by the entrance, so they were obviously a big deal.

'Come,' said Natty. 'Let's find seats.'

They made their way towards the seating and away from the dance floor. Natty had almost finished his brandy, his eyes alight with something that Spence couldn't quite decipher. It was like looking at the old, wilder Natty, but not quite. There was a seriousness underneath that told the true story.

'Why do I get the impression you needed this as much as I did?' Spence asked. Natty chuckled, shaking his head.

'Maybe.'

It made sense, Spence mused. He and Natty hung out, but it was mostly in and around business spots, occasionally sharing a drink and some conversation. The last time they'd gone out socially, they'd gone to a local party, and someone had shot at Natty. The time before that, they'd been in another club, a favourite of their old friend, Cameron. Despite what he'd done to them, they'd shared stories and drinks, celebrating his birthday and the memory of the good times.

Sombrely, Spence wondered if they would celebrate Cameron's next birthday too.

'Talk to me,' he said, after letting the silence go on. They'd picked a good night to go out. Spence was a fan of modern-day R&B, but the old joints the DJ was spinning were familiar and appreciated.

Natty sighed. 'Mitch wants a meet.'

Spence frowned over the top of his glass.

'Any indication why?'

Natty shook his head. 'One of Clarke's people made the call. Two days time. They pick the location.'

Spence glanced around, but with the general noise and music, over-hearing them would be extremely difficult.

'Think there's any way we could trail you?'

'Probably, but it's risky. Part of me is curious about what he'll say. There's more.' Natty briefly filled in Spence on his conversations with Clarke and Stefon.

'It could be worse,' Spence said in response. 'Clarke sounds like he's struggling with his loyalty. That could be good for us. Same with Stef potentially getting close to Mitch.'

'Possibly,' Natty said. 'One for more discussion when we know more. How are you doing in general?'

'Why?' Spence's brow furrowed.

'A lot's happened lately. You and Rosie. What you did for Clarke. I know that all must be weighing heavily on you. If you wanna talk about it, I'm here.'

Spence smiled, feeling a little tension lifting. 'I appreciate that, fam. It's difficult at times, but I stay busy. That helps. I spoke with your girl the other day, though.'

Natty's eyes widened.

'How come?'

'I was having a moment,' Spence admitted. 'Rosie was on my mind, and I was miserable. Somehow, I knew Lorraine would know what to say.'

Natty smiled despite himself. 'She's good at that.' A wave of sadness came over him, but he pushed through it.

'She is. We spoke about Rosie, and about you. She definitely misses you. I think she's just still trying to figure things out.'

Natty sighed, sipping his drink before speaking.

'I know she needs space to figure them out, but I just don't want it to drag on, bro. I've told her it wasn't like that between me and Lisa, but still . . . I let the flirting go on longer than it should have.'

'It will work out, Nat. Just keep up the faith. We've got a lot we need to do in the meantime.'

Natty nodded, enjoying the comfort of hanging out with his friend. He wondered if they should have invited Stefon, but brushed it off. The pair needed this time together.

'We're gonna win, Spence,' he said, still staring out at the dancing, happy crowds. 'I know it doesn't seem like it, and we've got everything against us, but we're gonna win.'

'I know,' Spence admitted. 'I'm with you all the way, but I can't help thinking of all the things that could go wrong.'

'That's your job,' Natty joked. 'You keep me on the right path. Your job has doubled with my cousin being around, but you can handle it.'

Spence chuckled. 'I'm glad you two are on good terms, and I'm doubly glad he's on our team.'

'Me too. He's a prick at times, but his heart's in the right place.' Natty grinned. 'Slight subject change, but I'm surprised you didn't reach out to Anika again, especially if Rosie's moving on.'

Spence finished his drink, holding the glass, tapping the rim with his free hand.

'Anika and I are done. I miss Rosie. It's like . . . I haven't *not* had anyone around in a while. How I was feeling was the driving factor behind speaking to Lorraine.'

'I get it.' Natty shrugged. 'I'll get us more drinks, then we can get you out on the dance floor with some of these young women!'

'I don't dance,' Spence called after Natty, chuckling as Natty pretended he couldn't hear him.

The night progressed, and the club's energy seemed to intensify, with people dancing more passionately, the DJ showcasing his skills with seamless song transitions and a remix of an old *Faith Evans* song that Spence had forgotten about. True to his word, Natty got Spence on the dance floor, and Spence danced with a few women, keeping his moves simple, not wanting to embarrass himself. He spoke with a few, and bought drinks for one, but went no further.

———

'How long have you been with him then?'

Natty sipped his drink, waiting for the woman to reply. They'd shared a friendly dance, and he'd struck up a conversation with her by the bar. She had a boyfriend, and he had a Lorraine, so it was interesting to hold a conversation with her, knowing he had no intention of taking it further. She was attractive, with alluring brown eyes, light brown skin and full lips.

'Two years on and off,' she replied. 'We seem to fight a lot, because I guess we're both passionate people. How long have you been with your girl?'

'I . . . don't know,' Natty said, after thinking for a moment. The woman's eyebrows rose.

'How can you not know?'

'I've known her most of my life. There's always been something between us, but I can't put a timeline on exactly when it turned into something else.'

'That's an . . . interesting way of putting it.' The woman sipped her drink. 'Is she likely to be in the club tonight?' She asked, looking past Natty. He frowned in return.

'I don't know.'

'I'm asking because there's a woman glaring at us.'

Natty turned, noting a group of people further down the bar, with one of them indeed glaring. She was attractive, with a group of people, and after a moment of staring, Natty recognised her.

'Sorry, I need to go and speak to her.' Natty left the woman, walking toward the group. It was a mix of half a dozen men and women, with one of the guys, a strongly built, well-dressed man, seeming familiar. Ignoring that, Natty focused on the woman.

'How's it going, Poppy, you good?'

Poppy let him give her a brief hug, but her expression hadn't changed.

'Doesn't look like I'm doing as well as you are,' she said, arms folded and her expression frank. Natty knew she was a good friend of Lorraine's, and had likely got the wrong impression of what he was doing.

'I was just talking,' he said.

'Are you sure? Because my girl is sat home every night moping over you, while you seem to be out here living your best life.'

'Poppy, it's his business,' the familiar-looking man said. Poppy shrugged him off.

'Curtis, I don't want to hear that. Where my friend is concerned, it's my business too.'

Natty respected her loyalty, enjoying the fact that Lorraine had people like Rosie and Poppy by her side.

'I appreciate what you're saying, Poppy,' he said. 'I worked too hard to get anywhere with Lorraine to throw it all away. Like I said, I was just talking. I've got a girl, she's got a boyfriend. It was just an easy convo.'

Poppy's expression seemed to soften. 'It better be, Nat. She loves you.'

'I love her too. If it was up to me, I'd be in the house with her and Jaden right now, but I'm working on it. I'm working on my friend too.' He jerked his thumb over at Spence, who was dancing with a woman, a smile on his face.

Poppy chuckled.

'Rosie would be happy to see him smiling, though I doubt she'd like the fact he's dancing with another woman.'

'She made her decision,' Natty said. 'Back to Lorraine. Tell her to let me out of the cold.'

They laughed, and Natty bought a round of shots for everyone, making conversation with Poppy. Before he could leave them, the familiar man — Curtis — asked to speak to him. Surprised, Natty agreed, and they moved a few steps away from the group.

'I wanted to apologise. A while back, I ran into you and Lorraine, and I kinda ran my mouth a bit. I just wanted to make sure things were cool between us.'

Natty remembered him now. He'd almost got into a fight with him and his friends when he and Lorraine had been on a date.

'We're cool, man. No harm done.'

Slapping hands with Curtis, Natty left them and went to go locate Spence.

By the end of the night, the pair traipsed from the club, tipsy and telling jokes. Laughing as they staggered past people and approached the taxi, Spence patted Natty on the shoulder.

'Thank you for this, bro. I needed it more than I thought.'

They both had, Natty thought to himself, as he climbed in after Spence, drunkenly giving the address to the driver.

CHAPTER EIGHT

OTIS PICKED Natty up two days later at a Dunn spot on the corner of Cowper Street in the Hood. He was in a blacked-out Range Rover, nodding at Natty as he climbed in the back. He was a tall, gangly man with a greying beard and plump cheeks that looked out of place on his face.

'Good to see you, boss. Everything good?' he asked.

'Yeah. Take it Clarke has you guarding Mitch?'

Otis nodded as he drove away.

'We've been moving things around. Clarke recommended me, so he's been keeping me close. Have you seen Clarke lately?'

'A few days ago. Looks like he's going stir crazy sitting around.'

Otis chuckled.

'He gets like that. Paula will be keeping him under manners too. I might go and see him when I get time off. That woman can cook.'

The pair made steady small talk as they drove into the city centre. Natty wondered if Otis could be flipped to their side, but instantly dismissed it as too risky.

When they arrived in the city centre, the car led him down a series of roads, before pulling into a car park outside an office building.

Natty and Otis climbed out and approached the entrance, walking inside.

The lobby area was spacious, with tasteful grey furniture and a selection of magazines on a dark coffee table. Several men waited for them, all of them armed. They approached the pair, and Natty instinctively tensed.

'We just need to check you,' one of the men said, sensing his nervousness. Again, Natty didn't recognise him or any of his colleagues, but they were all large and well-built, which he imagined was by design. Otis hung back to watch.

After he'd been searched, Natty was led to the third floor, nodding to Otis, who remained. The man who'd spoken to him knocked on the conference door, then walked away after a curt voice called for Natty to enter.

Mitch Dunn was looking out of the office window at the city below. When Natty closed the door, he give no indication he was there, continuing his surveillance. Natty's blood immediately boiled at the sight of him, and he had to dig deep to control his anger. Remaining in place by the door, he knew now was not his moment. Even if he followed his desire and immediately strangled his uncle, he'd never make it out of the building alive.

Part of Natty wondered if Mitch's apparent lack of attentiveness was a test. As soon as he thought this, another man entered the room behind him, not bothering to hide the bulge of a gun in his waistband. He motioned for Natty to step further into the room as Mitch turned around.

They locked eyes, a long moment passing. Natty couldn't tell what Mitch was thinking, and he hoped the same was true when his uncle looked at him.

As Mitch looked away, Natty surveyed the conference room, which was dominated by a large light brown circular table, with numerous chairs. Behind the head chair was a large monitor, and alongside that was a whiteboard that took up most of the wall. There were bits of writing and diagrams on it, some of which appeared to have been hastily rubbed out at some point. Natty focused his attention back on his uncle, who took the head seat and motioned for Natty to sit down.

'Drink?'

Natty shook his head.

'Vince, get me a coke, then wait outside. I'd like to talk to my nephew alone.'

Vince left, and Natty almost rolled his eyes. Mitch was trying to lull him once again into a false sense of security. He recognised the truth; Mitch didn't want Vince listening to what he had to say.

After a minute, Vince returned, handing Mitch his drink, before leaving. Unscrewing the cap, Mitch took a long swig of the fizzy drink, smiling.

'I don't drink much Coke, but it tastes refreshing every time I do.'

Natty didn't respond. Mitch placed the bottle on the table.

'How are things going?'

'Steady,' said Natty, picking his words carefully. As he surveyed his uncle, he wondered whether Mitch would address the rumours that had been circling. Focusing, he continued. 'People fell in line after Roman went, and our business has been relatively smooth since. People are a little worried now after what happened with Devon. That and the other robbery are what people are talking about.'

Mitch nodded, reaching for his drink again and taking another sip.

'I'm glad things are going relatively well. I'm aware of Devon's murder. He was a good worker. The ambush too was terrible, but luckily, Blade was able to get away and let us know the situation.'

Natty knew that Blade had been let go to deliver a message, and he was equally sure that Mitch knew that as well, but simply nodded rather than refute it.

'The investigation into Devon's murder is ongoing. Jakkar, however, is definitely behind the ambush.'

'Why?' Natty asked, intrigued and wanting to know more. He too, believed Jakkar was behind it, but the reasons still eluded him. It related to his uncle, and there was a high probability it was a response to his attacks, but he craved the finality of knowing.

'I don't know,' said Mitch, focusing his attention on the bottle. It was obvious he was lying.

'Devon, then. I heard he was doing a deal on the side. Think it was that?' Natty asked, interested in what his uncle would say.

Mitch waved his hand. 'The why's aren't important. What we need to do is stop the threat, before others get ideas.'

'I'll track them,' Natty said. Doing so would make Mitch less guarded. 'Do we have any leads?'

'Have you spoken to Blade?' Mitch asked. Natty shook his head. 'He said there were two of them. He described them as skilled and ruthless. They killed an entire house of people without hesitating.'

Natty nodded, wondering if Sanjay would be able to help. The times in the past they'd spoken about Jakkar, he'd seemed reluctant to get involved, but if Sanjay didn't, there were others Natty could try.

'The men I've mentioned previously . . . Mustafa and Ahmed. Do you recall them?'

'I do,' said Natty. 'Jakkar's distributors that backed Roman.'

Mitch nodded. 'If we get a solid bead on them, their elimination would cause more problems for Jakkar.'

'Understood,' Natty replied. He didn't see the logic in removing them. They were simple yes-men who did what Jakkar told them to. They weren't a threat, especially with Roman and the other major dealers they dealt with having been killed. It wasn't his hill to die on, though. He stood and went to leave. Being in the room with Mitch was still frustrating, knowing what he had done, and what he had taken away from Natty.

'Nathaniel.'

Natty turned, facing his uncle again, noting the penetrating look on Mitch's face.

'Yeah?'

'Is there anything else on your mind?'

Natty smiled tightly.

'Nothing urgent, unc. I'll get to work.'

As Natty left the room, his fists clenched and unclenched. Sharing the room with his uncle made his skin crawl, a feeling he couldn't—wouldn't—tolerate much longer. It was becoming increasingly clear: time was running out for both of them.

CHAPTER NINE

THE BRIEFING ROOM in the Leeds police station was spacious, with a large table surrounded by ergonomic chairs, and a wall-mounted screen that allowed for multimedia presentations and easy sharing of information.

Detective Chief Superintendent Johnathan Harding stood in front of a group of officers. He was a lean man in his forties, with greying dark hair, wearing a charcoal grey suit, a crisp white shirt and polished Oxford's. Everyone in the room had their eyes fixed on him, all at attention. This wasn't by accident. Harding was both feared and respected, and knew how to command a room. After a few moments, he began to speak, standing over the congregation.

'For obvious reasons, we've said little about the murder of Detective Inspector Brown. You've all read the documentation prior to the meeting, so nothing I'm telling you is new information. He was found alongside several senior officers, along with a selection of local gangsters, namely Roman Fielding. Roman was known to us, not long out of prison, and managed to immediately get himself back involved with the drug trade on a major level.

'Roman's main rivals were the Dunns. I won't speak to you as if you're children, but if you're a police officer, you know exactly who this family are, and what they've managed to achieve. They moved into the light after the former gang chiefs disappeared in 2015, and they've ruled since. A gang war has managed to grow out of control on our watch, leading to a shocking number of murders, all of which remain unsolved. This is unacceptable.'

Harding took a sip of water and continued, his dark eyes flitting from person to person.

'The problem begins and ends with the Dunn organisation. They have been allowed to ply their trade for too long, and the murder of police officers cannot and will not be allowed to stand.

'So, what are we going to do about it? We're going to take them out.' Harding pressed a button on the screen, bringing up the first page of a presentation, with numerous names in bold. 'Information is our friend. We know of the head, Mitch Dunn. We know of Nathaniel Dunn, and those they keep close. We have details on them in the packet which has been made available. We need more.

'I want us to know and identify everyone associated with the organisation, along with an understanding of the scope of their activities. Your groups will be decided and assigned by the end of the day. By the end of the week, I want your preliminary plans, and we will take it from there.'

With the meeting ending, Harding waited for everyone to leave, ending his presentation. After ensuring the room was tidy, he returned to his office.

Closing the door behind him, he powered up his computer, loading the file of Mitch Dunn they had on record. He scowled. He'd already checked it, so he wasn't sure what he was expecting, but the scant detail infuriated him. They had Mitch's date of birth and some other cursory details about him, but there was no meat to it.

Rubbing his eyes, Harding closed the file, glancing around the room, debating what to do next. There was tremendous pressure to act. Brown's murder had inflamed people, and the murky circumstances had everyone on edge.

Harding had been brought in to take the situation by the horns and steer it in the right direction. His office was a reflection of his personality: a well-organised desk with no papers out of place. A computer, various case files, and a bookshelf with numerous law enforcement manuals. Harding wasn't one for personal effects, not even keeping photos of his family around. When he was on the job, it was all he focused on.

It had served him well.

A knock at the door stole his attention.

'Come in,' he called.

A jovial, fleshy man bounded into the room, closing the door behind him. He had a ruddy face, a patchy grey beard, and sparkling blue eyes. Unlike Harding, DS Daniels's suit had more wear and tear, stretching tight across his considerable stomach.

'Heard your briefing went well. You lit a fire under them,' Daniels said, sitting opposite Harding.

'You should have attended. You're meant to be involved in this too.'

'I work better in smaller circles,' Daniels said, yawning. 'Are you ready? Going after the Dunns is a major move.'

Harding steepled his fingers. 'We should have acted earlier, instead of allowing them to infect our station. Brown and his. . . . *cronies* being caught around drug dealers was extremely embarrassing. We can't allow that to stand.'

'Harding, this is me you're talking to now. Do you really think Brown is the only one on the take?'

Harding's eyes narrowed. 'Is that supposed to make it better?'

'It's supposed to give you some perspective. You've been to a few different stations. I've been here, and I've seen how things have changed over the years. In that time, I've seen people try to make their careers trying to bring down organisations similar to Mitch's, and most of them scuppered those careers instead.'

Harding knew Daniels was right, but it didn't change what he needed to do.

'It's necessary,' he replied. 'We've seen an influx of murders and gang-related attacks in the past year, and enough is enough.'

Daniels shrugged. 'Can't say I didn't try. Am I gonna have to read the brief for you to give me the overview, or what?'

'As I said, we need more information,' said Harding. 'We know the main players, but we have no idea how to get them. The Dunns are deep, and they're insulated. Mitch has been around a long time, and he knows how to operate. He's kept himself out of the limelight for years, but he's vulnerable.'

'How do you work that one out?'

'The sheer number of murders connected to his organisation has shot up exponentially. If he was trying to send a message to the other gangs, I'd understand it, but he's not. That suggests that he has enemies and is being forced to engage them.'

Daniels scratched his chest. 'It sounds good, I'll give you that. Feels a bit thin, though. That Roman fella that got splattered . . . he was at war with the Dunns, according to our informants, right?'

'Right,' said Harding. The common rumour was that Roman had left prison with connections, and used them to carve out his footing in the drugs trade again, going head to head with the Dunns.

'So, if Roman is their biggest rival, and he's dead, who are they warring with now?'

'That's what we need to find out,' said Harding, locking eyes with Daniels. 'The time for them getting away with this is done. We're going to bring everyone down.'

CLARKE AND LISA walked around the local park not far from Clarke's house. Both were well-wrapped up against the chilly day, in warm coats, scarves and gloves. They were in no hurry, walking at a steady pace.

'Are you sure you're okay?' Lisa asked. Clarke scoffed.

'I'm fine, Lis. You don't need to keep asking me.'

'Yeah, I do. Paula will murder me if anything happens to you.'

'Bollocks. She probably loves you more than she does me,' Clarke said.

Lisa chuckled. The park's path was filled with leafless trees, their branches reaching up towards the sky. There were benches strategically placed throughout the park, but none were in use today. Other than the two of them, they'd only seen an older man walking his dog, most people having the sense to remain indoors.

'Have you spoken to Natty lately?' Clarke asked.

Lisa shook her head.

'Not since he did Roman. I've been on sabbatical.'

Clarke rolled his eyes. Only Lisa could make taking a break from killing people sound like being on a summer holiday.

'I have something to tell you then, and I need you to stay quiet until I'm finished.'

Recognising how serious Clarke was, Lisa nodded.

'Mitch came to see me a few weeks ago, just after the Roman thing. He told me Natty believes that Mitch had his dad killed.'

Lisa blinked, unable to hide her surprise. 'Really?'

'Mitch said it isn't true, but Natty heard it from his mum. Apparently, they're not getting along, because she knew about it.'

Lisa paused. 'That's . . . mental. Isn't it?' Her eyes flicked to Clarke, who continued looking ahead. When he didn't respond, she continued. 'What do you think?'

'I'm worried. I don't mind admitting that to you. The last thing anyone needs is a civil war. Natty has a lot of support in the crew, especially among the lower ranks. It'll be bloody, and no one will win in the end.'

'When I asked you what you thought, I mean, do you think Mitch did it?' Lisa asked, her face uncharacteristically serious.

'You think Mitch Dunn had his own brother taken out?' Clarke stared at Lisa, a guarded expression on his face.

'Some families aren't straightforward,' Lisa replied darkly. 'If Mitch did it, he deserves what he gets.'

Clarke shook his head. 'You're sounding like you believe it.'

Lisa shrugged. 'Natty is a lot of things, but he's not stupid. If he thinks it's true, then he must have good reason.'

'It's not that simple. I spoke with him about it, and he didn't give me much, which means he's probably up to something.'

'You still haven't told me what you think,' Lisa pressed. By now, they were moving again, the hard ground crunching under their feet.

'I think that Mitch is the boss. He's worried about his nephew, and we need to prevent things from escalating.'

'You've avoided what I'm asking, which shows me how seriously you're taking this. The fact is, whether Mitch is the boss or not, Natty is his blood. If it's true, Natty has a legitimate beef, and if he made it public, people would probably support it.' Her expression turned shrewd. 'If you really believed there was no truth to it, you wouldn't be speaking to me about it.'

Clarke chuckled. 'I want you to be safe.'

'I'm not the one who got shot, old man,' Lisa said sweetly.

Clarke huffed. 'I don't know why I bother with you. You're too stubborn. No wonder you and Natty get along.'

Lisa smiled. 'You get along with him too. I know you've taken him under your wing. Like I said, he's not stupid. If you really want to stop things from spiralling out of control, you're going to need to work out what really happened.'

'What do you mean?' Clarke asked as they turned a corner in the park, proceeding up a slight hill.

'Who killed his dad? He was obviously high profile. You were around back then, so who was claiming the hit?'

'No one. We were beefing with some Yardie gangs, or at least Ty was. They must have done it.'

Lisa stopped, causing Clarke to stop with her, as she stared into his eyes.

'Something about this whole thing doesn't smell right. People don't take out a big dog like Tyrone Dunn and not say anything, unless it's in their best interests to stay quiet. I'm not saying Mitch really did have his brother killed, but if he did, he's the most likely to keep it quiet.'

Lisa carried on walking again, Clarke staring after her. He had only told her about the situation as a warning to stay out of trouble, but now he wondered if he'd had the opposite effect. Lisa had given him a lot of food for thought, and that surprised him. As sharp as Lisa was, she didn't take many things seriously. The fact she was already poking holes in the situation was jarring, and made him wonder if she was in too deep with Natty, or if he was simply not looking objectively at the situation.

Tyrone Dunn had been murdered nineteen years ago. At the time, his death was major news, but the more Clarke considered it, the stranger the circumstances seemed. Mitch had retaliated against the gang they suspected of being behind the murder, but the gang never claimed it, and despite the action, Mitch never seemed angry about Tyrone's death. He wasn't emotional, mournful, or particularly vengeful, and it wasn't until now that Clarke had truly considered that.

'You're falling behind, old man,' Lisa called out to him.

'Just for that crack, you owe me a cuppa when we get back to the house,' Clarke said, as Lisa laughed. He would return to his thoughts another time.

CHAPTER TEN

THE NIGHT AFTER MEETING MITCH, Natty was drinking at Amanda's. She wasn't working, the replacement bringing him drinks and leaving him to it. Everyone else in the vicinity knew the same, and Natty welcomed it.

His conversation with Mitch had been rattling around his head, but he was pleased he'd kept his composure. Mitch seemed determined to keep things from him. He hadn't mentioned Morgan, nor did he provide any other details about Jakkar's people.

Natty wondered how much of the puzzle he was missing.

'I heard you were here,' a deep voice said from next to Natty. He'd sensed their approach, but hadn't faced them. He did so now, recognising Tommy's voice. He wore a fleece-lined hooded top, jeans, gloves and boots, his hair cut neatly with a moon-shaped pattern at the front.

'Lorraine send you to kick my arse?' Natty signalled to the bartender to get Tommy what he wanted. Once Tommy had ordered, Natty paid for the drink, stuffing the remaining notes into his pocket.

'Honestly, she'd probably rather do it herself,' Tommy said, once he'd thanked him. 'My mum spoke to me, though. Said I might want to speak to you directly and learn what's going on.'

Natty straightened, letting out a deep breath.

'We need to use your backroom,' he said to the bartender, who froze for a moment, then nodded. Amanda was diligent, and Natty was sure she'd made it clear who he was, and the respect he had around the establishment. While Natty wouldn't take advantage of that status by disrespecting the place, he also wasn't going to freely discuss business with Tommy where they could be overheard.

They were led to the backroom, one that Natty had used before. It had a single unused table, a sofa, a television, and a private bar. There was usually a cost to rent it out, but Natty wouldn't be expected to pay. Despite that, he would anyway, even though Amanda would give him hell when she found out.

Natty sat at the table, messing around with a pack of playing cards that had been left there. Tommy sat on the sofa, sipping his drink.

'Make sure this is my last one,' he said. 'The missus will kill me if I go home drunk and leave her to watch the kids.'

'How are they doing?' Natty asked. He'd seen Tommy's kids a few times, mostly at family events or parties. They were well-behaved, energetic children, and Natty definitely credited them and Tommy's partner with turning his life around.

Just like Lorraine had for him.

'Too cheeky for their own good, but I wouldn't change them,' Tommy admitted. 'Jaden looks like he's doing well too. I heard he's got a girlfriend. Is that your doing?'

Natty laughed despite himself. He filled Tommy in on Jaden's short-lived crush, and how that kickstarted his interest in the opposite sex. Tommy chuckled, shaking his head.

'About time he got started. With a known gyalist like you teaching him, he's gonna be deadly as he gets older.'

'*Retired* gyalist,' Natty corrected. 'I'm only interested in one woman.'

Tommy nodded.

'Probably a good time to get around to all that. What's going on? I didn't even know there was an issue until I stopped by my mum's and saw Lorraine and Jaden there.'

Natty didn't immediately reply, weighing up just how honest to be. Tommy knew the game and had done dirt of his own, but Natty was still taking a tremendous risk by sharing what he was about to.

After a few moments of deliberation, he decided it was worth it. Tommy was Lorraine's blood, and Natty trusted him.

'This doesn't go beyond us, Tom.'

Tommy scowled. 'What do you think I'm gonna do? Blab your business?'

'I'm giving you the same words you'd give me if you had some real shit to say.'

Tommy shrugged. 'Fair enough. What's happening?'

'I don't even know where to start. That thing that happened to Raider . . . your sister did it.'

'What?' Tommy roared. 'Where the fuck were you?'

Natty briefly summarised the situation, watching as Tommy grew angrier. Tommy stood, breathing hard, clenching and unclenching his fists, glaring at Natty.

'You should have been there.'

'I should have been. Still, that messed with your sister's head. She was worrying about me, and it was playing with her mind. She followed me to a spot and saw me with another woman.'

Tommy leapt forward, fist raised.

'Calm the fuck down,' Natty snapped, not leaving his seat. 'I wouldn't ever cheat on your sister. I love her.'

'Loads of people say that shit,' Tommy growled, though he'd ceased his attack.

'They do, but there's a respect between us, and that's why I'm coming to you straight up. She thought I was creeping, but she got herself caught up in a shootout. I got her out of there, but I wanted her to stay at your mum's.'

'What if the people that went for you, got her there?' Tommy said, his tone still frustrated.

'They're taken care of. I also have people watching the house. I needed to be free to handle the problem, and I did. Your sister said she needs space. I'm guessing she's worried about the lifestyle. There are things I can and can't control, Tom. You know the game, and you know how it is. The only thing that matters is my family. I want Lorraine and Jaden to have the life they deserve, and I want Jaden to grow up with a dad that cares about him.'

Tommy rubbed his forehead. 'I can have a word with my sis if you like. Make her see sense.'

'She said she needs time, and I'll do my best to respect that. There's a lot more street shit going on right now. It's probably best if she keeps doing what she's doing.'

Tommy sat back on the sofa, letting out a deep breath.

'That's some heavy shit,' he said. 'No wonder you were drinking by the bar and looking all miserable.'

Natty chuckled. 'I know.'

'Do you need anything from me? I can move back in for a bit if you think there's gonna be some trouble.'

'I'm good, Tom. I appreciate it, though. Come, let's go get another drink. You must have some other lighter shit we can talk about.'

'If I don't, I'll make it up, fam,' Tommy said, both men laughing as they left the backroom.

———

MITCH GRUMBLED to himself as he climbed out of bed in the middle of the night. Looking back at the comfortable mattress, his eyes went to the young woman still lying there, sleeping. Otis knew her from the Hood, and had brought her around to spend some time with him. She was twenty-five years old and knew her job. She'd made conversation, but hadn't overplayed her position, just the way Mitch liked it.

After a few moments, he put on his dressing gown and slipped out of the room, moving downstairs.

Mitch had yet to return home, but had transferred numerous amenities into the well-protected spot he was currently staying at, having moved from his Shadwell compound. The house was empty, but had guards stationed outside, and men on standby in cars on the street. No one would be able to approach without them being aware. For the first time in a long time, he felt truly secure.

When he'd narrowly avoided an assassination attempt a while back, Mitch took it as a sign he'd grown too lax. He had people watching his house in Moortown to see if anyone showed, but so far, no one had. He was considering returning home if things stayed as they were.

It wasn't a decision he needed to make yet.

Mitch poured himself a glass of water and sat in the kitchen, considering the meeting he'd recently held with Nathaniel. He was unsure when his nephew had become so difficult to read, and that irked him. Especially now.

He needed Nathaniel to lead the charge against Jakkar and his men, before their attacks intensified. At present, they were simply probing defences, sending a message that they were watching and waiting. The second they kicked it into overdrive, it would get dangerous for everyone, himself included, and he couldn't have that.

If Nathaniel couldn't be controlled, though, what could he do?

Nathaniel was powerful. He was ascending into the man Mitch had always known he could be; a natural leader with a strong reputation. Mitch didn't feel comfortable that Nathaniel was his weapon anymore, and that was worrying.

There had been a moment in the office where he had seen contempt in Nathaniel's eyes, but Mitch wasn't sure if he was over-exaggerating things.

Sipping his drink, Mitch tried to centre his thoughts. He needed to know what Nathaniel was thinking, and whether he truly believed he had killed his father.

If he did, he couldn't be kept alive.

As Mitch sat there, he considered just having it done. Nathaniel was family, but also a potential enemy. Resolving the situation by simply having him killed would fix that problem. Mitch considered who would be best for the job, his mind shifting to Stefon. It would be a test of his loyalty and a reward for his work.

Stefon was the one who had clued Mitch into the fact that Nathaniel and Tia were on the outs, after all.

It was a play, but he didn't think it was the best one at present. Waiting and gathering more string was the most prudent move. If he told Stefon to kill Nathaniel, and Nathaniel survived, it would tip his hand and leave him vulnerable.

Yes, waiting was the best move, he decided.

For now, he had other things to deal with.

Taking his phone from his dressing gown pocket, Mitch called Morgan.

'Boss.'

Mitch was pleased that despite the late hour, Morgan sounded wide awake and alert.

'Do you have an update?' He asked, moving straight onto business.

'Nothing concrete, but things are moving as planned.'

'Are you still exercising all the proper protocols?'

'I am,' replied Morgan. 'No one knows anything. I've been careful, and I'm double-checking piece by piece, just in case.'

Mitch nodded, despite knowing Morgan couldn't see him.

'Good. Stay vigilant. It's vital that we succeed. There can be no fuck ups.'

'There won't be,' said Morgan calmly. 'I'm taking full responsibility. Are you still on the move?'

Mitch's eyes narrowed. Morgan was extremely talented, but he was overstepping his bounds and needed to be reminded.

'That's not your concern. Don't worry about my moves. Worry about the tasks you've been given, and what's at risk if you fail.'

'Understood. I'll be in touch.'

Mitch hung up, draining the glass of water, staring at his phone screen. Everything seemed so complicated lately. As he looked around the lavish safe house, he considered his fortunes. Although the property was his, it was not his home. And yet, it had been meticulously prepared and furnished. It was more of a home than most families could even dream of.

Mitch Dunn had the resources to be happy and content wherever he chose to hang his hat. If he retired tomorrow, he'd never need to work another day in his life, and yet, here he was.

Unable to return to his home with enemies popping up everywhere.

As he climbed to his feet, Mitch shrugged off the thoughts. He wanted to leave on his own terms, and was determined to do what was necessary to make that happen.

Nobody would force him out. Not Jakkar, not Nathaniel. Not anyone.

CHAPTER ELEVEN

THE GROUND CRUNCHED below Natty as he ran around the cold park in Roundhay. Last night he'd intended to survey one of Mitch's suspected hideouts in Adel, but his meeting with Tommy had run longer than anticipated.

Natty hadn't spoken to the others yet, but it was likely they would have to come up with another approach.

With only the three of them, they couldn't keep indefinitely watching the safe houses Devon had given up.

Natty's breathing intensified as he approached a hill, legs pumping as he kept up his pace, accelerating sharply, welcoming the burning sensation coursing through his muscles as he reached the top.

Natty had contacted Sanjay about Jakkar's distributors, but he'd yet to get back to him. They needed more information on Jakkar's organisation, but in the meantime, Natty would ensure everyone remained on high alert.

Stopping for a break, Natty placed his hands on his head, expanding his chest as he sucked air in. Opening his bottle with his teeth, he chugged some water down, taking a seat on a nearby bench. Natty placed the bottle on the bench beside him, taking out his phone.

Instinctively, his hand guided him to Lorraine's name in his contacts, pausing momentarily before he called her.

'Hello, Nat.'

'Hey, Lo,' he said, noting that Lorraine sounded happier than she had when they'd spoken before.

'Is everything okay?' she said.

'Not really. I'm hoping to sort that out now.'

'How do you plan on doing that?' Lorraine asked, sounding intrigued.

'I want to see you. I miss you, and I miss Jaden. You must know that.'

'Even if I do, nothing has changed. You understand why I'm doing this. I told you when you last came to see me.'

'You did, and I've been thinking about it ever since. I'd still like to see you for a while. That's all I'm asking. You can sound off and say whatever you like, but that's what I want.'

Lorraine didn't respond. Natty's heart raced. He didn't expect everything to be resolved immediately, but he wanted to at least know they were going in the right direction.

'Come to my mum's for dinner. We can talk afterwards.'

A surge of warmth spread through Natty's body as he grinned.

'Thank you, Lo.'

'Don't thank me yet. We're just talking, and part of that conversation is going to involve you explaining to me what you were doing dancing in a club and having the time of your life.'

With that, Lorraine hung up. Natty chuckled. He'd known Poppy would say something to her, but he didn't mind having the conversation. Ultimately, he hadn't done anything wrong.

Taking another breath, he stowed his phone and then carried on with his jog, planning on at least another two laps before he finished. He considered whether to plan what he was going to say, or if he should just speak from the heart, ultimately deciding to do so.

It had worked for him in the past

ZAYAN AND GHAZAN were at their safe house, cleaning their weapons and checking ammunition. It had taken a while, but they had finally mined the intel Conrad had given them. Natty was well-respected and highly placed in the organisation. When they took him out, his murder would throw things into disarray.

'Is everything in order?' Ghazan asked, brow furrowed in concentration as he held the pistol.

'Yeah. We know the main spot, so we can just wait for him there,' Zayan replied.

'I still think we should snatch him and go to work. He'd have more information than anyone else we've dealt with so far,' Ghazan said.

'If we can catch him slipping, then we should. There's a reason the times we've tailed him have failed, though. He moves like he knows people are watching him.'

'When we trap him, he'll sing any tune we like. Jakkar is going to want an update, and that would be much better than admitting we don't have enough yet.'

Zayan considered his partner's words. He wasn't wrong. They'd experienced some success thus far, but he'd expected to have the situation resolved by now.

Zayan and Ghazan went where they were told, killed who they were supposed to kill, then went about their way. The Dunns were deep and well-insulated, though, which was surprising.

Zayan and Ghazan hadn't expected much, assuming the organisation was overrated. It was easy to gain a rep these days. Some good fortune and well-placed contacts were often enough to hoodwink people. To their surprise, it appeared the Dunns didn't fall into this bracket.

Jakkar wouldn't care. He'd given them a directive and expected it to be carried out. Nothing but the murders of everyone pertinent would satiate him.

'We'll capture him if there's an opportunity. If there isn't, we'll kill him and move on. Deal?'

'Deal,' said Ghazan. He slid to his feet and stepped away from the table. 'I'm going to wash my hands and then look for some food. What's your plan?'

'I've still got some work to do here.' Zayan motioned to the guns. 'I'll warm up some food when I'm done, then I'm going to sleep. I want to be well-rested for what comes next.'

THE NEXT NIGHT, Natty left the Dunn's main spot in the centre of the Hood, heading for his car. He'd spoken with a few people inside, getting a feel for how the crew was doing. He'd seen Spence earlier, noting his mood seemed better.

Stefon hadn't been around, and Natty intended to call him later on and get an update. He was buzzed over seeing Lorraine and Jaden, and was wondering how he should play it.

The best thing he could do was approach the situation with an open mind, he mused. Lorraine had always appreciated when he spoke his mind and took what she was saying into consideration. He hoped history would repeat itself.

'THERE HE IS.'

Zayan and Ghazan were in their car, parked down the street from the main spot. They knew that many of the Dunn crew hung out here. Conrad had said business was occasionally discussed, but that everything was kept clean. The place was often checked for bugs and surveillance, and no contraband was kept on the premises. That was likely why Natty Deeds felt comfortable there.

Ghazan surveyed the Dunn Family Underboss. He was a tall, powerfully built man, who had an edge, and reminded Ghazan of the British Boxer, *Anthony Joshua*. He didn't have much respect for black criminals, finding them to be flashy and loudmouthed, but Natty Deeds was an impressive figure. He seemed to be in his own world as he walked to his car.

'We're on.'

Zayan nodded, sliding out of the car, gun at the ready. Two steps, then he aimed. Just as he pulled the trigger, Natty ducked.

'Damn!' Zayan cursed, firing off another round. He lunged forward, gun poised for the kill shot. But Natty sprang up, letting loose a rapid burst of gunfire. Bullets whizzed past Zayan, one grazing dangerously close. He dropped to cover.

At that instant, Ghazan flung the car door open. Reinforcements spilled out from the main spot.

'Get in!' He told Zayan, who back-pedalled, climbing into the car and driving away as Natty and the other men fired shots at the retreating vehicle. Ghazan erratically span the car around and zoomed away down the street.

Natty stared after the car, breathing hard, his heart pounding. They had almost got him. He'd been in his own world when he'd noticed the car out of the corner of his eye. When he felt the man's attention on him, he'd gone with his instincts and ducked, finding cover behind a car.

'Natty? What's going on?' One of his men asked. He had a smoking gun in his hand and a serious expression.

'Someone tried to pop me. Lock down the spot. You two, come with me.' Natty ran to his car with two men following. They jumped in, and Natty peeled off, driving after the shooter.

––––––––

'ABSOLUTE MADNESS.'

Natty tuned out the words, staring at his phone. There were a myriad of missed calls and text notifications, none of which he cared about. He was sitting with Spence and Stefon, having finally caught up with them.

Two hours had passed since the Asians had attempted to shoot him. He'd got word to Mitch about what had transpired, and everyone remained on alert.

It was a sign for Natty that he needed to be more vigilant with his movements. He had come too close to dying once again, and only freak reflexes had saved him. There was no guarantee he would get a second chance in similar circumstances.

Hovering by Lorraine's name, he took a deep breath and tried calling again. His call was sent straight to voicemail.

Sighing, Natty attempted to hide his devastation. He had missed his shot, and was painfully aware of the fact. Lorraine had given him a chance, and he'd blown it.

After the shooting attempt, Natty and his men had driven around for nearly an hour. Unsure of the direction the shooters had gone in, they'd spun the block on a few streets, finding nothing. With all the stress afterwards, getting people in line, evacuating the spot and relocating people, time had gotten away from him. It was a poor excuse, but that was all he had.

'Nat?'

Natty glanced up. Stefon and Spence had undoubtedly finished their conversation, both looking at him. Stefon had a glass of whisky in front of him, the bottle within reach. Spence had a glass too. The only person not drinking was Natty, though he mused that he probably should have been, after the night he'd had.

'Yeah?'

'What's the plan? People are out for blood. They tried to hit you outside one of our spots. Half the crew want to go to war with every Asian man they see. The other half wanna keep their heads down and stay out of the fray.'

Natty had expected this. Shaking off his thoughts about Lorraine completely, he focused on business.

'No retaliation unless I deem it necessary. We're not trying to start a race war here. Spence, get word to the chiefs. If anyone does anything dumb, I won't be happy.'

'Got it.' Spence nodded.

'There has to be some sort of retaliation, though,' Stefon said. 'We can't let them get away with it.'

'We're not going to, don't worry about that. The problem is that I didn't get a proper look. There were two of them, though. One was driving, the other was shooting. If they'd had their way, they'd have popped me and got clear before anyone realised what was happening. Either way, we need to find out who they are, and then take them out.'

Stefon grinned. 'Good. We'll take care of them. Just have to narrow them down. What about the other thing with your unc? We can't be everywhere at once with just the three of us.'

Natty had been thinking the same thing.

'My unc goes on the back burner for now. We can't leave this threat unattended, and he isn't making moves against us right now. We'll neutralise the shooters, then we can regroup. We can't fight a battle on two fronts. Not with the resources we have. If you get the chance, though . . . do what we discussed, and see if you can get him to trust you.'

Stefon slowly absorbed this, finishing his drink.

'I've left a few messages. I'll keep you posted when I hear more. I'm gonna go rest up, anyway. Shout me tomorrow, Nat. We can go hunting when you have a plan.' Stefon slapped hands with the pair, then left.

'Are you okay?' Spence asked Natty, watching him grab the whisky bottle and take a swig. Taking a second to savour the burning feeling in his chest and throat, Natty shook his head.

'No, not really. The shooting I can deal with. It's fucking common-place for me nowadays.'

'What's the problem then? You've looked out of sorts all evening,' Spence said.

'I was meant to meet Lorraine earlier,' Natty said. 'In fact, I was on my way to her mum's to have dinner when it all popped off. I got so caught up in tracking the shooters that I lost track of time and didn't get in touch.'

Spence nodded his understanding. 'I'm guessing that you looking at your phone before was you trying and failing to get through to her?'

Natty blew out a breath. 'Yep. Back to square one.'

'Just go and see her. Explain the situation, and she'll understand. I'm not saying she'll like it, but she'll understand.'

'I shouldn't. Not right now. If these guys are on me, I need to keep my movements as simple as possible. I can't let them get anywhere near Lorraine or Jaden.'

Spence watched Natty take another swig, feeling his pain. The streets didn't want him to have an easy run at the moment. To him, it

THE DEED IS DUNN

seemed that every move Natty made was being blocked at multiple ends.

Reaching out, he took the bottle from his friend.

'No more drinking, Nat. You've got a busy day tomorrow. Get your head down and get some sleep. Any problems can wait until then.'

It was a sign of how exhausted Natty was that he didn't argue with Spence. Patting him on the shoulder, he left the room. Spence watched him go, finishing his own drink, analysing everything the trio had discussed.

There was an angle he was missing. He was sure of it.

———

'THAT DID NOT GO WELL.'

Zayan's nostrils flared at Ghazan's words. They were back at their spot, having disposed of the car they'd used. Both men were furious. In their years of wet work, they had never failed to execute a target. They'd made things harder for themselves now. The Dunns would be on full alert, and Natty would be there to lead the charge.

'No. That's an understatement,' Zayan said. 'I don't know how he knew I was about to shoot. If it wasn't only the pair of us in the know, I'd think he was tipped off.'

'He moved like he'd had training,' Ghazan said. 'Nothing in his dossier mentioned that.'

'It mentioned that he'd killed before, though,' Zayan pointed out. 'It just didn't clarify that he had real skills.'

'We needed to know that sort of information. If we had, we could have planned differently.'

'We should have done that anyway. We underestimated Natty Deeds, and we paid for it. Next time, we'll have to be better,' Zayan said.

Ghazan checked his phone, sighing.

'C'mon. He's waiting.'

———

THE CAR HUMMED in silence as they reached the meeting spot, a secluded back street in Seacroft. Jakkar sat in the back of a Range Rover, sharply dressed as ever but with a scowl etching lines into his face. The air thickened with tension as they climbed in beside him.

'Talk to me,' he said, sparing any greetings. Two men sat in the front of the vehicle, neither paying attention to the conversation.

'We picked our targets. As mentioned before, we sent a message by burning the money at one of the main Dunn stash spots, and leaving a man alive to tell the tale. We also got hold of a major facilitator, who has given key intel on the movements of the organisation,' Ghazan said.

Jakkar shook his head.

'These aren't the bits I am interested in, and you're aware of that. Don't tell me what you've done. Explain to me what you failed to do.'

'Natty Deeds managed to slip away.'

'Did he? Slip away, that is?' Jakkar's voice remained quiet, but it was thick with anger. 'The word on the street is very different. It makes him sound like Superman, defending himself against two armed men . . . men that were forced to flee. You failed to get the job done, and you exposed yourselves.'

Both men silently took the rebuke. Arguing back would only make things worse. After a long moment, Jakkar spoke again.

'I'm putting a clock on it. You have two weeks to finish the entire operation, or you will be replaced.' Jakkar signalled for the pair to leave. They climbed from the Range Rover, which motored away.

Zayan watched after the Range Rover as it sped away, shaking his head.

'We've got work to do,' said Ghazan as he glanced at his partner.

'Yes,' Zayan replied simply.

The pair headed for their vehicle, already deep in thought about what to do next.

Jakkar had laid down the law. If the Dunns weren't eliminated in two weeks, Zayan and Ghazan would be.

CHAPTER TWELVE

'LO, WHY ARE YOU SITTING OUTSIDE?'

Lorraine looked around at her mum, who stood in the doorway. She had been so lost in her own thoughts that she hadn't even noticed it had started to rain. Now that she was back on earth, she realised just how cold it was, and stood

'I just got carried away thinking,' she said, rubbing her arms. Her mum stepped aside to allow her in, locking the door behind her.

'Sit,' she said, pointing to the kitchen table. Lorraine almost rolled her eyes. Her mum couldn't help treating her like she was still a child. She found it endearing, knowing she meant well. Lorraine watched in silence as her mum made her a cup of tea, then slid into a seat opposite her. Lorraine thanked her, holding the cup and taking a tentative sip, appreciating the warmth.

'You need to think about the baby, Lo. You can't be outside freezing half to death for no reason.'

'I know, mum. It won't happen again.'

'It better not. Shall I take a guess at what you were thinking about?'

'I'd rather you didn't,' Lorraine said.

'Have you told Natty yet?'

Lorraine shook her head.

'He rang me the other day. Sounded sincere and like he really wanted to talk to me, so I agreed to see him.'

'And?' Her mum surveyed her, waiting for the answer.

'And nothing. He didn't show.'

'How come?'

'Was I supposed to ask?' Lorraine's grip tightened around the cup.

'You're supposed to ask if you were curious, or if you really wanted to see him. I know that you were, and I know that you did, so yes, you're supposed to ask,' her mum said.

'He stood me up, mum. Maybe that's his way of showing he's ready to move on?'

'Is that what you want? To move on, I mean?'

'Why are you asking me so many bloody questions?' Lorraine snapped.

'Watch yourself.' Lorraine's mum shot her a hard look, and Lorraine sighed.

'Sorry. I didn't mean that.'

'I know you didn't. Just like you know I'm right to ask. What exactly do you want to do, Lo? And don't start with that nonsense about moving out or whatever. You can stay here as long as you like . . . you and that ladykilling grandson of mine.'

'He's not a *ladykiller*,' Lorraine said. 'He's an upstanding young man, and he's going to treat ladies with respect.'

'With his stepdad whispering in his ear and telling him how to get women, I doubt that.' Her mum sniggered at the expression on Lorraine's face.

'This isn't about Jaden. Jaden's a good boy, and he will be fine.'

'I know. Natty's a good boy too. We both know that. He cares about you.'

'I care about him too, but he hurt me. I don't know where I stand with him. I don't know why he stood me up, or what he's involved in. There's so much I don't get, and I'm tired all the time, and I'm stressed, and—'

'And, you should speak to him. Properly and openly. On your own terms. He needs to know what you've got growing inside you, and you need to think about what type of life you want to have for your child.'

'Mum . . . you're not silly. You know exactly what Natty does . . . what he's into. Are you telling me you want me around that . . . that you want your future grandchild around that?'

'I want you to be happy, Lo. I trust you to make the right decisions. You have good instincts,' her mum said, shooting her a fond, reassuring smile.

'Good instincts got me saddled with Michael,' replied Lorraine, her stomach lurching as she thought about her ex, eyes closing as she imagined his twisted expression looming over her. Her eyelids clamped down tighter as the scene played out in her mind. When they finally flickered open, they set on her mum.

Lorraine was suddenly thankful she wasn't home alone. *In that living room. The scene of a crime she felt sure she would never forgive herself for.*

She took a deep breath, exhaling audibly.

'You made a mistake. We all do. The important thing is that you learned from it. You had an amazing son, and you found a man that loves you both. Natty has never treated Jaden any differently. In fact, he's always been there for him. That has to count for something, no matter what his faults may be.'

'What would you do if you were in my position?' Lorraine asked. 'Natty's out there, doing dangerous things. There's all this crap going on, and I . . .'

'Take a deep breath,' her mum instructed. 'To answer your question before you go off on a tangent, I would think about what I knew about the man I loved, and I'd ask myself a simple question.'

'Which is?'

Lorraine's mum stood, leaning over and taking Lorraine's hand into her own, giving it a slight squeeze.

'Would he no-show a meeting with me, without a really good reason, and how badly do I want to know what that reason is?'

Lorraine didn't say anything. Her mum gave her another fond smile.

'Seriously. Talk to the man. Make the decision you think is right, but bloody talk to him, and tell him he's going to be a dad. Turn off the lights before you go upstairs, and remind my grandson that I'm not silly. I know when he's been up half the night playing on that silly computer.'

'I will, mum. And thank you.'

'Anytime, darling.'

When her mum closed the door, Lorraine sipped her lukewarm tea, still mulling over things in her mind. Despite knowing that her mum was right, it didn't make Lorraine's thoughts any easier. She hadn't felt like she was at full capacity for a while, and this ongoing situation wasn't helping matters.

Slipping to her feet as gracefully as she could, she emptied the remains of the drink down the sink, then shuffled out of the kitchen, turning the light off behind her.

———

MITCH SIPPED A GLASS OF WINE, deep in thought as he always seemed to be nowadays. Events were moving far quicker than he had anticipated. The fact that someone had again taken a shot at Nathaniel was telling, and made him wonder once again if it was a sign he should move on. With every one of these instances, the mystique Mitch had worked so hard to attach to his name seemed to dissipate.

They were becoming far too accessible.

In the past few months, Nathaniel had been the target of multiple attempts, and someone had attempted to kill Mitch, as well. Someone who remained at large.

It boiled Mitch's blood to imagine some faceless man, laughing to his friends about getting one over on him. He felt like sending his men to kill people at random, as a warning, a way to re-associate fear with his name.

He stopped himself before he delved too deeply into that scenario, though. He needed to be smarter than that. Rushing out impulsively was his brother's way, not his. Tyrone had lit fires everywhere and left them to burn. He took offence at everything and wanted the world before they were in the position to take it. For all his toughness and strength, he possessed little long-term thinking.

Mitch sipped his drink, imagining Tyrone fitting into the world he had built. He'd made it to the top, and had outlived all of his rivals. Not only that, he'd done it his way, walking the political tightrope and acting only when necessary.

If Tyrone was alive, Mitch would have had fewer problems right now. He doubted Rudy would have turned on him, and he certainly wouldn't be worrying about his nephew.

The fact he was still unable to truly deduce what his nephew was up to, remained a sore point. Nathaniel was supposed to be a blunt object. He had potential, but he often gravitated towards impulsiveness, hitting first and asking questions later.

Just like his dad.

Then there was Nathaniel's other side. His calculated, methodical nature. His way of getting things done, not always cleanly, but effectively. He was liked, respected, feared nowadays, since Mitch had given the go-ahead for Clarke to train him.

Had he made a mistake?

He needed to make a decision, and he knew it. He'd flirted with the idea of binding Stefon to him. Nathaniel's cousin was solid and could fit into a lot of the roles that Nathaniel occupied.

On top of that, he'd been attempting to contact Mitch for days, wanting a meeting. It seemed the stars were aligning.

Finishing his glass of wine, Mitch made up his mind. Nathaniel would be occupied with the Asians — more so than ever after their attempt on his life. He wouldn't be able to focus on Stefon, so Mitch would.

Sliding to his feet, he grabbed his phone, ready to make the call.

———

'TALK TO ME.'

Harding was behind his desk, watching Daniels. The investigation wasn't moving as swiftly as he liked. His teams had gone out as ordered and begun compiling intel on the Dunns, but he had nothing concrete, and nothing he didn't already know.

In Harding's view, it was the fault of those in charge of the purse strings. In dealing with numerous cuts and layoffs, they'd been forced for too long to simply maintain, with not enough money made available for quality policing. With Harding's record of getting results with shoestring budgets, the higher-ups had shoehorned him in with a specific mandate: Slow down the local crimes, and stop the killings.

'Someone took a shot at Natty Deeds.'

Harding's eyebrows rose.

'Takes balls to go at the heir to the throne. Who's our money on?'

Daniels shrugged. 'Fuck knows. People have said it's some Asian gang looking to take over, but I've heard nothing else to back it up. No gangs I can think of seem to fit the profile, and no one is claiming the hit.'

Harding frowned and continued to survey his relaxed colleague.

'Didn't someone take a shot at Natty a few months ago?'

'I think it was nearer than that, but yeah, they did,' said Daniels. 'He was at a house party, and some cowboy tried to get him. They didn't hit him, but someone else at the party was shooting. We had someone in custody, but we couldn't link him to the scene.'

'Did anyone ever follow up with him?' Harding asked. Daniels shook his head.

'We didn't have a case. I think Brown was working on it, but I'm not sure. I'd have to check the paperwork.'

'Check it, please. If Brown was involved, based on what we know now, there's likely more to that situation than meets the eye.'

Daniels yawned.

'Right, I get that. How's it gonna get us closer to taking these lot out, though? Natty's never gonna cooperate with us against his uncle, and he's hardly gonna share who tried to kill him.'

'If we can get something on him, he might not have a choice,' Harding said. 'We need to get results. That means we have to reach out and try things, and we have to be willing to get out there.'

Daniels shrugged. 'You're the boss. I'll get it sorted and see what I can put together.' He checked the time on his watch. 'It's getting late. What time are you heading out?'

'It'll be a while yet,' Daniels absentmindedly said, already opening a document on his computer. 'See if you can find that paperwork before you head out.'

'Got it.'

When Daniels closed the office door behind him, Harding took a sip of his lukewarm coffee, seeing it as a blessing. He'd had six cups throughout already, and it was getting to be a problem. He looked around for his water bottle, but couldn't see it. The more he considered it, the more he realised that Natty Deeds was perfectly placed to cause maximum damage to the organisation. It was imperative that they found some way to reel him in.

Harding clicked open DI Brown's file. He would need to request the notes from the cases he'd been working on, he mused. Maybe that would show whether they had anything tangible on the Dunns. He couldn't prove it, but he suspected Brown had been working with the Dunns, before he became surplus to requirements.

There was an angle here. He was sure of it.

CHAPTER THIRTEEN

MITCH WAITED for Stefon to be shown in to see him. He sat behind the makeshift desk in the office he'd had set up. He'd had little chance to use it, as most of his business meetings had been done over the phone lately. He needed to get back some sense of normality. Before things spiralled too far out of his control.

Stefon had a frown on his face as he stood in the doorway. He was a strapping man, similar to Nathaniel. The more Mitch saw him, the more he approved. There was a place for him, as long as he could continue to conduct himself appropriately.

'Sorry about the cloak and dagger,' he said, signalling for Stefon to take a seat. 'As you can appreciate, it's vital that I remain out of sight for now, with everything going on.'

'I get that,' Stefon said, shaking his head when Mitch offered him a drink. Mitch took a sip of the white wine he'd brought in. He used the seconds to further assess Stefon, noting he didn't squirm or appear nervous.

'I've been meaning to speak with you for a while, Stefon. We had quite an illuminating conversation a while back. Do you recall?'

Stefon nodded, not giving anything away. Mitch mentally marked it as another positive. He liked people who were calm under pressure.

'You spoke about Nathaniel, and some of the issues he was having with his mother. I reached out to Tia, and we had an interesting conversation.' Again, he checked Stefon, and again he showed nothing. He would need to be more direct. 'Did Nathaniel say anything to you about his father . . . namely, the circumstances behind his murder?'

There it was. Stefon tried to hide it, but there was a slight flicker. He knew what Mitch was talking about, but Mitch continued, ready to twist Stefon to his way of thinking.

'What were the circumstances?' Stefon did an admirable job of side-stepping the question, and Mitch allowed it.

'There are two sides. There's the side Nathaniel may believe, and then there's the truth. I love my nephew, but his father was taken from him just when he needed him the most. I was busy building my empire, and I didn't have the time to school him the way I should have. That meant he was raised by an emotionally damaged woman.' Mitch paused, taking another sip, noting that Stefon had leaned forward slightly, ready for more information. Inwardly, he smirked.

'Tia was tough on Nathaniel. She was also less than complimentary about his father, and she committed what Nathaniel clearly viewed as a sin when she became involved with one of my subordinates. You remember Rudy, right?'

Stefon nodded.

'Rudy turned on us. He was removed because of that. He was disloyal, and nothing he said or did could be trusted, including the information he fed to my sister-in-law. . . information she fed to Nathaniel.'

'You're saying that Natty believes something happened, that isn't true?' Stefon's frown deepened.

'Precisely. The 2000s were wild, and I know you're old enough to recall just how many conflicts and beefs there were at the time. You had Teflon's team vying for power. That shit with Wisdom. Delroy and his people. We were doing our thing, and then you had the Yardies, running around shooting and stabbing everyone. It was a melting pot, and unfortunately, all of that led to the death of my brother.'

'And that's the truth?' Stefon asked. Mitch nodded.

'Yardies killed my brother, Stefon. Nathaniel believes that I ordered his murder, but that isn't true. I would never have done that. Do you know what I did do, though?'

Stefon shook his head.

'I had the crew responsible for my brother's death eliminated. A Yardie named Snypa was a big deal back then. He was warring with my brother, and they killed him and his crew. I retaliated in kind, and had them and their allies wiped out. It was a costly, arduous battle, but they touched my family.' Mitch stared into Stefon's eyes. 'I put my family before everything. I always have and always will.'

Stefon swallowed. 'Why are you telling me this?'

'Because you're working alongside my nephew. That means you need to pick your moves carefully. I don't quite know what he has going on, but there's a lot on his plate. So . . . help him. Provide counsel. Find out what he needs, and if there's anything you think I need to know, then tell me.'

Stefon's eyes widened for a brief second, as if Mitch's words had jolted him. Then, his brow furrowed, and his jaw tightened. 'You want me to spy on Natty?'

Mitch shook his head. 'I want you to protect him. Whether from himself or others. Things are changing, and we have to change and adapt with the times. You've come back to Leeds at an opportune time. There's a lot up here for you to get stuck into, and the right person could rise just as quickly as my nephew . . . I think you fit that path well.'

Stefon didn't say anything, but Mitch knew he was digesting everything he had been told.

'Take some time, think things over. My men will give you a private number for me. Anything you think I need to know, share it with me. In the future, we can have another talk about your path . . . if events play out correctly. Sound good?'

'Yeah, that sounds good, Mitch.'

Mitch smiled.

'I said it before, and I'll say it again. You were always a good kid. My men will take you home, and we'll speak again soon.'

———

STEFON PULLED up outside the temporary hangout spot the team had moved to after Natty's shooting attempt. Climbing out, he checked his gear in the wing mirror, ensuring his appearance was neat.

Mitch's words had stuck with him, and it had definitely clouded his thinking a little. Mitch had sounded sincere, like an uncle who was concerned about his nephew. At the same time, Natty had sounded confident, and Stefon had chosen to believe him.

Despite telling Natty he'd update him once he'd made contact, Stefon had yet to do so. There was still a lot he needed to unpack. He'd come to speak with Spence, to gain his thoughts on the situation. Spence was in a similar predicament; he too had pledged loyalty to Natty, no matter the opposition. It was likely he would be able to relate.

Heading inside, Stefon greeted the guys that were hanging around, heading for a backroom to see Spence. He entered the room with a spring in his step.

'Yes, Spence. What's happen—'

He stopped short. Spence was there, but he wasn't alone. The backroom was fairly roomy, and had a sofa, a love seat, two wooden chairs and a small table.

Spence was sitting on a wooden chair, and a beautiful woman was sitting on the sofa, her legs crossed, with an expression that tinged on amusement on her face. Her eyes met Stefon's, and he took the opportunity to continue checking her out. She was slender, with alluring features, dark hair, and a strength to her demeanour that he dug.

'Stef, good to see you. Have you two met before?' Spence asked, his eyes alight as he took in the vibe between the pair.

'You seem familiar, but I'm not sure,' Stefon said, his eyes remaining on the woman.

'Lisa, this is Natty's cousin, Stefon. Stefon, this is Lisa. She's a key member of the crew.'

'Nice to properly meet you,' Stefon said, remembering. Lisa had been there when they took out Roman and his men, but with the urgency of the situation, and the high stakes, he hadn't paid much attention to her. Lisa nodded, eyes still studying him.

'You too, Stefon. You were in Leicester, right?'

'Yeah, I thought I'd come back up here and fuck my cousin's world up,' Stefon joked. Lisa giggled.

Spence simply watched the byplay between the pair, struggling to keep the grin off his face.

'Anything that involves unravelling Natty is fine with me. I think you met one of my friends at that party you went to ages ago, with Spence and Natty. It's good to be on proper speaking terms with you,' Lisa said.

'It's good for me too. If you'd been at the party, I'd have definitely got you a drink.'

'Just one?' Lisa's eyes sparkled.

'For starters.'

Lisa's smile widened, her tongue tracing the bottom of her upper teeth. She slid to her feet in one movement.

'I'll leave you alone, Spence. I can see that you have business to attend to.'

'Don't leave on my account. The more, the merrier, as far as I'm concerned,' Stefon said.

Lisa shook her head.

'I have other things to do, but I'm sure we'll see each other again,' she said silkily.

'Sooner rather than later. Count on that,' Stefon replied. Lisa's smile remained on her face as she said her goodbyes to Spence and left. When she did, Stefon finally noticed Spence, who was beaming.

'Fuck's wrong with you?' he asked. Spence chuckled.

'Are you okay? Do you need a minute to yourself after all that?'

'All what?'

'You two trying to burn the house down with the looks.'

'It's nothing. We were just talking. She's sexy, though,' Stefon said, thinking again about the mysterious beauty. 'What's her story?'

'Nothing you don't already know. She's a specialist. Clarke trained her too. She's dropped plenty of bodies.'

Stefon scratched his chin.

'Do you think I should watch myself if I'm getting involved?'

Spence nodded. 'I'd advise it. She's lovely, but she marches to her own beat, and you never know what direction that's gonna lead her in. Anyway, forget Lisa for now. What did you want?'

'I wanted to talk to you about Natty and his unc.'

Spence straightened in his seat.

'This might be a conversation to have at the safe house. Shall we get some food and head over?'

———

STOPPING at Maureen's restaurant on Roundhay Road, they ordered jerk chicken and dumplings, then drove to the safe house. Natty wasn't there, and Spence hadn't heard from him since earlier. Organising the food and taking seats, Stefon spoke.

'I met with Mitch, at Natty's behest.'

Spence nodded, pulling a face as he ate his chicken.

'This is strong,' he said, letting out a breath. 'Yeah, Nat mentioned something about that. He thinks you could spy for us.'

'That was the plan.' Stefon filled Spence in on the conversation he'd had with Mitch, Spence listening and continuing to eat.

'You two said a lot,' Spence finally said. 'Do you think he was telling the truth?'

'I don't know,' Stefon admitted. 'I trust Natty, but what if Mitch is right?'

Spence sighed.

'I can't tell you how to think, Stef. There's a lot on the line, but you need to make sure you're in all the way, no matter which side you go with.'

Stefon frowned.

'Aren't you worried about my loyalty?'

Spence grinned.

'Not at all, fam. I trust you, and I trust Natty too. More than anyone. He is positive Mitch was involved, and that's enough for me. I've weighed up all the facts, and frankly, I believe Mitch ordered the hit.'

Stefon placed the remnants of the food on the coffee table next to Spence's.

'You're right, bro. I appreciate you listening. I'll keep doing what I'm doing, and see what I can shake loose.'

'If you ever need to talk some more, I'm here. For now, let's talk some more about the love connection between you and our beautiful killer.'

Spence laughed as Stefon elbowed him.

CHAPTER FOURTEEN

HARDING STRAIGHTENED his shoulders as he entered the room. Levelling Barry Stryde with a look, he took a seat in front of the dishevelled man, trying to keep his disapproval from his face. Barry had squirmy features, a thin nose and crooked teeth. He wore expensive designer clothing, but with no panache, the jacket he wore appearing overly washed and dull. He looked at Harding obstinately, then looked away, casting his eyes around the room.

'Do you need a reminder about why you're here?'

'I know that you can't hold me for nothing,' Barry replied, baring his discoloured teeth. Harding folded his arms.

'Maybe I should make my position clear. Based on that response, you obviously don't understand,' he said primly.

'Are you saying I'm dumb?' Barry scowled.

'Even if I was explicitly saying it, you couldn't do a thing about it. I've seen your type many times before, and that's why I know exactly how this conversation will go.'

'I told the last guy you sent in here. I dunno anyone called Natty Deeds.'

'Barry, I know that you know. That's already been established,' said Harding, shaking his head. 'By lying and pretending otherwise, you're simply wasting both of our time. I suggest you get with the program and share what I want you to share.'

'I'm not saying a fucking thing. When my solicitor gets here, you're fucked.'

'Gets where?' Harding gestured around the small, boxy room. 'This isn't an interview room. This is simply two people talking, one of whom is far more powerful than the other. I know you've dealt with my subordinates before. Maybe the name *Detective Brown* means something to you. The fact is that I outrank them all, and right now, I have my eyes firmly placed on you. That's not a good position for a criminal like yourself to be in.'

Barry opened and closed his mouth, gulping, clearly trying to maintain his composure. It had been a while since Harding had conducted such an investigation. He usually liked to oversee them and comment on the interrogator's technique, but he was glad he'd decided to do this one. He'd continued digging into the Dunns after the shooting attempt on Natty Deeds, and using what Brown had noted, along with the words of confidential informants, he'd linked Barry Stryde to a shooting attempt several months ago.

Barry had been picked up and taken to a small room in the police station. It was used for witnesses and family members to gather themselves during intense situations, but Harding had commandeered it for his use, not wanting to use an interview room, where he would have to explicitly follow procedure.

'I don't know anything. Keep telling you, but you're not listening.' Barry tried again, but it was clear his heart wasn't in it.

'Let me tell you what I know. Someone hired you to shoot at Natty Deeds. You heard he was at a party, and you went with the intent of killing him. Not only did you fail to do so . . . you were also wounded at the scene. Honestly, it's shocking that my officers weren't able to make charges against you stick.'

'Probably a sign you're wasting your time too,' Barry said, a smug look appearing on his face.

'You think?'

Barry nodded.

'I don't know shit. Didn't do shit. I'm not arrested, so I don't even have to be here.'

'Leave if you want,' Harding started, watching Barry immediately stand and move towards the door. 'When you do, though, there's no going back.'

Barry paused. 'What does that mean?'

'It means that I will focus my considerable resources on you. Everything you're doing. Who you're doing it with. I believe you're linked to *Kirk*, a criminal well-known to us. When we started tearing apart his operation with targeted raids, I'm sure he'll treat you fairly when he learns you're responsible.'

'You can't do that!'

'This isn't an official interview. You haven't been charged, yet. Help me, and then, quite frankly, you can go back to your pathetic existence.'

Barry's lips trembled as he looked around the room, as if searching for instigation. He placed his hands on the small round table in front of him, then sighed.

'I tell you what I know, and that's it, right?'

'That's it for now. As I said, you won't be my focus. I don't care much about what you do, but there are things that need to be fixed in Leeds, and right now, you can help me do that.'

Barry wiped his face. 'Look, all I know is that Deeds has got enemies. Get me? They told me to do him. Paid good money for it too.'

'Who told you?'

'Asians. I don't know any of their names, but they weren't English ones.'

That piqued Harding's interest. The men who'd attempted to kill Natty Deeds recently were rumoured to have been Asian men. Harding was sure there was a connection, but he needed to find it.

'How much were you paid?'

'They offered me twenty-five grand,' Barry said.

'Why you?'

'They thought I could get close to him.'

'What happened?' Harding asked.

'You know what happened. I messed up. Couldn't get the job done.' Barry fidgeted, cheeks pink with embarrassment.

'How?'

'I took my cousin along. He was watching out for Deeds and his people. Sent me a text when they were in place, and then I went in.'

'You took a live pistol into a party full of people?'

Barry quaked at Harding's stern tone.

'I didn't take out the gun until I saw Deeds. I didn't even aim it at anyone else. When I went to shoot him, though . . . I dunno.' Barry's gaze drifted away for a moment, as if replaying the scene in his mind.

'What does that mean?'

'He was quick, that's all.'

'So?'

'So, I've never seen anything like it. He moved like one of those assassins in the films. I missed my shot, and then one his guys shot me. I got out of there in the confusion, and went to get my arm checked out.'

'Which one of his men shot you?' Harding leaned forward. Despite Barry's shooting being mentioned, no one had stated he'd been shot by Natty Deeds' people. If they could learn who, they could leverage them against Natty.

'I dunno. Honest, I don't. He was a big guy, though. Didn't get much of a look at him, but he wore a lot of jewellery. Had on a white t-shirt, I think.'

Harding noted the details, determined to learn who the man was. Tracking him down would be a priority.

'What happened after?'

'Nothing. I had to give back the upfront fee, and I went back to my business. After, though, Deeds caught up with me. Dunno how he learned I was involved, but he gave me a beating and made some threats. I told him that the Asians paid me, and he let me go.'

'Just like that?'

Barry nodded.

'That's all I know. I swear.'

'Okay,' Harding said. 'I might contact you to verify some points of the story, but for now, you're in the clear. I suggest you make the most of the second chance you're being afforded. I promise that if you're caught again under any circumstances, you're finished. Understand?'

Barry nodded, standing and shuffling to the door. Harding remained seated, going over the facts in his head. The investigation so far had borne little fruit, and it was a sad state of affairs that none of the people on the case had dug into the files to locate witnesses, as Harding had. A weasel like Barry shouldn't have been able to go under the radar.

Sighing, Harding finally stood. He would need to locate Natty's shooter, shed light on the party shooting, and then plan his next move accordingly.

———

TOMMY RICHARDS LED his kids up the path to his mum's house, listening to their chatter. His conversation with Natty had been on his on his mind and despite Natty advising he didn't need the assistance, Tommy had decided to speak to his sister, and see where her head was at.

Knocking on the front door before opening it, he instructed the kids to take their shoes and coats off.

'Tommy, I didn't know you were coming over,' his mum said, allowing Tommy to kiss her on the cheek.

'I've been meaning to come for a while, but I've had a lot on,' Tommy said, his voice full of affection.

'It's nice to see you now, anyway,' she replied. They entered the living room, where Jaden was watching television, and Lorraine was reading a book. She smiled at her brother, and he gave her a quick hug, then bumped fists with Jaden.

'How's it going, sis?'

Lorraine shrugged, then greeted her niece and nephews, before focusing on Tommy again.

'Everything's blessed. You?'

'All good,' Tommy said. 'Can we have a little chat in the kitchen?'

Lorraine flinched, but quickly gathered herself.

'Sure.'

Their mum looked between them for a moment.

'Take your time. I'll spend some time with my grandkids.'

Lorraine followed Tommy into the kitchen, wondering why he was acting so serious. They hadn't spoken in a while, but they were on good terms. Things had been prickly when they were younger, but they had worked past it.

Lorraine sat at the worn oak kitchen table, debating whether to make a drink, but deciding against it. She glanced around the kitchen as Tommy rooted around the cupboards, finding their mum's stash of wine and pouring himself a glass. He looked so funny standing there holding his wine stem, Lorraine had to force herself not to laugh.

The current subject would likely distract her, she mused. It had taken a few minutes, but she'd gathered why Tommy was here, and it wasn't to enquire about how she was.

'What do you want to know?' she asked.

'Don't play dumb, sis. I know why you're here. What I wanna know is why you're not with your man?'

Lorraine's nostrils flared. She should have seen it coming. Natty wasn't the kind of guy to leave things to chance. When Lorraine stopped responding, he'd switched tactics and gone after her brother.

'What did Natty say to you then? Did he tell you about me following him and what I saw? Or did he tell you about the fact he arranged to come and see me so we could talk, and then didn't turn up?'

'I ran into him a while ago, and yeah, he told me about the shit at the house, and what you saw him do.'

'What do you think about that?' Lorraine shot her brother another measured look as he sipped his wine.

'I'm not happy you were caught up in it, but I know Natty. He'd never let anything happen to you if he could help it.'

'What about the fact he was at the house with another woman?' Lorraine strongly believed she'd made peace with what she saw between Natty and that Lisa woman, but it didn't stop it from popping back up to the surface every once in a while.

'A woman that works for him. You don't know the game, sis.

You're best off out of that, but he's your man. You can't punish him for some shit like that.'

'You weren't there. You didn't see how closely they were sitting together,' said Lorraine, gripping the cup tighter in annoyance.

'So what? Who cares? Natty's your man. Do you think he'd step out on you?' Before Lorraine could open her mouth to reply, Tommy spoke again. 'That man loves you. He's always loved you. Even when you were both younger and bullshitting, messing around with other people, you still loved each other. If you'd got serious back then, that dickhead Raider would have never been in the picture.'

Loraine closed her eyes for a moment. She hated the moments where she was forced to think about Jaden's dad, and the trauma he'd put her through.

'We can't change the past. Still, I can't just roll over and pretend everything is okay. How did he seem when you spoke to him?'

'Stressed,' Tommy admitted. 'He carries it well, though. Natty's a real dude.'

'You used to hate him when I was younger,' Lorraine pointed out.

'I hated any dude that was trying to fuck my little sis. Natty's grown up, though. You can see it in how he carries himself, and you had a lot to do with that shit.'

'I guess,' Lorraine replied, her eyes sweeping across the room. Tommy observed her intently.

'So are you going to forget all this shit and move back home with your man?'

Lorraine paused, gathering her words. Before she could respond, Jaden burst into the room.

'Mum, can we have pizza for dinner?'

'Jaden, we were talking,' Lorraine scolded.

'Sorry, mum. I didn't mean to.' Jaden looked so chastened, that Lorraine felt bad.

'It's okay. Just be careful next time. When me and uncle Tommy are finished, we can order something. Ask your cousins what they want.'

'When we're finished, we can have a few games on Fifa too, Jay. I've heard you think you're good,' Tommy said.

While Jaden laughed and agreed with his uncle's assertion,

Lorraine went over what she and her brother had discussed. Deep down, she liked the fact he had taken up for Natty and was speaking on his behalf. They'd clashed when she and Natty were younger, but over time, a mutual respect had developed between the pair.

When Jaden headed back into the living room, Lorraine locked eyes with her brother again.

'Well?'

Lorraine shook her head. 'I can't give you a simple answer, bro. I'm still working things out.'

'While you're doing that, he's suffering. He needs you, Lo.' Tommy poured the rest of his wine into the sink, then headed into the living room, lightly gripping Lorraine's shoulder as he did so.

Lorraine sighed, finishing her own drink, then trudging to the sink to do the washing up.

It would pile up again later, but washing up was good for collecting her thoughts, and she needed that right now. She wondered if Tommy knew even more than he'd let on about the situation. It seemed he did.

'Mum?'

Lorraine turned. Jaden was watching her from the doorway.

'Can we order now? Uncle Tommy said to ask you.'

Lorraine nodded, smiling.

'Okay, baby. I'll be there in a minute.'

CHAPTER FIFTEEN

'WHAT IS THE MEANING OF THIS?'

Zayan brooded in the corner of the social club. The house had been built in the forties and had been well-maintained over the years. In the nineties, one of Jakkar's subordinates bought the property, then proceeded to do nothing with it. Now, it was used for the occasional private gathering, and for specific meetings such as the one taking place. It had several chairs against the far wall, a thick dark brown table, and a light yellow sofa to the side.

Zayan sat on one of the chairs. Ghazan remained on his feet, a glass of sparkling water in his hand as he glared at the two men sitting at the table.

'A situation has cropped up in Nottingham.' Ahmed gestured to a file on the table. 'Jakkar wants you both to handle it.'

'What situation?' Ghazan asked. Zayan's usual approach was to provide no verbal backup. Ghazan had been annoyed with this approach when they both started working together, but over time, he'd realised that it was to their benefit. If Zayan started speaking his mind, they often ended up in trouble, and they were already on the cusp of it.

'One of our agents down there was killed. The man who did it needs to be eliminated,' Mustafa said.

'We have a job up here.'

Ahmed nodded. 'As we said, this situation has transpired. Jakkar has stated it takes priority. Handle it efficiently, and maybe he'll remove that timeline he put on you handling the Dunn job.'

'How do we know this isn't a ploy to get us killed?' Ghazan asked. He didn't like Ahmed and Mustafa. He trusted in their ability to follow Jakkar's orders, but didn't trust them directly.

'The pair of you are meaningless to us. This is a lucky situation for you. The way things are going up here, the Dunns will likely track you down and kill you both, based on your blundering of the attempt on Natty Deeds,' Mustafa said.

Ghazan's eyes flashed, but he held his tongue.

'Who is the target?'

'Everything you need is in the dossier there. We have links that can get you weaponry, and we've booked train tickets for you both. You leave in the morning, so get some rest.'

———

NATTY STEPPED into the house located opposite Saville Park in Chapeltown. He always had mixed feelings in the area. Months ago, he'd been lured to an ambush, managing to escape by the skin of his teeth after shooting one of his attackers. Despite the fact those who had ordered the hit were dead, he remained wary.

'Just this way,' said Sajid, his voice light as he led Natty through the hall. Natty was armed but hoped he wouldn't have to use it. He could hear voices coming from various rooms, but paid them little attention. Stefon and Spence knew where he was. It wouldn't prevent anything in the short term if it was an ambush, but he would have to deal with that if it occurred.

Sajid and his contemporaries had their hands in a lot of pies. They worked in and around Chapeltown, with both legal and illegal ventures, selling drugs, running fraudulent scams, and offering protection to others in exchange for lucrative cuts.

'We've been working on this place for months,' said Sajid. 'This place used to be two separate houses, but we got permission after we bought them, and knocked out the walls between them. We've got these spots all over the place. Tell you what . . . if you're ever looking to get involved, I know a few houses you might be interested in. Buy them cheap, then do what you want with them.'

'I might take you up on that, bro. For now, let's stick to this,' Natty said.

Sajid chuckled.

'I can't believe you're like this now,' he said, shaking his head.

'Like what?'

'Like a boss, man! You always had skills, but you were small-time. Now you carry yourself differently. It's mad to see.' Sajid's eyes widened, and he leaned in closer, as if unable to contain his excitement.

That made Natty grin, despite himself. He'd known Sajid for years. They'd gone to the same high school, remaining close despite the racial tensions between the blacks and Asians at the school. It wasn't uncommon for vicious attacks to take place after school, and it often spilled into the streets, with assaults becoming commonplace.

Being a Dunn, Natty was largely protected from the skirmishes, but still had his fair share of fights. He and Sajid had been paired together in a few classes and realised they had similar interests. They'd gone in separate directions after school finished, but like Sanjay, Sajid remained a valuable associate, and the pair had done business together several times.

'Whatever, man. Just took me a bit longer to get here.'

'That's cool,' Sajid said. 'You did it. That's all that matters. Anyway, they're in here.'

The room Sajid led Natty into was nicely laced. There was a large leather sofa, several comfortable-looking armchairs and several random paintings on the walls.

Two men were sitting, smoking and talking amongst themselves. They looked up when they saw Natty, giving him sharp nods. At first glance, they didn't seem like much. Both were shorter than Natty, with average builds and features. Their eyes were hard, though, and Natty could see the slight shifts in their demeanour as they gave him the same quick assessment, pegging him as a potential threat.

'Natty Deeds, meet Urfan and Nadeem. Guys, this is Natty Deeds. I know you've heard the name.'

Both men again nodded, but said nothing. Natty returned the gesture.

'Take a seat, Nat,' Sajid urged. Natty sat on one of the chairs, facing the pair. He couldn't see any weapons within sight, but his was within reach if things got messy. He assumed the pair would have taken similar precautions.

'How is it you think we can help?' Nadeem asked, taking another drag of his cigarette. 'Sajid didn't give us much. Just said he wanted us to meet a friend of his.'

'I had a recent situation. Two dudes tried to kill me when I was leaving a house. I shot back and they ran off. We looked for them, but they were in the wind. They were both Asian.'

'You think it was us?' Nadeem asked.

Natty shook his head.

'Sajid has vouched that you two are proper. All I want is some information about where to look, and who to focus on.'

'What makes you think we can help?' Urfan spoke for the first time, his voice deceptively light compared to his partners'.

'I don't know if you can, but I'm hoping so. I'm willing to pay for information. Cash or favours, whichever is easier.'

The pair shared a look, silently communicating. Natty waited them out, understanding how to play the game. If he rushed for a response, he would only alienate them further.

'What's the plan when you get them? They were probably hired, which will only tip off the people who did it,' Nadeem said.

'I'm pretty sure I know where the order came from, but I require proof. Either way, they've affected my business, and I need to stop them . . . one way or another.'

Nadeem continued to smoke his cigarette. Urfan reached for a nearby bottle of Coca-Cola and took a swig, sighing.

'It's dangerous getting involved in these situations, so you need to leave our names out of it. The favours can come later,' Urfan said. 'There's a few different people doing contract work at the moment. Some of them are exclusive. Others go wherever the money is.'

'These guys have attacked my business three times. They attacked a stash spot, killed one of our major facilitators, and then they tried to attack me. Does that narrow it down for you?' Natty asked.

'A little. Like I said, there's a few different people, but I'd put my money on Zayan and Ghazan,' Urfan said.

Natty sat forward, rolling the names around his mind and coming up with nothing.

'Tell me about them.'

'Not much to tell. They've worked for different people, but they're highly recommended and ruthless. I've heard they're on retainer, but I don't know who for. They don't just do tap jobs to the back of the head. When they need to, they're willing to maim and torture to get what they want.'

'Where can I find them?' Natty asked.

'You can't, really. They don't have a fixed address. They roam, and do what they need to do. Honestly, the best way to find them is just to do what you're doing. If they tried to kill you once, they'll try again, so stay on guard.'

'I will. Thank you for the assistance,' Natty said. It didn't seem like they had given much, but he had potential names now, and he could use that to acquire more information.

'Don't rush off,' said Sajid. 'Let's have a drink, and we can talk some more about my sidelines. I think you'll like what I have to say.'

Natty shrugged. He didn't have any urgent meetings to attend, and he was definitely intrigued.

'Let me make a quick call, and then I'll be right with you,' he said, reaching for his phone to call Spence and Stefon.

————

Leeds City Centre was a vision at night.

Something about the lights all around as winter approached seemed to do something to people. Despite the chilly weather, couples were out in droves, holding hands, laughing and listening to one another's stories as they walked along.

Inside a nearby restaurant, Stefon noticed little of this. He was far too focused on his current company. The soft glow from the sleek, modern interior of the restaurant seemed to illuminate the night. A soft hum of conversation filled the air, accompanied by the clinking of cutlery and the occasional laughter.

Lisa sat across from Stefon, sipping her wine, eyes twinkling as she looked at him. After they'd bumped into one another, Stefon had convinced Spence to get her details so he could contact her. They'd flirted via text and when he'd asked her out, she'd agreed.

Stefon ate some of his food, weighing up what he wanted to say, and how to get to it. Lisa was definitely worth the effort. He noted that immediately. Stefon had a way of dominating women, using his charm and magnetism to get what he wanted. He had a feeling that Lisa might be different, but he wanted to see what happened.

'What do you think of everything that's happening at the moment?' he asked, again looking into her eyes. Lisa was enjoying her meal, and he liked that she didn't appear self-conscious about tucking in, in front of him.

'I think there's a lot I don't know.' Lisa's head tilted slightly as she appraised him, and Stefon smiled. She suspected he knew something, but likely also knew there were things he couldn't tell her. He knew she was a killer and a honey trap for the organisation. She was deadly and in the wrong hands, not someone he'd want to test his skills against.

Still, he wondered how loyal she was to Mitch.

'You and me both. Feels like I've only been here two minutes. I'm still trying to work things out. The scene is different from Leicester, that's for sure.'

'Tell me about it.' Lisa leaned forward, a warm, yet teasing smile on her face, the sight of which made Stefon's blood thrum.

'Not much to tell. I had my little piece of what was going on down there. Lived good, but not too good. People were always watching, but I was known, and I had a good rep.'

'Why come to Leeds then?' Lisa's eyes twinkled with interest, her brows lifted in anticipation. The teasing smile had turned into a look of sincere engagement, and she bit her lip slightly, eagerly awaiting his reply.

'I felt like an outsider down there. As decent as I was doing, I wanted more. I've got kids down there. Mums are around, but they stay quiet as long as the money comes in.'

'I didn't know you had children,' Lisa said.

'You're still getting to know me, aren't you.' Stefon winked. There was a brief silence as they both ate. The waiter came and asked if they wanted more drinks, both choosing to have another glass of wine.

'Tell me about your children.'

'I have two girls. Both young. Their mums knew one another, so that caused a lot of hassle that I had to sort out. Towards the end, it was nonstop stress, so I thought about it, and decided Leeds might be the place to get it done. I used to be active up here, and I knew Natty was doing his thing, so I came back.'

'How are you finding it?'

Stefon wasn't sure how to answer. His time since returning to Leeds had been interesting, and turbulent. From clashing with Natty to pulling guns at parties in defence of the crew, to getting on board with Natty's vision and pushing it forward. It felt like he'd been back for years.

'Feels like I never left. Shit moves differently up here. I knew Natty was doing well, but not this well. He's changed a lot.'

'How has he changed?'

Stefon was surprised at the interest in Lisa's voice, but wrote it off as her simply wanting to know more about someone she worked with.

'He was a hothead before. Full of himself, not wanting to listen to orders. He's done a lot of growing up now, and it shows.'

Lisa nodded, seemingly satisfied with his response.

'So, you're up here to make more money and look after your kids. I like that. Far too many parents find it easier to abandon or neglect them.' A dark look flashed across Lisa's face for a moment. 'You spoke earlier about the unrest. What do you think is causing it?'

Stefon finished his food, wiping his mouth and gathering his words. He had no intention of revealing any details about the plan, but that didn't mean he couldn't at least feel Lisa out to see where her head was at.

'A few things,' he started. 'Natty and his uncle . . . maybe they've reached the end of the road.'

'What makes you think that?'

'The decisions that have been made lately. That business with Roman, for example. Mitch pushed that. Everyone else was cool with just doing business and making money, but he insisted on a dangerous course of action that led to all the shit happening.'

'You think Mitch was behind it?' Lisa asked.

'I know he was. We both do.' Stefon wondered if he was burying Mitch too much, and pulled back. 'There's just a lot going on. People aren't really sure what's gonna happen next, and that can mean bad news for everyone. Spots getting attacked. Natty getting shot at again . . .' his voice trailed off.

'You've said some interesting things,' Lisa said softly. Stefon laughed.

'Yeah, you've been happy to let me do most of the talking.'

Lisa grinned.

'It's not by design. We just all have our roles, and mine doesn't involve thinking too much about the politics.'

'I get that, and I respect it. Do you ever worry about what's coming next, though?'

Lisa shook her head.

'One thing at a time . . . that's my motto. It makes dealing with things much easier.'

'I'm guessing that includes relationships too?'

'What makes you think that?' There was a teasing lilt to Lisa's voice as her eyes roamed over his frame for a moment.

'Just a feeling. You do everything on your own terms. I doubt there's a man or woman on the planet that could dictate to you, or tell you what to do.'

'I don't know about that. We all answer to someone, but I'd like to think that if I truly didn't like something, I'd say no.' Her eyes met his again, seemingly beckoning Stefon forward. For a moment, he was lost in the beautiful, glittering dark pools, but he composed himself. He was stronger than this. *Than her.*

'That's good to know.' He took another sip of his wine. 'I'm glad there's no other men I'm competing with. We could definitely have some fun together.'

Lisa nibbled her lower lip for a second, beaming.

'I'm sure we could.'

The night went on. They had a few more drinks, then dessert, before Stefon paid the bill and they left the restaurant. Both moved easily through the city centre, unencumbered by the cold.

Stefon stopped short, dramatically sighing as Lisa raised an eyebrow.

'I have a dilemma,' he said, a smile creeping to his lips as he tried to remain serious.

'Oh?'

Stefon reached into his pocket, pulling out his wallet and opening it.

'It's empty. I spent all my money on that delicious meal we just had, and now I can only afford one taxi.' His eyes gleamed as he surveyed Lisa. 'Guess you'll have to come back to my place.'

Lisa's eyes sparkled as she leaned in close, pointing to the credit cards in his wallet.

'No need to pay attention to those,' he said, smirking. 'What do you say?'

Lisa assessed him for a long moment. He felt his heart racing in a way it hadn't previously. Stefon couldn't remember the last time he was nervous about being rejected. There was definitely something about Lisa. He kept up appearances, though, outwardly looking confident.

Finally, Lisa grinned.

'I think we definitely have more *learning* to do.'

CHAPTER SIXTEEN

CLARKE WAS in the kitchen washing up. He'd spent a lot of time on his feet over the past day, and it felt like his body was finally handling the strain better. He was taking longer trips to the park and had even done a few short barbell workouts to get his strength back up.

Paula was still worried he was overdoing it, and it was difficult to work out when she was around, but Clarke wanted to be back to full strength as soon as possible. If that meant keeping his daily routine from Paula, it was worth it in the long run.

'Do you want a hand?'

'No, lad. I've got it covered,' Clarke said as he picked at a persistent stain on a plate with his forefinger. Danny stepped into the kitchen, grabbing a bottle of water and uncapping it, standing close to Clarke, but not impeding his movement. 'Everything okay?'

Danny glanced around, making sure he'd closed the door behind him.

'What's going on?' he asked shiftily, his eyes darting left to right.

'With what?' Clarke finished washing the final bit of cutlery, wondering if it was worth investing in a dishwasher. He'd lived without one all of his life, but he was getting older, and was more geared towards convenience.

'The streets,' Danny said, as if that was obvious.

Clarke wiped his hands, then went to sit at the kitchen table, signalling for Danny to sit with him. They heard loud voices from upstairs, along with footsteps, but paid little attention.

Clarke liked Danny a lot. He'd taken him under his wing from an early age, and was proud of the man he was growing into. Danny was diligent and attentive, took his boxing seriously, and was always respectful.

To hear him asking about the streets was surprising, but Clarke forced himself to remember that it was a different world nowadays. Youngsters were far more in tune with the streets, and social media had taken it to a whole new level.

That being said, it wasn't a subject he intended to discuss with him. He was a good boy, and the further away from the streets he was, the better.

'Nothing.'

'I'm hearing differently,' Danny said. 'No disrespect. I'm not trying to crowd you, but look at you. You got hurt. Mum doesn't say much, but I've heard her crying a few times. I just wanna know what's going to happen.'

Clarke respected the approach. Paula remained terrified that he was going to get himself killed, and he couldn't convince her otherwise. She had stuck by him through a lot, and had seen him get himself into some scrapes in his younger days. For a moment, a wave of guilt surged through him. He resolved to sit her down and have another conversation as soon as possible.

'Nothing is going to happen, and there's nothing to worry about, Dan. I just want you to focus on your schoolwork and your boxing. Leave everything else to me.'

'Clarke . . .'

'Seriously, Dan. It's nothing. Answer me something now: Was it your girl who asked you about me?'

Danny frowned. 'Why would you ask that?'

Clarke paused, wondering if he'd put his foot in it. Deciding to keep going, he internally shrugged it off.

'I know she's been around some street guys. I've never asked you whether you're doing any dirt out there, but if you are, it needs to stop.'

'I'm not,' said Danny hotly. 'Rachel's spent time around some of those dudes, but that's behind her. She thought it was exciting, but something happened that scared it out of her. She won't tell me what, but it was enough to show her she shouldn't be hanging around with those people,' Danny said.

Clarke hid his smile. Rachel had fallen foul of Natty Deeds a while back. He'd rushed one of Roman's stash spots, scaring the life out of those in the house. Rachel was one of them. Natty had delivered a more thoughtful and compassionate message to her, but it had done the trick regardless. Clarke was pleased she had taken those warnings to heart.

'Good. Look, I won't lie to you. There's a lot going on, but to reiterate, it's nothing you need to worry about. You have enough on your plate already.'

Sighing, Danny nodded, lightly patting Clarke on the shoulder. Grabbing his bottle, he left.

Clarke watched after him, hoping he could back up his words. He needed to speak with Natty again, and gain some more insight into what was going on from his perspective. He'd always seen the younger man as easy to read, but he couldn't get a fix on him nowadays.

Slowly, over time, Natty was becoming much more effective, and Clarke wondered if that would be a problem. Standing, Clarke was about to make a cup of coffee when his phone rang. He pulled it from his pocket, peered at the number for a moment, and then answered.

'Yes?'

'I'm outside. We need to talk.'

Mitch hung up before Clarke could confirm. Instantly, Clarke tensed, his street senses alert. Mitch hadn't contacted him so abruptly in a while, and when he did, he always asked Clarke to come to him.

Wondering what could have changed the protocol, he pulled on a jacket and headed out.

A black Range Rover with tinted windows idled by the curb, not a sound coming from it. Clarke climbed in the back, noting his boss rubbing his knuckles and staring down. Mitch glanced up at Clarke and nodded as Clarke closed the door behind him, and settled on the leather seat.

In the front, Morgan was in the passenger seat, with Otis driving. Otis nodded, smiling at him, hands resting on the steering wheel.

'How's the recovery coming along?' Mitch asked. Clarke wondered why he had come with Morgan to ask him this. He'd worked with Morgan in the past and found him to be diligent and very analytical. He had his strengths, and they were being put to work making Mitch more money. He had numerous financial connections and was skilled at putting the crew's money to work. He wasn't as active in the street side of their business.

Morgan based out of an office in Armley. The location was discreet, and only those Mitch truly trusted were privy to its whereabouts.

The concept was simple, but smart. In the event of an attack, Morgan was far enough away to ensure Mitch's money was safe. This made him crucial to the long-term ambitions of the crew.

'Day by day. I'm doing more exercise, trying to stay on my feet more. I have a checkup next week.'

Mitch nodded again, looking away from Clarke, checking his phone.

'I'm asking because I need you back in the fold as quickly as possible.'

'Is there something happening?' Clarke asked quickly.

'We're at war, Clarke,' Mitch said slowly, as if speaking to a child.

'We've been at war for a while. Your nephew is on top of it, right?'

Mitch stared at Clarke, who met his gaze unflinchingly. There was more going on here, he was sure of it. *Why wasn't Mitch including Natty in battle planning?*

'Nathaniel could benefit from your experience. His focus is on numerous things at the moment, and you can offer some much-needed structure. If your recovery allows that, of course . . .'

Clarke nodded.

'I'll speak with him. See what I can work out.'

Mitch smiled, but it didn't meet his eyes.

'Excellent. If there's anything going on that you think I need to know, tell me. Okay?'

'Understood.'

'Good man. Give my love to Paula and the kids.' Mitch didn't explicitly say it, but the meeting was over. Clarke climbed out without a word, and the vehicle motored down the street.

Clarke watched the Range Rover disappear, frowning. He didn't know what to make of it. Mitch had seemed rattled and almost annoyed by Clarke's presence. Morgan being at the meeting and not saying anything was also strange.

Clarke headed into the house, moving to the kitchen to finish making his drink.

There was a lot to unpack, but he would be sticking to his word and speaking to Natty to find out more.

————

NATTY PEERED into his empty cup, wondering if it was worth going to make some more coffee. It was after midnight, and he had been up for hours, trying to make sense of everything that was going on.

He'd made multiple calls and floated the names *Zayan and Ghazan* among people, but nobody seemed to know them. Not who they were, nor who they were connected with. This shocked Natty. In his position, he had the resources he needed to pull information on almost anybody. The fact he couldn't find anything on Zayan and Ghazan was telling.

Sanjay was also proving more difficult to get ahold of, which concerned Natty. They hadn't been particularly close in the past, but they could always count on each other for honest and open conversation. Natty had never struggled to pin Sanjay down for a meeting, so he found the current struggle to do so frustrating, but intriguing. Big things were happening in the city, and battle lines were undoubtedly being drawn.

Natty hoped Sanjay's lack of presence wasn't a sign he had chosen his side.

What *side* that was, remained to be established. With all roads seemingly pointing to Jakkar, it was clear to Natty he'd inherited more of his uncle's problems.

A small smile curled the corners of Natty's mouth as he considered the situation. By now, Mitch was no doubt aware of the dual threat Natty and Jakkar posed to him. Remarkably, those threats were now focused on each other, rather than their original target. His uncle had positioned himself exceptionally, and Natty couldn't help but admire the play.

Mitch had warned Natty about Jakkar in the past. The chilling caution cemented an image in Natty's mind of a man not to be messed with. The fact that his uncle appeared to have outmanoeuvred Jakkar so effortlessly was surprising. Jakkar's men had failed in their attempts to take Natty out for the second time. Their approach had seemed as disjointed and inconsistent this time as it had the first.

So much of the situation made little sense to Natty.

Despite his confusion, some things were clear. Natty was sure Jakkar's men wouldn't stop hunting him until they completed their task. Given his uncle's warnings, he expected future attempts to be more thoughtful and thorough.

Now, more than ever, he needed allies.

Natty tapped his fingers against the porcelain rim of the cup, weighing it all up. Releasing the cup, he grabbed his phone and checked the notifications. There was still nothing from Lorraine, but she'd seen a message he'd sent her earlier. She hadn't replied, which tore at him.

He didn't want to pull back completely and make her think he didn't care, but attempting to keep close seemed to be having the opposite effect.

Natty navigated the contacts in his phone, analysing the names as he went. With pressures mounting, he needed to speak to somebody who could help him make sense of the situation.

As he approached the end of his contacts, Natty's thumb hovered over Spence. His best friend was often the perfect sounding board. He was grounded and intelligent, and his opinion was something Natty valued above most things.

Natty's eyes darted from his friend's name to the time at the top of the screen. It was late, and Spence had worked a long shift. His sensible friend was likely asleep, and Natty didn't want to unsettle him.

Natty's eyes returned to his contacts list. Tracing down from Spence, they landed on Stefon. Pushing out his bottom lip in consideration, Natty shrugged and called his cousin.

It took longer than he had expected for Stefon to answer, and Natty was sure he could hear giggling and shuffling in the background as he waited for his cousin to speak.

'Stef?'

'Shit . . . yes, cuz. You good? Summat happening?' Stefon sounded distracted and tired. Natty's eyes narrowed as he attempted to get a read on the situation.

'Sorry. Did I wake you?'

'Yeah . . . kinda . . . shit. I'm ready, cuz. What's up?'

'I just wanted to run some stuff by you, but if you're tired, it's cool,' Natty said.

'I'm not tired . . . I mean, I am, but. Ouch!'

Natty heard the laughing once more. Finally understanding the situation, he relaxed, rolling his eyes before smiling. Stefon had company, and Natty was intruding.

'Are you at it again, Stef? You need to chill, bro. You're going to pull a muscle.' Natty smirked.

'Nah, this is different,' Stefon replied. Natty rolled his eyes once more.

'It's always different, bro. I'll leave you to it anyway. Have fun.'

'I will, cuz. Speak to you in the morning.'

As Natty pulled the phone away from his face and motioned to end the call, he heard a third voice. It was silky and seductive. It was . . . familiar. As his phone beeped three times, signalling the end of the call, he stared off into the room, deep in thought.

After a moment, his eyes widened.

Lisa.

Natty placed his phone on the table, glaring down at it, deep frown lines creasing his forehead. He could feel his heartbeat increasing and an uncomfortable warmth spreading throughout his body. Rising to his feet, he began pacing the room, attempting to piece together what he had uncovered.

The time of night, the close proximity of the two, the giggling and shuffling; it all pointed to one explanation, but it was a conclusion that Natty seemed unwilling to accept.

Lisa had become a thorn in his side since they had shared their kiss. An unwanted complication in an already complicated relationship. In moving on, Lisa was giving Natty everything he thought he needed to make things work with Lorraine.

It was a gift Natty coveted as much as he resented.

Natty stopped pacing, shaking his head.

Was Lisa playing him all along?

After a moment, he took a deep breath, exhaling audibly. *Of course she was*, he mused. Lisa played everyone.

Dropping his head slightly, Natty smiled as relief washed over him. This game appeared to be over, and he was happy that he'd given it as good as he'd got.

Natty grabbed a bottle of water, uncapping and draining half of it. Tidying the table, he picked up the phone and headed upstairs, going to the bathroom to get ready for bed.

The night pondering had surfaced more questions than answers.

Despite this, some things had become clearer, and Natty knew what he needed to do next.

CHAPTER SEVENTEEN

THE NEXT NIGHT, Natty headed to Jukie's spot. He'd bothered Amanda enough with his problems lately, and he didn't want people to get used to him hanging around the same spots. Lately, he suspected people were tailing him. He'd switched up his car, and had started driving in random directions, just in case. So far, nothing had come of it, but he remained vigilant.

Stefon had reached out to him in the morning, checking if everything was okay after Natty's call when he was with Lisa. He hadn't mentioned her, and Natty hadn't either, but both were aware he'd sussed it out.

Natty wondered what would happen between the pair. He considered speaking to Lisa and seeing what she said. If she was messing his cousin around, or trying to get under Natty's skin, he wanted to know. Hopefully, he was done with her games for good.

Jukie's wasn't as busy as Natty expected. There were a few regulars, drinking and playing cards and dominoes, and one or two faces he didn't recognise.

Nodding and greeting a few people, Natty scanned the room, looking for Jamie. He ran the spot on behalf of his uncle, and the pair had always got along. Despite the vaunted neutrality of Jukie and his family, Natty had often been able to get nuggets of intel from Jamie that had aided him.

To his surprise, Natty saw Jamie at the bar, but he wasn't alone. A well-dressed man was talking to him. Natty could only see his profile from the back, but couldn't immediately place him.

As he approached and Jamie saw him, Natty noted with surprise that Jamie's expression blanched. He filed the reaction away, not breaking stride, grinning and holding out his hand, which Jamie took and shook.

'Nat, how's it going, bro?' he said neutrally. When Natty's name was mentioned, the other man turned, and he and Natty surveyed one another.

Morgan.

Natty had met him enough times in the past to know him by sight. He hadn't changed since the last time they'd met. He wore glasses, had no facial hair and had his hair cut short. He wore a cream designer sweater, jeans and a pair of trainers. Morgan was around ten years older than Natty, but didn't look it. He had a confi- dent, worldly expression that befitted his status in the Dunn organ- isation.

'Nice to see you, Nathaniel,' he said, the pair also shaking hands.

'You too, Morgan. It's been a while.'

'Let me get you a drink.' Morgan was already signalling to Jamie.

'The usual, please,' Natty said, wondering what the pair had been talking about. Jukie's was a spot where anyone could go, without fear of attack, and the old man had worked hard to keep it that way. Long after his semi-retirement, the rules still applied.

Natty took his brandy and coke from Jamie, sipping it by the bar. He'd hoped that Jamie and Morgan would continue their conversation, but he seemed to have spooked them.

After a few seconds, Natty moved away. He'd planned to track Morgan down, but had been focused on his attackers. Seeing him now had caught Natty off guard. Sitting in the corner of the room, he nursed his drink, letting his thoughts wash over him.

Morgan was one of his pathways to Mitch, but Natty was unsure how that would even work. What he needed was more information on

Mitch's actions, but he would have to work Morgan over to get that information out of him.

He considered calling Stefon. Between them, they could overpower Morgan, but there was a risk they would be discovered. Jukie's spot hadn't earned its reputation for nothing; Natty was sure it would be kitted out with the best surveillance equipment possible.

'You look like you have the weight of the world on your shoulders.'

Natty blinked slowly, the blurry bar coming back into focus. He turned his head, looking up at the figure before him. Morgan had made his way over while Natty was deep in thought. He had a smirk on his face, motioning to the table.

'Mind if I sit?'

'Go for it,' Natty said.

'You and Jamie are close, right?'

'I've known him for years, yeah,' Natty said, wondering where Morgan was going with it.

'Is he trustworthy?'

If Morgan had asked Natty earlier, he'd have answered without question. Now, he took a second, still unnerved by the look on Jamie's face when he'd seen Natty.

'As trustworthy as he can be, running this place,' he finally said. Morgan smiled.

'Mitch always speaks about how sharp you are. Sounds like he wasn't exaggerating.'

'No disrespect, Morgan, but why are you over here?'

Morgan raised an eyebrow. 'Straight to the point?'

'Best way to be,' Natty said. 'If you have something to say, then say it. If you're over here to make friends, then the next drinks are on me.'

Morgan grinned. 'You've come a long way. I always knew you would. I won't lie and say I don't have an agenda where you're concerned, but I guess I'm more curious than anything.'

'Curious about what?'

'Honestly, I'm wondering why you've been asking around about me.'

Natty fought hard to keep his expression neutral, but Morgan's words shocked him. Natty had barely scratched the surface in his search for Morgan; early on, he'd asked around about Morgan, and the potential moves he might be making in Armley, but that seemed like a lifetime ago.

Maintaining his composure, he took another sip of his drink.

'I was curious,' he admitted.

'I figured. What do you want to know?' Morgan's smile grew.

Natty had to play it carefully here. His mind whirred as he considered what Morgan knew.

Did he know Stefon and Spence were in cahoots with him? Or would he naturally have presumed that? Where did he get his information from?

More questions circled his mind at a rapid pace until, finally, he went for it.

'What are you up to? I have sight of 90% of what's going on in the organisation. Guess you could say I'm curious about the other 10%.'

'Nothing nefarious,' Morgan replied. 'I'm trying to grow the organisation, same as you. That involves overseeing the monetary side of things along with your uncle, and reaching out into new markets.'

'New markets where?'

'There are a few places in mind. Beck Hill, maybe. On a small scale. You've done solid work in Little London that it would be nice to replicate, though it would be my intention to do it better.'

'Better how?'

Morgan grinned again. 'You haven't spoken with Jermaine in a while, have you?'

'What does that have to do with anything?' Natty hadn't. Jermaine had taken over the running of Little London after Carlton's murder. Natty hadn't heard much from him, and the money was still coming in, so he hadn't thought much about it.

Now, he was starting to.

'Speak to your subordinate. Maybe you and I can speak again in the future, see if we can put our heads together and come up with something better. After you've resolved that . . . problem for your uncle, that is.'

'Sounds good,' Natty said, trying not to grit his teeth.

'Excellent. I'm sure we'll run into each other soon. Oh, and Nathaniel?'

Natty looked at Morgan, whose smile finally vanished.

'Don't ask around about me again. You want to know something, ask me straight up. Got it?'

Natty's eyes narrowed. Rising to his feet, he stepped in front of Morgan.

'Mind how you speak to me,' he said. 'I don't take orders from you.'

Morgan smiled slightly. Picking up his drink, he drained it, placing the glass on the table.

'Not yet.'

Morgan patted Natty on the shoulder and, without another word, turned and left. Natty's eyes flitted between his shoulder and the door, nostrils flaring. He wished he had messaged Stefon earlier. They could have captured Morgan so Natty could teach him some manners.

Taking a deep breath to steady himself, Natty sat back in his chair. Giving the door one last glare, he finished his own drink.

There was a lot to unpack. Running into Morgan had been interesting. Natty wondered why Mitch was excluding him from the operation, and whether he should ask his uncle about it. There was a reason Morgan had brought it up. The line about Little London had been interesting, and he resolved to find out what was going on there.

Sliding to his feet, he glanced at the bar, noting that Jamie had been replaced with another man. Putting it from his mind, he said his goodbyes to a few people, and then left.

CHAPTER EIGHTEEN

NATTY REMAINED keyed up the day after his conversation with Morgan. While he acknowledged he had been taken by surprise, it still felt like Morgan had won the exchange. Natty didn't know who'd told Morgan he'd looked into him, but it reinforced his decision to limit who he divulged certain information to.

Clearly, not everyone could be trusted.

Natty had told Jermaine he would be coming to see him in the next few days. Jermaine hadn't sounded nervous, and Natty wasn't sure if that was due to his composure, or because Morgan had exaggerated his comments about Little London. He wasn't as involved in the day-to-day as Spence, but Natty was sure he would have heard if Little London wasn't performing as expected.

Natty had even considered going back and approaching Jamie about what he and Morgan had discussed, but didn't want to overplay his hand.

After a quick workout and a shower, Natty sat at his kitchen table, eating a quick meal. Spence had spoken to him about only using the safe houses when necessary, and Natty agreed it was likely a smart move. If he was right about the fact he was being tailed by people, leading them to the boltholes they'd set up would be foolish.

In general, things seemed to have quieted down on the streets. There had been no attacks on any of their spots, and if Zayan and Ghazan were still out there, they'd seemingly retreated.

As Natty finished his food and washed up, his phone vibrated. Wiping and drying his hands, he unlocked it, surprised to see a response from Lorraine to the message he'd sent.

> Hey Nat. Sorry for the late reply. Me and Jaden are good. Hope you are too xx

It was a short response, but Natty still smiled as he read it, before firing off a quick reply.

> Glad to hear it, Lo. We should talk again soon. Anytime you need me, just shout me.

Lorraine replied a few moments later:

> I will xx

That was enough for now. Natty viewed it as a step in the right direction. It had a marked impression on his mood, and he felt his smile widening as he finished tidying. His thoughts turned to another subject: Lisa and Stefon. He'd quickly made peace with the idea of the pair hooking up, but the more he considered it, the more Lisa's motives intrigued him. He'd been meaning to speak to her anyway, and with that in mind, he invited her over.

———

LORRAINE POTTERED AROUND THE HOUSE, deep in thought as she always seemed to be these days. Since speaking to her brother, she was trying to put things into perspective. Despite her irritation when they'd been speaking, she was touched that her brother was so loyal to Natty. Deep down, it reinforced the idea she'd picked the right man this time.

Whatever problems her brother and Natty had in their younger days, she knew they viewed the other with respect now.

Lorraine was thinking about the street life. Tommy had commented that she didn't understand. Being around Natty, she'd picked up the odd bit, but Tommy was right. She compared this to Lisa; how she'd moved, and how ruthless she and Natty had been when they'd laid waste to the men who attacked them. At first, it had sickened her. When Lorraine compared this to her struggles to push past what she'd done for Raider, it only intensified. It seemed so much easier for the pair, and every time she'd seen Natty after, he'd seemed fine . . . almost at ease with the murders.

Lorraine wanted to relate to Natty, but wasn't sure how. Pregnancy and their relationship aside, she wanted to be an asset; someone he could rely on, rather than someone he felt like he had to protect all the time.

As Lorraine considered her place, an idea came to her, and she smiled. Sitting down in the living room and grabbing her phone, she called Spence.

'Hey, Lo,' he answered. 'Everything okay?'

'Yeah. Are you busy? I have something I want to run by you.'

'Course,' said Spence. 'You caught me at a good time. Want me to pass through?'

'Yes, please,' Lorraine replied.

'No problem. I'll see you soon.'

———

LISA GRINNED when she entered Natty's place. Stefon had mentioned he suspected Natty knew about them, and she was looking forward to the conversation. He sat on the sofa, a bottle of water within reach on the coffee table, his hair a little longer and not quite as sharp as Lisa was used to. His facial hair had also grown out a little, leaving an even five o'clock shadow across his face. He wore a plain white t-shirt and black jeans.

Lisa's eyes surveyed Natty, taking in the unfamiliar image. It was different to what she was used to, but she liked it. It gave him a rugged, dangerous edge.

'How are you doing?' she asked, standing in the doorway.

'You can sit down if you like,' Natty said. 'I'm not going to bite you.'

'What if I want you to?' Lisa teased, placing her pinky finger on her bottom lip. Natty stared straight ahead, not noticing the gesture.

'I don't think Stef would like that.'

'Oh . . .' Lisa smirked. 'Is that what this is about? You want to interrogate me about your cousin?'

Natty shook his head. 'I'm curious, don't get me wrong. You both know what you're doing, though. In fact, you might even be good for each other.'

Lisa shook her head now. 'We're just having fun.' She surveyed Natty, wondering if he was being honest. 'Are you seriously telling me you're not bothered?'

'I didn't say that. But, truthfully, no. I felt a bit weird about it at first, but that annoyed me more than finding out what you two were up to. I had no right to feel like that. I'm with Lorraine,' Natty said.

'Why did you feel weird?' Lisa finally moved to sit down. She picked up the bottle of water, taking a long sip as she waited for his reply. Despite himself, Natty smiled.

'I don't know. At first, I was worried it was jealousy.'

'At first?' Lisa pressed.

Natty nodded. 'As I said, I have a girl, Lisa. I love her. That might sound weird to you or whatever, but it's the truth, and I already got far closer to you than I should have, and that fucked things up for me.'

'You're talking about what happened at the safe house?' Lisa tapped the knuckles on her left hand, still smirking.

'I'm talking about all of it. I shouldn't have kissed you. Shouldn't have flirted and played along, but I did, and I have to live with that shit. Lo and me are barely clicking, so you got what you wanted. But you moving onto Stefon is good for me. Despite what I felt when I first found out, I think it'll help her realise we were never a thing.'

Lisa's smirk faded. 'I told you. We're just having fun. Besides, it's not my fault that your girl's insecure.'

Natty avoided the obvious attempt to bait him.

'I can't really blame her. Before she gave me a chance, I was a bit of a dog. I got around, and I slept with my fair share of women. She took a chance on me, so when an attractive woman like you shows up, she's bound to feel a certain way.'

Natty picked up the bottle, taking a swig and staring straight ahead. Lisa watched Natty out of the corner of her eye, a smile spreading across her face.

'You think I'm attractive?' she said, her voice soft and sweet.

Natty scoffed.

'We're not playing those games, Lisa. You know you're beautiful, and you don't need me to reinforce that. Now, let's move on.'

'Fine. For what it's worth, I never wanted to cause trouble between you and Lorraine.'

Natty shot her a look, showing he wasn't convinced. Lisa giggled.

'Well, maybe a little trouble. But I liked you, Natty. I still do . . .'

Natty placed the bottle on the table, turning to face Lisa. He watched her eyes trace from his own, down to his lips. Shaking his head, Natty blew out a breath.

'Whatever you say. Listen, there's a lot going on. I know you heard that some people tried to rush me. I've got some names. We haven't heard anything from them in a while, but they're out to do a job. Everyone needs company. I want you to tell me if they reach out to any women you know, looking for some fun.'

'I'll handle them. No problem.' Lisa rubbed her hands together.

Natty shook his head.

'Keep them alive. If you get the drop on them, drug them and keep them there until I arrive. I need to know more about the man behind them.'

Lisa frowned, leaning forward. 'Which man?'

Natty scratched his chin.

'Our boss has beef with a man named Jakkar. The Asian bigwig whose people supplied Roman and Keith. Mitch's dealings with them have spilled over, and now we're having to deal with the mess.'

Lisa nodded.

'Okay. I'll see what I can do. Is there anything else you want to tell me?'

'Like what?' Natty looked nonplussed.

'How about, the stuff that's going on with you and your uncle.' For a moment, Natty saw the hurt flash across Lisa's face.

'Guessing Clarke told you about that . . .'

Again, Lisa nodded.

'What does he think?'

'I don't think he knows what to think. Are you sure, Natty? Like, really sure? It's a big accusation to be throwing around.' Lisa looked surprisingly earnest, and he found it touching.

'I'm positive. He had my dad killed. They couldn't control him, so they killed him, and Mitch gave the order.'

Lisa reached out to touch his hand, then seemed to think better of it, pulling back.

'So . . . what are going to do? The Natty I know wouldn't let something like this go.'

Natty was sure Lisa could see the alarm in his expression. His mind whirred as he struggled to formulate a response. The situation was spiralling out of control. He didn't want to overplay his position and have his uncle focus directly on him.

'Let's say I still am the *Natty you know,* and I had something up my sleeve. Would you follow me?' he finally asked.

'Would you want me to?' Again, Lisa met his eyes. Another long moment passed, Natty weighing up his words. The conversation was dangerous, and he knew his answer would move from talking in hypotheticals to actuals, and he wasn't ready to take that step yet.

'For now, see what you can find out about those dudes, and get back to me please.'

Lisa slid to her feet and headed for the door. Pausing, she turned to look at Natty again.

'You can trust me, Nat. I mean that.'

Natty said nothing as she left. Despite his words, he still felt the electricity between them, and wondered if it would ever subside. Taking a deep breath, he reached for the bottle of water and took another sip, happy to dip back into his thoughts and assess his next moves.

———

'THANKS FOR MEETING ME.'

Spence sipped the tea that Lorraine had made him. The pair were sat in her mum's kitchen. Jaden was playing on his PlayStation, and her mum was out running errands.

'Anytime. How are you doing with everything?'

Lorraine blew out a breath.

'Short answer, I've been better.'

'I can imagine. I know I've said it before, but I think it needs repeating. Natty would never hurt you.'

'Of course you'd say that. You're his friend,' Lorraine said, though there was no heat in her voice.

'I am. He's my brother, and I'd do anything for him. I'd even lie for him if I thought that's what he needed. But you know me, Lorraine. You're a good judge of character. So tell me, do you think I'm lying?'

Lorraine let out a harsh laugh. 'Am I? You know about my ex, right?' Lorraine ignored his question, gratified when Spence nodded.

'That was necessary. I know you've been beating yourself up about it, but you shouldn't.'

'I did something wrong,' she said softly. 'Something heinous and unforgivable.'

'We've all done it. Me, you . . . Nat,' Spence said. 'Sometimes you have to do it, and there's no going back after that. Your life was on the line, and that's the only thing you need to take into consideration.'

Lorraine shrugged. Natty had said similar in the past, and just like then, it didn't make it any easier. Slowly, she felt like she was coming to terms with it, but not fast enough for her liking.

Lately, Lorraine's sleep had become more consistent. She had more of an appetite and strangely, more energy. Sometimes, it seemed like she was prowling around the house, searching for things to do.

She'd been meeting with a counsellor her doctor had referred her to, and found the conversations mostly pointless. Lorraine couldn't be honest. She couldn't write anything down either, so a lot of the things in her head, she needed to come to terms with by herself.

She was sick of leaning on Rosie or her mum. She wanted to be brave and strong, but it was hard. She'd reached out to Spence in the hope he could provide a different perspective, one that could help her heal and grow.

Then, maybe she would be able to get her life back on track, she mused. Her mind flitted to her work. Angela had left several messages, and had indicated she wanted a meeting, a *friendly catchup* to see how she was feeling.

Lorraine knew this wasn't the case. She had worked with Angela long enough to know she didn't have her best interests at heart. She didn't have to go back to work. The doctors were happy to keep giving her sick notes, and work couldn't force her to go in.

The longer it went on, the more her sick pay would be affected, but Lorraine wasn't a splurger. She had savings she could dip into long-term if she needed.

The concerning factor for Lorraine was that she didn't want to go back to work. It wasn't just Angela. The more she thought about the job, the less appeal it held. After all her hard work to succeed, to push ahead in her chosen career; she just couldn't switch off and get back to it. Something else was calling her, and she wanted to work out what it was.

'Spence, how do you do what you do?'

'What do you mean?' Spence's eyebrows shot up.

'The life you're in. The risk. Mixing with certain elements . . .' Lorraine picked her words carefully.

Spence mulled over the question for a moment. It had surprised him. He hadn't had an agenda when Lorraine called him, but he'd assumed she wanted to speak about Natty or Rosie.

'I guess I'm just used to it. Like Natty, I've been around it all my life. I think, unlike Natty, I didn't grow up wanting to be exactly like my dad. It was exciting. Still is, but mostly, it's something I'm good at. Something I truly understand. I have my outlets, and what I do plays well into those.'

'By outlets, you mean investments?'

Spence nodded. 'I haven't put as much effort into it recently, but yeah. I have a fair few long-term investments that are ticking over nicely. Short-term, my success is reliant on doing research and staying up to date, so I haven't been as effective.'

Lorraine leaned forward, finding this fascinating. It surprised her that Spence was so financially astute. The more she considered it, the more she felt they were similar in that fashion. Lorraine had wanted to avoid the trappings and stereotypes of the streets. She wasn't just going to be some gangster's girl, or nothing but a mum. It had driven her to push forward with her chosen career.

Somewhere down the line, she had lost that part of herself, likely after what went down with Raider. Between that and the relationship with Natty, she was being drawn closer to the streets. It seemed to her as though she had a choice; walk away or embrace the chaos.

'So . . . investments,' she said, after a moment. 'What tips would you give a beginner?'

'I'd save up six months' worth of wages before I even considered getting involved,' Spence said, a twinkle in his eyes as he began talking about something he clearly loved. 'Mutual funds are a good place to start, or even a decent ISA. I can send you some books, links, and recommendations, and you can take it from there.'

Lorraine nodded, her excitement growing. 'What about if I wanted to be more advanced, and go beyond just the basics?'

Spence grinned.

They spoke for over an hour, and Spence shared some of his insights. To his surprise, Lorraine soaked up what he was saying, asking insightful questions. They agreed that after she'd got started, she would come back to him for guidance, taking it bit by bit until she'd built up a sizeable portfolio of her own.

'Have you helped Natty with his investments?' Lorraine asked.

'A little. Like I said, we're pressed for time at the moment, but he's definitely taking it more seriously. For years, he didn't.'

'What changed?' Lorraine asked. Spence grinned.

'He fell in love.'

Lorraine smiled, a rush of warmth for her wayward partner flushing through her body. Spence watched her.

'Lo, he really does love you. He fucks up sometimes, but he would never hurt you. He'd take a bullet for the people he loves, and that includes you and Jaden.'

'I know, Spence,' Lorraine said, her hand instinctively going to her stomach for a moment. 'This is complicated, okay? I know it is, and I wish it was more simple, but I'm all over the place right now.' Lorraine opened her mouth, the urge to tell Spence she was pregnant almost overwhelming her. She managed to stop herself, though. It wouldn't be fair to tell him before Natty. It was bad enough that other people knew.

Closing her mouth, she shook her head.

'I'm just saying, just in case you needed a reminder. Put the man out of his misery soon, won't you? I'm sick of seeing him shuffling around,' Spence said.

'Duly noted. I'm surprised you've gone this long without asking about Rosie.'

'There's nothing to say,' Spence said, shocking Lorraine with his coldness. Her eyebrows rose.

'Are you sure?'

'Positive.'

Lorraine frowned, wondering about Spence's reaction. She wondered if he had simply come to terms with the fact they were over.

'She misses you, Spence. What you did . . . what happened . . . it's confusing.'

'I know it is. The situation was fucked up, but I just wanted to help Anika, that's all. I never wanted to get back with her, but I didn't make that clear enough, and it cost me.'

'I think Rosie has calmed down now. Everything is still a little raw, and—'

'And, Rosie knows what she's doing. She wants us to be done, and I have enough to focus on. My shit would only worry her,' Spence said.

Lorraine assessed him. His demeanour had shifted, now steelier and more resolute.

'So that's it then? There's no way back?'

Spence scratched his chin, taking a moment to think before responding.

'It's hard, but it's for the best.' Spence smiled, but it didn't reach his eyes, the look of sad acceptance etched on his face. Lorraine nodded.

'Okay, Spence, that's fair enough, I suppose.'

Glancing at his phone, Spence's eyes widened.

'I didn't realise it was so late,' he said, rising to his feet. 'Sorry, I've gotta go. I'll get you that investment stuff sent over.'

Again, Lorraine nodded.

'Thanks, Spence.'

Spence made his way to the gate, swinging it open and exiting onto the street.

CHAPTER NINETEEN

NATTY WAS in the kitchen at the main Dunn spot, drinking coffee and staring into space when Jermaine entered, closing the kitchen door behind him.

'What's going on, fam?' Natty asked, slapping hands with him. He searched Jermaine's face for any signs of anxiety, but there were none. Jermaine had definitely come into his own, and walked with an assured confidence, his head high.

'Same old,' Jermaine said. 'People in Little London know their role. There's a few little shits that shout their mouths off from time to time, but we've got them in our sights. They're not harming anyone.'

Natty nodded. Little London had a special place in his heart. It was where he'd worked to establish himself after being given the opportunity to set up territory in the area. A bully named Warren was the big dog back then, but had been removed. Since then, things had remained quiet.

'People have been saying we have issues down there . . . Keep me posted. Let me know if you need anything handling.'

'I've got it covered, boss. Trust me. Who's talking shit? Anyone I know?'

Natty shook his head, happy to put Morgan's words to rest. He remained intrigued about the plans Morgan and Mitch had, but had other things to deal with first

'Seriously, don't worry about it. I'm here if you need anything. If not me, Spence.'

Jermaine nodded.

'You hungry? I'll get us some food if you like. I missed lunch.'

Sounds good,' said Natty.

———

JERMAINE BROUGHT BACK some food from a local Caribbean takeaway, and they ate and caught up on minor street talk. Natty was making another drink when Jermaine said something that got his attention.

'Oh shit . . . totally forgot to ask earlier. Do you know a woman in Little London called Julie?'

Natty frowned, searching his mental database. Eventually, the mist subsided, and he remembered the woman he'd used as an informant. She had been essential to their early plans.

'Yeah. She's not taking, is she? She was clean before.' He turned to face Jermaine.

'She's clean,' Jermaine replied. 'She's in trouble, though. Came to see one of my young dudes asking for help. He was telling her to fuck off when she said that you knew her. Said you'd been in her house.'

Jermaine had a strange look on his face, which made Natty laugh. He was assuming Natty had done something with her, which he found hilarious.

'It's not like that. She's not really my type,' Natty said, still chuckling. I used to pay her for intel when we were getting set up back in the day. What's going on?'

'People have been going to the door demanding money. There's problems with her son. Couple' of the local gangs are grooming him.'

Natty frowned again. He remembered her mentioning her kids. When Warren had been eliminated, he'd gone to Julie's with a football, saying he'd keep the streets safe so they could play.

'I thought you said you had the local gangs locked down,' he said, his tone suddenly sharp.

'I do,' Jermaine said. 'These lot are harmless. They do their business, but it's strictly small-time. That's probably why they're patterning this kid and trying to get him webbed up with them. One more yout they can use.'

'What did Julie want? You said she needed help?'

'Yeah. She wants the gangs to leave her son alone. Asked if I'd speak to you, and see what you could do. I wasn't even sure about bringing it to your attention, boss. There's a lot going on, and her problems aren't our problems, right?'

Natty considered that. For the most part, Jermaine wasn't wrong. Julie was a civilian. He'd tapped her up for intel, and had paid well. On top of that, he'd made her streets safer by getting rid of Warren, who'd terrorised Little London when he was on top.

He couldn't shake the guilt, though. He'd made Julie a promise, and now gangs were circling her son. It was more work, but he couldn't turn his back on her.

'Julie's cool. She was useful to us. Stand down, and I'll take care of it.'

'You sure?' Jermaine asked. 'I can sort it out for you if you want.'

Natty shook his head. 'I'll speak with her. For now, get me the details on these little gangs.'

Jermaine shrugged. 'It's sorted, boss. I'll have it for you, ASAP.'

———

TRUE TO HIS WORD, Natty drove to Little London the next day, spinning the streets and getting a feel for the area. Little London wasn't like Chapeltown. Despite its reputation, Chapeltown was community-oriented. Neighbours were like family, and local businesses were supported like high-street shops in a city centre.

Little London was devoid of that community spirit. People kept to themselves here, the obscurity providing a sense of protection.

Nobody questioned what was happening behind the doors and windows of neighbours' houses.

For a long time, Little London represented the perfect example of untapped potential.

Natty and the others resolved that issue.

He saw a few younger boys and girls, dressed in tracksuits with moody looks on their faces. Other than that, he saw the rank-and-file locals, some with kids and pets, but all of them in their own worlds, not focusing on the people around them.

In general, it definitely seemed better off, which backed up Jermaine's words. Natty made a mental note to reward him as he pulled up outside Julie's house.

Locking the car, he approached the house and knocked. When he didn't hear anything after a few moments, he knocked again. Eventually, the door slowly opened, and Julie peered out at him. The nervous suspicion on her face vanished when she recognised Natty, her eyes widening.

'N-Natty? You're here.'

'In the flesh,' Natty said, giving her an easy smile. 'Can I come in?'

Julie nodded, and let him in, leading him to the living room. It had been over a year since he'd been there, but it looked even shabbier. There were gaps in the room where things were missing, and he guessed she'd had to sell them for money. He contrasted it to the last time he'd visited, when the room had been cluttered with toys. It shocked Natty to see how things could have fallen apart in such a short space of time for Julie, but he tried hard not to react.

When Julie invited him to sit down, Natty did so, the sofa immediately creaking under his weight. He glanced at Julie, who was playing with her hands, a look of embarrassment on her face.

'Do you want a drink or anything?' she asked, her eyes flicking between Natty and the floor.

'I'm good, Julie. You don't have to worry about me *dying of thirst* this time,' Natty responded warmly. It received a brief smile.

'I'm sorry for reaching out to your guys. I know you said you'd always help, and I wasn't sure, and I just —'

'Julie.'

She stopped, chest heaving and mid-word. Natty shook his head.

'Take a deep breath, calm down, and tell me what's going on.'

Julie nodded gratefully, taking a moment to gather herself.

'I don't know where to start.'

'Start from wherever you like. My people said shit was rough, and they mentioned one of your kids being in some trouble. Just start where you're comfortable, and we'll go from there.'

Julie nodded.

'Okay . . . I don't . . . The money I get every month was stopped for a bit. They believed I was claiming incorrectly, and it was tied up in some crap for a while. While I was trying to sort it, my son was spending more time on the estate. A few of his mates have started dealing, and when he saw some of the things they were buying, he was tempted.'

Natty nodded for her to continue.

'I fell behind on the bills. I had letters coming out of my arse demanding money, and I had to scrimp and scrimmage to get the money just to eat. I've been down to the offices seemingly every day, trying to get it all fixed. Even now, with the investigation over, they've yet to backdate everything that I'm owed. I don't know why they're dragging their feet, but it's killing us.' Julie's eyes darted around the room, pausing at several dust-filled gaps. Natty followed her eyes, before he spoke again.

'And your son?'

Julie hung her head, taking a second before she looked up and faced Natty with tear-filled eyes.

'Julian's a good boy. He tries his hardest at school, and even though we don't have much money or stuff, he's always tried to help me. Never given me any trouble. He's older now, though, Natty. He's seeing how the world works, and what the struggle really means. When you've got flash dealers showing you stacks of money and wearing nice clothes, promising you can do the same, it's hard to resist the lure.'

'Is he selling for these people yet?' Natty asked, absorbing Julie's comments about the culture. He couldn't argue with any of them.

Julie shook her head. 'He's hanging around them, and it's only a matter of time. He's not listening to what I'm saying anymore. He looks at me, and he sees a mess, and I don't really blame him.' Julie broke down, tears streaming down her face as she noisily cried.

Natty watched awkwardly, not knowing what to do. Finally, he reached for a nearby kitchen roll, tearing off a strip and handing it to her. Thanking him, she wiped her face.

'Sorry about that.'

Natty shook his head.

'What do you need from me?'

'I don't know,' Julie sighed. 'I know none of this is your problem, but things have been better around here with you guys doing what you do. You've made it safer for my kids to play, and your people keep to themselves. When they've got a bit lairy, they've been shut down.'

Natty listened, again realising just how sparse his reports coming out of Little London had been. Despite that, Jermaine had clearly been sorting out issues with little to no fuss, which Natty was pleased with. He felt a moment of annoyance at Morgan for attempting to cloud his vision, but it quickly dissipated.

'The problem is, I guess, that people have got comfy now, and people like my son are being caught in the middle.' Again, she met Natty's eyes. 'There's no hope for me. This is the life I have, and I'll make do, but my kids deserve a better opportunity.'

Before Natty could reply, there was a loud banging on the door.

'Julie! We know you're in there. Open the fucking door.'

Julie went pale, freezing where she sat. Natty's brow furrowed.

'Who's that?' he asked, as the banging grew louder.

'His name's Drew. When I was desperate, I took money from him, and—'

'Julie! I'll fucking kick it down if you don't answer.'

Natty's shoulders tensed. He liked Julie, and he didn't like the fact she was clearly in a bind. Even if Drew wasn't banging on the door, he would have still helped her, but right now, he felt compelled to nip this in the bud.

Standing, he looked to Julie.

'Stay where you are.'

Natty sauntered to the door and unlocked it. Without saying a word, he looked out at the men assembled there.

'No need to knock so loud, Drew. We're aware you're here,' he said, keeping the annoyance out of his voice.

Drew's fists were clenched by his side, his nostrils flaring and his breathing heavy as he glared back at Natty. He had muscular arms and broad shoulders beneath his navy blue tracksuit, a gold earring and a chunky Rolex on his wrist that immediately reminded Natty of the kind of watches Cameron used to wear.

Further down the path were two more men, both slighter and ratty-looking. Natty couldn't see them, but he presumed they were the muscle and were likely armed.

'Who the hell are you?' Drew asked, his glare intensifying.

'Does that matter?'

'Where's Julie? I dunno who you are, mate, but this has nothing to do with you. She's been ducking me, and it needs sorting.'

'Fair enough,' Natty said. 'How did you plan on sorting it?'

'What's it to you?' Drew said, stepping closer.

'Julie's a friend.'

'So what? I wouldn't give a fuck if she was your sister. She owes me.'

Natty grinned, knowing it would drive the man crazy. Inside, he was boiling. Natty had no illusions about what he did, and the effects it had on people, but he certainly wasn't forcing people to buy his drugs, and never had. Men like Drew preyed on the lowest people, got them further into debt, then bled them with crippling interest.

Part of that, Natty understood. It was the game, but something about turning up at the house of a single mum accompanied by two men that clearly weren't there to talk, didn't sit right with him.

'I'm not going anywhere.'

'Are you sure about that?' One of the other men moved forward, his hand hovering near his pocket.

'I'm positive,' said Natty. 'You might want to look behind you before you do something stupid.'

When the man turned to look, Natty moved, slamming his forearm against his temple, causing him to crumple to the floor. His companion shouted in alarm and lunged forward, but Natty grabbed him by the throat, then dropped him with a vicious headbutt.

Drew froze in place, stunned by the quick movement, his associate moaning on the ground and holding his bloodied nose.

'You wanted it like this,' Natty said. 'I don't like the way you approached Julie. Now, we're gonna talk, and if your guards get involved, they won't make it out of Little London. What does Julie owe?'

———

Julie felt like she was dreaming.

She'd been dealing with a host of problems for so long, she'd given up ever getting a positive resolution. When the problems with her benefits continued to intensify, she'd contacted Drew, having heard his name from one of her friends. She'd borrowed one thousand pounds to tide her other, accepting the 20% weekly interest without really under-standing what it meant.

When she couldn't pay the first instalment, the interest continued to mount, along with Drew's threats.

If Natty hadn't shown up today, she shuddered to think what would have happened.

But, he had.

Julie remembered Natty as a cocky man who'd visited last year, helped her out, and cracked jokes to put her at ease. He'd disappeared after that, and she hadn't given him much thought.

Now, he seemed different. Less jocular, firmer in his words, with a more dangerous element that remained throughout his talk with Drew. After Natty laid out his men, Drew didn't have a leg to stand on. Some tough-looking guys that Natty seemed to recognise had shown up. One of them had given Drew the initial money she'd borrowed, then Natty warned him about troubling her or anyone else in the area, before sending him packing.

'Natty?'

Natty turned to face her.

'Are you okay?' he asked. Julie hesitated, then nodded.

'I . . .' she took a deep breath. 'How the hell am I going to pay you back?'

'You're not,' said Natty, waving his hand when she tried to protest. 'You did right by me last year. I could have been full of shit when I turned up at your house that day, but you still let me in. You made a choice then, and I've made a choice now.'

Tears pooled in Julie's eyes. Sniffling, she wiped them.

'I must look like such a state,' she said.

She did, but Natty wasn't going to tell her that.

'Let's go back inside and get you sorted out. Make yourself a drink, and then we can chat.'

———

LESS THAN TEN MINUTES LATER, Julie had composed herself and was sitting on the sofa, staring down at her cup. Natty figured she would be happy to sit in silence if he didn't speak.

'You're gonna need to get all your stuff back,' he said, looking around the room.

Finally, Julie looked up.

'What stuff?'

'All the stuff you've obviously sold to pay your debts. Buy it all back, so you don't have these silly gaps where they used to be.' Natty pointed around the room.

Julie chuckled. 'Do you think it's that easy? I'm getting my benefits again, but I get less now, and every penny counts. I have no idea how I'm going to get myself ahead.' She shot him a defeated look. 'Life's hard.'

'I get that. I'm not gonna patronise you by pretending your problems don't mean shit. I'm not even gonna pretend that I've ever had the sort of problems you've had, but I know something about having my back against the wall. Last year, after getting set up around here, it all nearly got taken away from me. I lost my role, I had people out to get me, and had no one in my corner,' Natty said.

Julie's eyes widened.

'What? But . . . look at you? You're obviously doing well.'

'Because I refused to stay down. I'm not gonna let you stay down either. I look out for those who look out for me, so tomorrow, one of my people is gonna drop off some money, and you're gonna use that to get yourself set up. After that, you'll get a little bit every week. It's not gonna be millions, mind. But, if you do right with it, the sky's the limit.'

Julie's mouth opened and closed. Natty got it. Life had ground her down, and the idea that someone would come along and help her was a lot to take in.

'You're not turning it down, Julie. It's done.'

She burst into tears again, the cup in her hand shaking. Leaning over, Natty took it from her and put it on the table. Reaching for the kitchen roll once more, Natty unravelled a piece, tearing it off and handing it to her.

'I'm sorry,' she said, still trying to compose herself.

'You don't have to be sorry. Next time, reach out earlier, and I'll do my best to help you.'

'Why?'

'Why not?' Natty shrugged. She shook her head.

'That's not good enough, Natty. I know what you do. I can't be the only sad sack hard-luck story you come across. Why me?'

Natty thought it over. Julie wasn't wrong. Natty did hear a lot of stories. Some genuine, some clearly made up. He couldn't help everyone, but he could do his bit where possible, and keep the pipeline smooth so that everyone could make money.

So, why Julie?

'Honestly, it's my girl,' he said. Julie frowned.

'What do you mean?'

'She has a son. His dad pretty much abandoned him, and I'm the closest thing to a father figure he's had. She's smart, driven, and even without my help, I've no doubt she'd have made something of herself, but even so, she has a solid support structure. She has a sibling, plus a mother who helps her. She has me. You have no one. Without all of that, she might be in the same position as you, and I guess it just reminds me of her, and makes me want to help you.'

'I'm not a charity case.' Julie's frown deepened.

'I don't want you to be. Just get back on your feet.'

'I'm gonna pay you back, Natty,' she insisted.

'If you need to do that, then fine. Go to any of my people around here, and they'll see I get it. I'll make sure they're aware. Don't pay me anything until you're sorted, though. No strings. No hidden interest. I appreciate it being something that you want to do.'

'Thank you, Natty. I mean that.' Julie's smile seemed to vanish all of her fatigue and ills for a moment, and Natty saw signs of the looker she might have been when she was younger.

'It's done. Now, let's talk about your son.'

Julie sighed. 'I can't tell him anything, like I said. He thinks he's doing the right thing, and why the hell would he listen to me? I'm a mess.'

'You're still his mum, and you're going through a hard time,' Natty said, a jolt in his stomach as he thought about his own mum, and the words they'd hurled at each other the last time they spoke.

She was different, though, he quickly mused before any lingering guilt could settle in. She'd known about the circumstances behind his dad's murder, and even if Natty didn't take that into consideration, he had always been an afterthought where she was concerned.

There was little love, just grim duty, criticisms, and comparisons to a man he truly understood how much she'd loathed now.

Natty tried searching for some happy memories between the pair, but struggled to find any. He'd adored his mum when he was younger, and tolerated her as he grew older, but he never knew where he stood. Even with Rudy around, it was as if it was guaranteed he would go down the street path. Natty had wanted it. He'd wanted everything he saw his dad with. The money, the nice things, the status and reputation; Natty wanted it all.

But the thing that stuck in his memory most was his dad's warnings. His insistence that Natty didn't have to live the same life he had.

'He wants to help, and he thinks this is the way to do it,' Julie said.

'I'll sort it,' Natty said.

'You've done enough,' Julie said softly.

'Maybe, but I'm still going to do more. Tell me about these people he's knocking around with. Everything you can about them. I'll do the rest.'

It took a while to coax the information out of Julie, but Natty reinforced the information that Jermaine had given him. Based on everything he knew, it was only a matter of time before the gifts and the money that the gangs had been giving him, would need to be paid back. They would lure him into the fold, and make him pay it off by slanging drugs or holding dangerous packages.

From there, it was difficult to break through. Not everybody had what Natty had. Street smarts people could acquire over time, but the reputation that came with a well-known name was priceless. Without Natty's surname, there was a possibility *Dunn* would have remained *Deeds* forever.

Regardless, he would give the information to Jermaine, and he would ensure they left Julie's son alone.

Finally, Natty left Julie's, noticing a curtain twitching across the road. He grinned, wondering what her busybody neighbour thought they'd been doing. Giving the neighbour a mocking wave, Natty laughed when they moved away from the window.

Blinking he realised he'd been stood on the spot, staring into space for some time. Natty looked left and right, ensuring the coast was clear. Pulling his jacket up, he obscured as much of his face as possible before stepping purposefully to his car.

His phone rang as he buckled himself in. Natty glanced at the number, straightening when he saw it was Lorraine.

'Lo, is everything okay?' he quickly asked.

'Everything is fine, Nat,' she said softly. 'Can you come over when you're free? I think it's time we had a proper conversation.'

CHAPTER TWENTY

LORRAINE WAS NESTLED in the living room, a fortress of solitude against the encroaching chill. A steaming cup of chamomile tea was perched on the glass coffee table, tendrils of warmth curling up and vanishing into the cool, book-scented air.

Stacked next to her were hefty tomes and slim paperbacks, a selection of Spence's recommendations; investment strategies, behavioural finance, plus the unfathomable depths of the stock market. The room was filled with the crisp aroma of fresh paper and ink, an unexpected nostalgic trigger, sending her mind drifting back to the caffeine-fuelled study sessions when she was first learning about software development.

On her lap lay her tablet, the screen dimmed to a soft glow, a beacon amidst the encroaching evening shadows. Web pages and PDFs flickered in the corners of her vision, an endless procession of information. Her fingertips brushed over the cool glass surface, tracing lines of text about emerging markets, investment success stories, and complex geopolitical impacts.

Nearby sat a notepad, a jumble of her thoughts and musings sprawled out across the pages. Scribbled diagrams and annotated questions punctuated her feverish notes, each stroke of the pen an echo of her focused thoughts.

Periodically, she allowed herself some respite, her gaze drifting towards the abstract painting adorning the far wall. She'd lose herself in the chaotic swirls of colour, a contrast to the structured world of investment she was navigating.

Yet, despite the tumult of information, a serene calm clung to her. This was not the breathless urgency of a job, but a chosen endeavour. She was in no race against time, she was simply immersing herself in a world of unexplored knowledge, digesting it at her own pace.

Her focus was unwavering, her determination unyielding. It was a reprieve from the relentless whirlwind of her life. For now, she wasn't Lorraine, the partner of Natty Deeds, a man with a foot firmly in the crime life. She was simply Lorraine, a woman braving the intricate labyrinth of investment.

Lorraine had taken advantage of the solitude, with her mum out of the house, and Jaden in his room. He'd checked on her earlier, made himself a drink, then retreated back to his room, a smile on his face.

Since her conversation with Spence, she had allowed herself to focus on the current task, happy to be able to lose herself in something worthwhile.

A knock at the door pulled her from her work. This was it.

Taking a deep breath, Lorraine stood and went to open the door, smiling when she saw Natty. He was dressed for the weather in a fitted black bomber jacket, jeans and boots. Lorraine let him in, smiling ruefully as he took off his boots before entering the living room.

'Do you want something to drink?' Lorraine asked. Natty's eyes flicked toward the chamomile tea drink, his lip curling.

'No, thanks. I'm good.'

Lorraine sat back down amidst her work.

'Is that the stuff Spence sent you?' Natty asked, sitting next to her, moving several books out of the way, and putting them on the coffee table.

'Yeah, it is. Take it he's spoken to you then?'

'It came up in conversation,' Natty said. 'He's been telling me for a while that I need to think more about investing.'

'He mentioned it. Though, from what he said, he made it sound like you had definitely stepped up and started making some positive financial moves.'

Natty nodded. 'I'm trying to. Sometimes it doesn't feel like there's enough time in the day to get it all done. He's right, though. I want to make sure you and Jaden are taken care of.'

'Why?' Lorraine reached out for her drink, taking a sip and savouring the unique flavour. She closed her eyes for a moment, inhaling the scent, loving the warmth emanating from the cup.

Natty's eyes widened momentarily. 'Because you're my family, and I love the both of you.'

Lorraine studied Natty, heart thumping against her chest at the sight of him. Something about him triggered that need for protection within her, and she both loved and loathed that idea. She wanted to be able to stand up on her own, and to be an asset to him. A true partner, rather than a damsel in distress.

'I felt we needed to speak, so I could understand more about what you're into.'

'What I'm into?' Natty said, his brow furrowing.

Lorraine took a deep breath.

'I know what you do. I always have. Rosie kinda implied you were in deeper than I thought, but I don't think it really became clear until that night . . . with you and Lisa.'

Natty said nothing, waiting for Lorraine to continue.

'You cut those people down. You were ruthless.'

Still, Natty waited.

'Is that the sort of thing you do all the time?'

Natty shook his head.

'No. They tried to kill us, and that was the only outcome. Just like you and Raider, when your life is on the line, you act. That's it.'

Lorraine nodded. She was slowly beginning to accept that Natty was right. The guilt and loathing over what she had done to Raider was fading over time. Though it remained lodged deep within her, Raider had harmed her, and without her defending herself, the outcome would have likely been fatal.

'I . . .' Lorraine took another deep breath. 'I want us to be equal, Nat.'

'We are equal, Lo,' Natty replied, his face betraying his confusion.

'We're not, and I get it. I don't want you to keep me on the outside anymore, though. I want us to be equals. I want to put everything behind us. That's why I'm doing this.' She motioned to the books.

Natty stared at Lorraine, and she could almost see the cogs turning as he weighed up the pros and cons of being honest with her. She didn't blame him, but still wondered how he would handle it. Finally, he cleared his throat.

'Okay. I'll level with you,' he started. 'There's a lot of shit going on at the moment. People are trying to kill me. That time I was meant to meet you . . . two men tried me, and I went after them, and got caught up in all of that.'

Despite the fact she'd been present when Natty had killed people, the fact he could talk so casually about an attempt on his life, was startling.

'Why are they trying to kill you?'

Ruefully, Natty smiled.

'It's a long story.'

Lorraine rested her hand on Natty's, signalling for him to start.

Natty told her about Jakkar's men, and the threat they presented. He told her about the situation with his uncle, and the decision he, Spence and Stefon had made. Lorraine listened in complete silence, fighting the medley of emotions surging through her. She'd seen Natty's uncle around, but they had never spoken. The idea of him ordering his brother's murder chilled her to the bone. Her heart went out to Natty. Underneath his tough exterior, he had been dealing with all of this, internalising it and trying to protect her.

She had to be there for him.

'I want to go home, Nat. I want you there with me.'

Natty smiled, but it was tinged with sadness.

'There's danger, Lo. I'm up against some dangerous people. The last thing I want is you lot in the line of fire.'

Lorraine's grip on his hand tightened.

'I want us to be together, Nat. We'll deal with everything, and you'll confide in me. You need me just as much as I need you.'

Natty couldn't hold back. He pulled Lorraine close, his mouth meeting hers as she responded with abandon, the distance between them vanishing, metaphorically and physically. When they broke apart, they were panting.

'I do need you, Lo. I won't let anyone or anything hurt you.'

Lorraine smiled at the obvious sincerity in Natty's voice. He deserved to know the truth. She doubted it would upset him, but somehow it would become even more real when she told him they were having a child.

'Nat, I have—'

'Natty!'

Jaden was in the doorway, wide-eyed, beaming as he saw Natty. He ran across the room and flung his arms around Natty, who gave him a tight hug, then ruffled his hair. Lorraine wiped a tear from her eye as she watched them roughhousing. It was a defining image for her. No matter what, no matter the trials and tribulations, Natty loved her and her son, and they both loved him.

That was the thing she needed to focus on.

'Look at you. You've definitely been training,' Natty said, grinning at Jaden. 'You still doing your press-ups every day?'

Jaden nodded. 'We need to do some more training, Natty. Are you staying for a while?'

'Yeah, course I am, little man. Go load up the computer, and I'll give you a lesson on *FIFA*.'

Jaden bounded from the room and hurried upstairs. Still grinning, Natty sheepishly turned to Lorraine.

'Sorry about that. What were you going to say?'

Lorraine shook her head, still smiling. The moment had gone, but there would be others. Jaden was just as important in this as her and Natty. He needed his dad.

'Nothing. Jaden . . . he's missed you,' she finally said.

'I've missed him too. That's my little man.' His grin turned cocky for a moment. 'Not *soldier* . . . *man*.'

Lorraine rolled her eyes, remembering when she'd flipped out on him for calling Jaden his little soldier.

'You really need to let that go.'

'Maybe.' Natty winked. 'Not anytime soon, though.'

'Whatever, Nat. You better go to him before he comes down and puts you in a headlock.'

Natty chuckled as he headed to find Jaden, Lorraine watching after him as he left the living room. It was hard putting into words the sense of relief she felt at being back on the same page with Natty. Picking up her books, she smiled at the thought of her boys playing together, then went back to work.

CHAPTER TWENTY-ONE

THE DAY after her talk with Natty, Lorraine found herself still in a good mood, sitting in the kitchen and staring into space. Natty had stayed for hours, hanging out with Jaden, then eating dinner with them. He'd left in the late evening, and the plan was that they would move back in together as soon as possible. Lorraine intended to go home and make sure everything was tidy, and she was looking forward to them going back to normal.

Lorraine hummed, fingers tapping the side of the cup of tea she'd made earlier. Making things right with Natty had been crossed off her list. Next, she had something else to deal with. With that in mind, she called Spence.

'Hey, Lo,' Spence answered, sounding at ease as ever.

'Hi, Spence. I wanted to ring you and say thanks. I spoke with Nat, and we got everything out in the open.'

'That's great.' Lorraine could hear the happiness in Spence's voice. 'I didn't do much, though. You two were always going to find your way back to one another.'

'Maybe so, but it might have taken longer, so just take the thanks.'

'Fine,' Spence replied, chuckling. 'How are you doing with the bits I sent you?'

'I have some things I want to go over with you, but I'll send you an email later.' Lorraine paused, gathering herself for the next thing. 'I need you to set up a meeting with Lisa, Spence. I also need you not to mention it to Natty.'

———

CLARKE WAS IN THE KITCHEN, making breakfast. Paula was still asleep, and none of the children were up. He loved the dynamic they had as a family, but he also appreciated his alone time, especially as of late.

Since his injury, Paula had been over the top about making sure he was okay, hovering over him to make sure he wasn't overexerting himself.

Clarke poured some oatmeal into a bowl, grabbed a spoon and sat at the table, blowing on it before tucking in. Between the oatmeal and frequent sips of piping hot coffee, the warmth surging through his body provided much-needed comfort. There was still some soreness, and he wasn't moving as quickly as he used to, but Clarke felt better. At the same time, he wasn't sure what he was walking into.

He hadn't spoken to Mitch since the last time, and had only spoken with Lisa a few times. He and Natty still needed to speak, but he remained confused about everything going on. Clarke couldn't follow the angles. Mitch had wanted him back on duty, but nothing had been said since. It made him feel like he was in the middle of a political struggle, and that didn't sit well with him.

Clarke was trying to consider both sides, but some of Mitch's moves had left him confused and suspicious. The way he'd handled the situation with the Asians had led to it snowballing into a bigger issue. He'd targeted dealers associated with Jakkar, using Clarke and his men to murder them. Clarke had little issue with killing. He played by the rules, and anyone involved in the life was fair game, but he struggled to understand the approach his boss had taken.

Clarke had some decisions to make. With the clock ticking and Mitch seemingly expecting him back to work, he had little time to continually ponder these issues.

But how effective would he be if he returned to the fold conflicted?

His role demanded decisiveness and commitment.

Placing his spoon down on the table, Clarke blew out a breath. He considered how he might resolve the issue and bring harmony back to the family. *Maybe he should speak to both sides again*, he mused.

As a last resort, he could arrange a meeting between the family members and get them to speak directly.

Lost in his plans and theories, Clarke frowned when his phone rang. He didn't recognise the number, but answered anyway.

'Yes?'

'We're outside. Big man sent us.'

Clarke's frown deepened. The protocol had been perfect. Very little had been said, no names were used, and if the call was being listened to, no one would get anything they could use. He didn't understand why he was being summoned, though. Mitch hadn't set a clear plan for him, and he'd yet to speak to Natty face-to-face.

Clarke had a unique role in the organisation, similar to people like Natty and Lisa. For he and Lisa, in particular, they didn't check in. Clarke dealt with the security side of the organisation, which essentially meant being on call for his team, and taking on necessary jobs when someone needed silencing. Lisa had taken a fair number of these jobs on in Clarke's absence.

There was no point speculating, though.

Clarke took his time finishing up, then brushed his teeth and washed his face. He grabbed a jacket and put on his boots, ignoring Paula when she sleepily called out to him.

Outside, a black Range Rover waited. Clarke remembered the vehicle from his last conversation with Mitch, and opened the back door. To his surprise, Morgan waited for him, grinning. Again, Otis was driving. Unlike last time, he gave Clarke a quick nod, his expression surly.

'Nice to see you, sir. Jump in,' Morgan said.

'Where's Mitch?' Clarke didn't move.

'He asked me to speak with you.' Morgan's grin widened. Clarke didn't like it, but climbed in regardless. He wasn't armed, but even at close range, he could disable Morgan before Otis could stop him.

'Are my people watching him?'

'Mitch is fine,' Morgan said. 'He's more protected than the Prime Minister, don't worry about that. How are you doing?'

'All due respect, Morgan . . . what am I doing here?' Clarke liked Morgan. The pair hadn't spent a tremendous amount of time working together, but Morgan was diligent, sharp, and had grown in power over the years. When Natty had turned down Mitch's offer last year, Clarke had expected Morgan to get the job, but Spence had stepped up instead, before Natty returned.

'I wanted to see how you were, and get a feel for what to expect. The team has taken some hits lately, and you were wounded in the line of duty. I've never been shot before, but that shit changes you, I've heard.'

Otis had taken off by this point. Clarke wasn't sure where they were going, but his attention was on Morgan.

'So, Mitch is wondering whether I'm still capable, is that it?'

'I'm here talking to you, not Mitch,' Morgan said, still smiling.

'I know you are. The fact is, you're his mouthpiece, so you're clearly doing his bidding. To answer the question you haven't directly asked, I'm fine. Yeah, I got hit. It's not the first time. Hopefully, it will be the last, but that's the risk.'

Morgan shook his head. 'There's no need to be so aggressive, Clarke. We're all friends here, and you can't blame us for wondering. After all, you're getting older. It's perfectly acceptable to slow down.'

Something about Morgan's smug attitude made Clarke want to break his face, but he maintained his position. Mitch had sent Morgan, and he had no doubt Morgan would be reporting every word back to Mitch. It irked him that Morgan was underestimating him, and he had no intention of taking it lying down.

'I appreciate your concern. Don't worry, I'll reach out to Natty and have a chat with him.'

Morgan's smile slipped. 'Why would you need to speak to Natty?'

'I said I would, last time I spoke to Mitch. He's in charge, remember? Mitch put him in charge of street business. I suspect my well-being would constitute street business. You're an office guy. You don't get in the streets, so I wouldn't want to waste your time by speaking about myself.' Clarke's words were polite, but dripping with sarcasm. It was a little more forward than the moves he normally made, but he wanted Morgan to know that he wasn't just a blunt instrument. He knew how to play the game.

'I can speak to you. Natty has other things to be doing.'

'So you say, but I'd like to hear that from him directly.'

The tension in the back was so thick that even Otis glanced at them. Morgan hadn't spoken yet, but his neck was flush, and he was gritting his teeth, his lips twitching with rage.

'This is just a friendly conversation. We're part of the same team, so I don't know what you're implying, or why you have a problem with me, but —'

'I don't have a problem with you. I guess what you need to understand is that I've been in this organisation far longer than you. I don't need to be micromanaged or *handled*. I know my role, and I know what I need to do. If something in my role has changed, you are not the one to tell me.'

'Are you sure about that?' Morgan hissed. Clarke met his eyes, hoping Morgan made a move so he had an excuse to bury him.

'I'm positive,' he said calmly. Morgan's nostrils flared, but he seemed to compose himself, nodding.

'If that's how you want it, I guess the big man will contact you directly. Pull up here,' Morgan demanded. Otis nodded, indicating and bringing the car to a stop. Morgan's smile returned as a puzzled look crept across Clarke's face.

'Where are we?' Clarke asked.

'I'm not sure, but it seems like we're done talking now, so you can make your way home from here.'

Clarke nodded, then smiled himself.

'Got it,' he said. Grabbing the handle, he opened the door and exited onto the street. Before closing the door, he crouched down so he could see Morgan.

'When you talk about the big man, are you referring to *Natty* or *Mitch*? Just so I know. Don't want any confusion, you know. Natty is your boss, after all.'

Morgan's face contorted with anger.

'Shut the door,' he said through gritted teeth.

Clarke's smile widened. Without another word, he did so, watching as the car sped away.

———

LORRAINE QUICKENED HER STEP, hurrying towards a coffee shop in the heart of Chapel Allerton. The window was adorned with hand-painted signs advertising the daily specials, and hanging baskets of flowers added a pop of colour. It felt like minutes after she'd spoken to Spence, he called back, having spoken to Lisa. As diligent as ever, he'd even sorted out the time, and the location.

Upon entering, the rich aroma of freshly brewed coffee enveloped her, mingling with the subtle scent of homemade pastries. Framed pictures of local landmarks and snippets of Leeds's history adorned the walls. An eclectic mix of tables and chairs filled the intimate space, a wooden counter at one end showcasing an assortment of freshly baked goods.

Lorraine was shocked to see Lisa had beaten her there. She'd secured a booth at the back of the room, upholstered in worn but well-loved leather. Lisa smiled at Lorraine as she sat down.

A short, beaming woman with a round face approached, her name tag reading *Meg* in cheerful script. The clinking of coffee cups and subdued chatter of other patrons added to the cafe's homey atmosphere.

Lorraine ordered her drink, eyes darting back to Lisa. She was beautiful and had unique features. She seemed so unassuming that Lorraine struggled to match her to the woman that had ruthlessly murdered a room full of people.

'Thanks for meeting me,' she said.

'I won't lie, I wasn't expecting it when Spence spoke to me,' replied Lisa, smiling.

Lorraine's mind flashed to the moment on the sofa, and how close Natty and Lisa had seemed. As she thought back, a sudden spike of fear spread through her body. In her annoyance and bluster, she had failed to take into consideration the fact that she'd burst in on two active killers, both of whom could have put her down without a second thought.

It was sobering to think back on.

Lisa was still looking at her, clearly waiting for her to speak. Lorraine's drink arrived, and she took a small sip, not taking her eyes off Lisa. She envied the other woman's composure. She was still smiling, totally at ease with the situation.

Lorraine didn't speak, taking in her drink, seeing who was around her. For some reason, she felt safe being around Lisa. The idea irked her, but she couldn't shake it. Despite everything she knew and inferred about Lisa, she'd seen firsthand what the woman could do.

If she'd had that sort of skill when it came to Raider, he would never have put his hands on her, she mused.

'I'm pregnant,' she finally said. Lisa's eyebrows rose, but other than that, there was little reaction to her words.

'Congratulations. Natty never said anything . . .'

'He doesn't know. I don't even know why I'm telling you, but there we are.'

Lisa frowned. 'Why haven't you told him?'

'I don't have a proper answer. We were on the outs for a while, so it didn't feel right to tell him. I didn't want it to look like I was using it as a weapon. But now things are looking up, there's no reason why I shouldn't have told him. I guess the right opportunity just hasn't presented itself . . .'

'I wish I had something I could say that could help, but I don't,' Lisa said. 'I think you should tell him, though.'

'I need to ask you something.' Lorraine was determined to get everything out in the open, and to ask any questions that came to her mind.

'I'm listening.'

'Would you have made a move that night if I didn't walk in on you both?'

'I don't know. I'd like to think I wouldn't have, but a lot of what I do is about looking for pressure points and taking advantage. If I'd seen one . . . I guess I would have,' Lisa said after a few moments.

Lorraine shook her head, sighing.

'I just don't understand you. I don't get what drives you, and why you do the things you do. That's why I wanted to speak to you, so I can gain some of that understanding.'

'There's nothing to tell you. I do what I want to do, and that's it. I take what I do seriously, but personally, I just go for it.'

'Okay . . . and what you do . . . how do you do *that*? What takes you down that path?'

For the first time, Lorraine saw Lisa flinch, before the woman instantly recovered.

'A hard life, and my back firmly against the wall. My options were limited, and the decisions led me here. I was lucky enough to find people who cared about me, and a man that trained me and made me the best version I could be.'

'A lover?'

'No.' Lisa smiled. 'Just a man that I really care about. He didn't take me on willingly. I needed to be strong, and he helped me get there.'

Lorraine nodded. There was a lot Lisa wasn't telling her, and she wasn't going to pry into what she imagined were very traumatic circumstances.

'I think I'm going to quit my job,' she started.

'Why?'

'Because it doesn't feel enough anymore. I don't feel like I had any control, and I've been in several situations recently where I was help-less. So, I took back control, but I want more.' She met Lisa's eyes. 'I want to be more like you.'

Lisa shook her head. 'No, you don't.'

'Yes, I do. I want to be an asset. I want to contribute and be treated as an equal. So, I guess I'm glad we had this conversation. I suspect it won't be the last one.'

Lisa blinked.

'I don't understand you.'

'I'll take that as a win,' Lorraine said. 'Please keep what I said to you to yourself.'

'I will. You have my word. I still think you should tell him as soon as possible.'

'Maybe.' Lorraine knew Lisa was right, though. She stayed seated as Lisa nodded at her and walked away. She wasn't sure what to make of the situation. It was clear they would never be friends, but Lorraine had the measure of her a little better than she had before.

Despite her skills and nature, there was a vulnerable little girl nestled beneath, hiding from the world because of various dubious circumstances Lorraine doubted she could ever relate to.

As she ordered another drink, she delved into it some more. She had her own circumstances that she had pushed past. Raider had beaten her up. Later, he'd come back and beaten her again, with the intention of killing her. She had survived, and though she would never be comfortable with the fact she had taken a life, but some of what Natty had said was finally seeping through. It was him or her.

That was a very Lisa way of thinking, she thought to herself, shaking her head and smiling.

CHAPTER TWENTY-TWO

'HE'S TAKING THE PISS, MITCH.'

Mitch watched Morgan pace around the room. Since the meeting convened, he'd been furious. Morgan stalked around the room, shouting, swearing and cursing Clarke out.

Mitch listened, but offered little, content to let his subordinate get it out of his system.

Truthfully, he liked this side of Morgan. He found him to be pragmatic and driven, but it was nice to know he had an angry side that could take over when necessary. Mitch found it to be a useful tool, when it could be controlled. He saw the anger as a weakness, similar to how his brother had been. When you could utilise someone at will, you could truly make the most of them.

'You've said, Morgan. Multiple times now. If you had spoken with me before you approached Clarke, I would have told you how it would go. You have to handle people like Clarke a certain way.'

'He works for the organisation. He should fall in line without question.' Morgan paused, folding his arms. 'He's not going to play ball, Mitch. This is just the start, I'm telling you.'

Mitch said nothing. Clarke had been in his service for as long as anybody in the organisation, but he had seen a change in him recently.

His lack of drive to return to work was one thing, but Clarke questioning Mitch about his brother was the kicker. It was clear that Clarke was conflicted.

It was, therefore, down to Mitch to assess the potential damage of that conflict. Clarke was too powerful a force not to fully have under his control. Left unchecked, the damage could be disastrous.

Mitch cursed himself for stupidly putting Nathaniel and Clarke together. It had seemed a good idea at first. A way to insulate himself from usurpers following Rudy's failed takeover attempt. Now it seemed like a misstep. Nathaniel had learned from Clarke. He had established an air of dependable calmness which was serving him well.

'People are looking at us sideways, Mitch. You don't see it, but I talk with people. No one is being upfront about it, but the mood is clear. They want to see your nephew running things.'

Still, Mitch didn't respond, mulling over Morgan's words as they mingled with his own plans. He wanted Nathaniel to be the lightning rod for the Asians and the police. If people thought Nathaniel was the main man, he would be the target, and that could leave Mitch to operate freely in the background.

Mitch needed a proper conversation with Clarke. He'd had Nathaniel reporting to Clarke, who would then report to him, but that setup didn't seem viable anymore.

One thing at a time, Mitch thought. He would focus on Clarke, while Jakkar and his minions remained quiet. Nathaniel's cousin, Stefon, was also on the hook. Mitch had lured him in, then hung him out to dry, wanting him desperate enough to reach out directly, allowing further manipulation.

'I will speak to Clarke.'

'But, it's Nat—' Morgan started to protest. Mitch held up a hand, silencing him.

'I will speak with Clarke, and I'll sort your situation. There are things I need to discuss with him. In the meantime, keep working on your tasks. If you want to rise above my nephew, keep working hard. Understand?'

Morgan's jaw jutted.

'Yes, boss. I understand.'

———

ZAYAN AND GHAZAN sat in their safe house. They had returned from Nottingham a few hours earlier, having handled their mission. The execution of the job had been simple enough. The preparation and build-up had taken longer than expected, with their target proving elusive for some time, before they finally got the drop on him.

Upon returning, they'd eaten, and informed Mustafa of their success. Now, they were back on their main job, and they had some catching up to do.

Ghazan was checking social media apps on his phone, making notes in a dog-eared notebook as he did so, face screwed up in concentration. Zayan was checking Netflix previews, trying to work out what he wanted to watch. Other than a collection of fizzy drink cans and empty packets of crisps on the coffee table, the space was relatively tidy.

'I definitely think this man Spence is our best option,' Ghazan said, glancing at his partner.

'Why?'

Ghazan's eye twitched. He had explained why to Zayan twice already, but he seemed determined to be obstinate.

Other than the first salvo against the stash spot, and the kidnap and murder of Conrad the facilitator, nothing about the job had been easy. Messing up the kill on Natty Deeds had led to a level of micromanaging that neither had experienced in years, and they didn't like it.

The Nottingham hit had bolstered the pairs' confidence, but the truth was, the elimination of the Dunns was far harder than Jakkar had made out. They were black gangsters, and Ghazan's stereotypical view was that black gangs were loud and unorganised.

The Dunns were different. They were deep, well-insulated, especially in Chapeltown, and well-trained. Natty had been proof of that. They had probed other areas, using the information that Conrad had shared, but even some of that was dated. Stash spots had moved, and collectors had changed in different sectors, making it hard to plan a comprehensive move against them.

Part of Ghazan wondered if they needed more backup, and how to go about getting it.

'Because, he's easier to get. He rarely travels with protection, and his routine appears more regimented than the others. Stefon is a loose cannon, and is far likelier to just shoot at us, and ask questions later. You read how he reacted when Ahmed and Mustafa tried having Natty Deeds eliminated at that house party. He just pulled out his gun and shot at them. No hesitation. If there is a choice between that and a relative babe in the woods, that's who we should go for.'

'Spence comes from a crime family, doesn't he?' Zayan finally turned from the screen, giving Ghazan his full attention.

'Not exactly. His father, Wayne, was a lieutenant for that old king-pin, Delroy Williams. He stepped back from the game long before Delroy was taken down. Probably the main reason he's alive,' Ghazan said, making another note in his pad.

'Do you think his father taught him anything?'

Ghazan considered this. 'I'd assume he did. Spence isn't a killer or anything like that. He has been linked to no murders, but he is smart, resourceful, and trusted. He went from working for Natty Deed's sub-crew, to one of the higher up's in the crew in less than a year. Even with potential nepotism, that's a significant jump. He could do a lot towards drawing out the rest of the targets.'

Zayan thought it over. 'It's better than stewing around here. We can begin intense surveillance, and from there, we can pick our spot. By all accounts, we could snatch him and move. If he's unlikely to be armed or protected, we could work him over like Conrad, and see what he knows, or better still, use him to lure Deeds into a meeting, so we can get them both.'

Ghazan grinned. He liked it when Zayan was locked in and on board. It made things so much easier.

'It's settled. That's the plan then,' Ghazan said. 'It should keep Ahmed and Mustafa from bothering us, and give us time to execute the rest of it.'

Both men grinned. Zayan turned his attention back to the Netflix screen, finally settling on an action film.

———

SPENCE QUICKENED his step as he left his car and headed into his dad's house. As always, his days had been spent keeping things in line. Though the threat level appeared to have reduced, it wasn't lost on him that their enemies weren't going anywhere, making every move still risky. Meetings with potential allies across Leeds were having mixed results. Not wanting any of Mitch's spies to get suspicious, they had to move coyly, and it was difficult getting people to commit.

He'd had a brief meeting with Natty earlier to go over some points, and he was elated that Natty and Lorraine were back on track. There had been a contagious energy about Natty, as if he were operating at a higher frequency and for Spence, that only meant good things.

Spence's dad stood up as soon as Spence entered the living room, holding out a glass filled with a radiant amber liquid. Spence took it, inhaling the smell of dried rose petals emanating from the Hennessy Pardis.

Every year on his mum's birthday, Spence and his dad would have drinks in celebration of her. They took turns buying a bottle of Hennessy Pardis, and they would sit and tell stories. Spence kept the celebrations to himself. Even Natty didn't know about them.

He closed his eyes, memories of his mum flitting through his mind. When he opened them, his dad was watching him, clearly fighting his emotions.

'She loved roses,' he said in a whispered tone. Spence nodded, swallowing down the lump in his throat. He took a sip, savouring the warm, smoky aftertaste of the liquor. The pair sat down, sitting in silence for several minutes. Spence thought about his mum, and what a force of nature she was. She ran their household, but was always happy and smiling. She liked to dance, and always encouraged him to follow his passions.

'I remember the day I heard,' Wayne said. 'When they told me about the accident, I just wanted to fall to the floor and stay there. She was my world.' He paused. 'I tried to stay strong for you, Spence. I dropped the ball at times, but I tried, son.'

'I know, dad.'

Wayne shook his head, taking a deep sip of the liquor.

'I'm damn proud of you, Spence. I know I talk a lot of rubbish sometimes, but I'm proud of you, and your mum would be too.'

'I love you, Pops,' Spence said, his voice breaking. They clinked their glasses, savouring another quiet moment, both thinking of the woman they loved, and how much they needed her.

CHAPTER TWENTY-THREE

LORRAINE HAD a smile on her face as she finished applying her makeup, ready for the day ahead. Jaden was psyched about going home. As much as loved his nana, he missed his room, and Lorraine too missed her house. It wasn't as grand as her mum's place, but it was hers, and going back represented a significant step forward.

Today, she intended to take another.

When she'd finished getting ready, Lorraine checked the time, then hustled to leave the house. She had a meeting with Angela, and didn't want to be late.

Lorraine drove into the office, parking in the company's underground car park, swiping herself into the building with her work ID.

The closer she got to her destination, the more Lorraine's heart raced. She made it onto the unit, everyone immediately staring. She felt her neck itching, the anxiety growing. Angela should have met her at the reception. She had a feeling this had been done on purpose, to make her uncomfortable.

Lorraine stood by the exit, waiting for Angela to realise she was there. She nodded to a few of her colleagues who were still gawping at her, disheartened when only one nodded back. She wondered what stories had been going around the office. She'd heard some of them before, and they were often exaggerated.

After a moment, she decided she wasn't going to let it bother her. *She needed this*, she mused. This wasn't her life anymore. These weren't her people, and it wasn't the right environment.

As of late, Lorraine had felt more focused, more confident in her surroundings, diving into the fundamentals of investing with a fervour. She had even moved some money around and begun her investing, trying to get out of the habit of looking at her investments every second of the day.

She was stronger than this, she told herself.

Five minutes passed before Angela stepped out of her office, striding across the unit towards Lorraine, her fleshy face quivering as she shot a few fake smiles at her staff. When she reached Lorraine, she shook her hand.

'Good to see you, Lorraine. Let's go to my office.'

Lorraine had anticipated a formal meeting room for their encounter, but brushed it aside, focusing her attention on the office surroundings.

The office was compact, bordering on claustrophobic, most of its space dominated by chunky, aged furniture. A large desk sat in the centre, flanked by a bookshelf on one side and a pair of soft chairs on the other, each fighting for their share of the cramped quarters.

Angela's personal life was on full display on the office walls. A framed certificate of achievement, the gold script standing out against a sea of beige, sat proudly behind her desk, a testament to her professional competence. Next to it, a gallery of framed photos provided a glimpse into her family life.

Lorraine found herself drawn to one particular photo of Angela's husband and children. His wide smile and the children's genuine laughter contrasted sharply with Angela's professional demeanour. Lorraine couldn't help but wonder if Angela's stony exterior at work masked a different persona at home.

The room hummed with a subtle, underlying tension. The quietness before their meeting was a testament to the intensity that was sure to follow. She steeled herself, ready to face whatever Angela had in store.

'It really is good to see you, Lorraine. This place hasn't been the same without you. Would you like something to drink?'

'No thank you.'

'Take a seat.'

Lorraine did so, waiting for Angela to shuffle into her chair.

'I'll cut right to the chase. We want you back, as soon as possible. Do you think you've had a sufficient break?'

Lorraine frowned. Angela made it sound like she had been on holiday.

'A break from what?'

'You tell me. I've obviously received your sick notes, and there was the time you hung up on me, but I'm willing to be magnanimous and move beyond that. The stress or whatever it was that you were feeling, are you over it?'

Lorraine was shocked at her audacity. There wasn't an ounce of sympathy in Angela's voice. She wasn't interested in Lorraine's plight, only how quickly she could return to work.

'No. I'm a work in progress. I've taken several positive steps, and I've refined some of my passions, to give myself something to focu—'

'What do *passions* have to do with anything? This is about work, Lorraine. You're a bright woman, and you have a lot of promise, so I know you can answer this question. What impact do you think your being off has had on your colleagues?' Angela's smile didn't reach her eyes.

'I imagine a negative one,' said Lorraine. 'But—'

'You'd be right. The targets have only grown harder. We don't have the budget to temporarily hire someone, so your team have been picking up your work in your absence. As you can imagine, that has led to increased fatigue. Surely you owe it to your colleagues to return, rather than focusing on *passions*?'

Lorraine was growing angry despite herself. She hadn't asked for any of the things she'd been forced to endure, yet had done her best to navigate the choppy waters and regain some sense of self. For Angela to try to emotionally blackmail her, whilst disregarding what she had been through, was infuriating, and it was hard to keep her composure.

'*I* come before work,' she said coldly. Any pretence of affability on Angela's side was dropped, and she turned her flint-like eyes onto Lorraine.

'That's not a very team-friendly attitude, is it?' she said. 'What makes you so special?'

'Nothing. I haven't claimed to be special. You're trying to twist what I'm saying, and make out like I've done something wrong. You spoke about the impact my being off would have. What impact do you think my being here, but being unable to properly focus or contribute would have? How would that have helped our stakeholders, or my colleagues, if I can't be relied upon?'

'You can't be relied upon, dear. The fact of the matter is that you ran away when things got difficult, and now I'm politely asking you to return, and you seem to have an aversion to it,' Angela said.

Lorraine wanted to reach across the desk and slam Angela's smug, self-satisfied face into it.

'You have no idea what I've been through, and do you know what? I think even if you did, it would change nothing. You see things one way. I haven't known you a long time, but what I do know, I don't like, and I have no intention of returning to work.'

'Excuse me?' Angela stuttered, eyes widening at Lorraine's words.

'You heard me, you miserable toad of a woman. I think this meeting was certainly the wrong move. In a matter of minutes, you've undone so much of the positivity I imbued into myself during my time away, so thank you and well done. Really stellar work.' The sarcasm dripped from Lorraine's voice as she glared at Angela, then hurried to her feet and exited the office.

She heard whispers and little pockets of conversation as she stormed across the office floor. She and Angela had evidently grown loud towards the end, and the team had overheard their argument.

'Excuse me, Lorraine Richards!' Angela called after her. 'I don't remember dismissing you.'

'Thankfully, I have the ability to dismiss myself,' Lorraine said, turning to face Angela after reaching the exit. She motioned to the work pass around her neck. 'Feel free to get this from reception. I quit.'

Lorraine left the office with a spring in her step, her emotions battling within. She hadn't been sure what she was going to do prior to the meeting, but she liked the decision she had made. Long-term, she and Angela would never be able to work well together, and the surge of positivity spreading through her was a sign she'd done the right thing.

As Lorraine headed to her car, her smile only grew.

———

'WHAT'S THE UPDATE THEN?'

Harding sat at his desk, looking at the detectives he'd ordered to have Natty Deeds tailed.

One of them, a short man with a well-groomed beard and a receding hairline, cleared his throat.

'Nothing exotic, that's for sure. We followed Deeds around, or at least we tried to. Didn't lead us anywhere. He's been spending time at a few gambling spots. We've raided them in the past. One of them is Jukie's place, but the old man is rarely there, and the charges never stick. Want us to organise something?'

Harding shook his head. He wasn't interested in gambling. He wanted to nail the Dunns for their laundry list of crimes, and by hook or crook, he would do it. It wasn't going to be easy. There were no suspects, and very little cooperation from the people they'd spoken to.

They were made of stronger stuff than Barry.

'Focus on the task at hand. Keep up the surveillance on Deeds for another three days. If nothing turns up, we'll go back to the drawing board.'

Recognising the dismissal, the men left the office. Harding sighed, massaging his temples. Stifling a yawn, he looked at the half-drunk cup of coffee that had gone cold. For a moment, he almost sipped it anyway.

Staring at the golden brown liquid, he tried to gather his thoughts. Brown was definitely a dirty officer. Harding had dug through some of his paperwork of previous crimes, and had even found a list of people Brown had used as informants. Their details were scattered and all over the place, which Harding didn't like. Anyone could have accessed his lists, which would have been a disaster for all involved if the information had been leaked.

Harding had reached out to several of them, and they spoke of threats and coercion, and Brown threatening to fit up the charges against them if they didn't cooperate.

It made Harding wonder if he had tried the same thing with the Dunns, or even with Roman and his organisation. Everything remained muddy, and Harding was having to fight to keep the investigation into Brown open.

Most people considered the matter closed, and though there weren't many in the station that had a higher standing than Harding, there were others with more political clout, and they were trying to use it to stonewall his investigations.

Harding couldn't work out why, but figured that Brown's antics made them all look bad. He doubted he was the only officer that had been on the take, but still.

Harding's thoughts returned to Natty. Natty had been the target of two different assassinations. One he knew Barry had been behind. The other had been more direct. On both occasions, evidence pointed to Asian males being responsible for the attempts. Now it was Harding's job to work out who they were and why they were targeting Natty.

As contract killers weren't exactly advertising in the *Yellow Pages*, it involved a lot of manual work to narrow down potential suspects, and so far, the only one he'd looked into had an airtight alibi, and no connection to the Dunns or to Barry and his associates.

Harding sighed. All roads were leading to nowhere at present, and it was disconcerting. He hadn't expected the investigation to be a slam dunk, but he had still expected to be further ahead than he was.

Reaching for a nearby folder, Harding went to remove the papers from it, but paused. Wiping his eyes, he weighed up his options. He was running on empty, and was experienced enough with investigations to know he couldn't keep pushing himself without breaking down completely.

Over the past two days, he'd had repeated headaches and little appetite, signs that he wasn't taking care of himself.

Finally, Harding stood up and tidied his desk, picking up his cup and leaving his office, locking the door behind him. Taking the cup to the kitchen and washing it, he wiped his hands and then left the kitchen.

There were a few officers dotted around, but it was late, and most people had finished hours ago. Walking past the desks, he nodded and said his goodbyes to those who remained, using his pass to unlock the main door and ensuring it was closed behind him.

Navigating his way outside, Harding climbed into his car and drove away. Tonight, he would get an early night, and tomorrow, he would come back into the office, fresh and ready to go.

The investigation wasn't over, and Harding was determined to stay true to his instincts, and solve the ridiculous puzzle he found himself in the middle of.

———

NATTY AND STEFON were at Stefon's place, sitting in the living room. Glasses of brandy sat untouched on the coffee table, and there was a lingering tension in the air. Stefon had come to accept that as something that would always be present when he spoke to his cousin. They both had big personalities and were used to dominating the room. Taking a step back and being more subservient had been difficult for Stefon, and he was definitely still learning.

He'd stayed busy, keeping on top of the streets, working directly with different crews and troubleshooting issues. He and Spence had coordinated several times, but he and Natty kept missing one another.

It had given Stefon more time to think about his position, and the offer Mitch had hinted at when they'd met. He'd heard nothing since from the man or his minions, but he doubted Mitch had any intention of forgetting about him.

Stefon glanced at his cousin, who was staring into space, and he wondered if part of the issue between them was Lisa. Natty had seemed strange when he'd heard them on the phone, and Stefon knew that he'd had a conversation with Lisa afterwards, where he was mentioned. Despite Lisa telling him they'd spoken, she hadn't told Stefon what they discussed, which had irked him at the time.

So far, they had slept together three times. Stefon couldn't get enough of her. She was gorgeous, fucked like she was born to do it, and she was low maintenance. She wasn't constantly calling and wanting his attention like so many other women he had dealt with. They just had sex. No dinner dates, drama or insecurity.

Yet, part of Stefon had grown accustomed to women chasing him down, and if he was honest, he wanted Lisa to do the same. She was calm, comfortable in her lane, so the fact she wasn't was no surprise to Stefon, but it made him wonder.

The memory of seeing Lisa when she'd been speaking to Spence that time flitted into Stefon's head. He remembered how amused Spence had seemed about the encounter.

Had Natty had a thing with Lisa?

Neither of them had said anything, and Stefon knew that Natty was loved up, but that didn't always mean anything.

Stefon blew out a breath. It wasn't worth thinking about at this moment.

'Stef?'

Stefon shook his head, focusing on Natty, who had a frown on his face.

'Sorry. I was just thinking. What did you say?'

'I said I'm sorry it's taken so long for us to sit down. Feels like everything is nonstop at the moment, but I wanted to touch base, and make sure everything was cool.'

'Is this about Lisa?' Stefon said bluntly. Natty raised an eyebrow.

'Not at all. This is business. You two's thing is separate from that,' he said.

'Fair enough. Can I ask you summat, though?'

Natty nodded. 'Course you can.'

'Have you fucked her?'

'No. Would it matter if I had?'

Stefon shrugged.

'I guess not. Didn't stop me being curious. I know you spoke to her about us.'

'It came up during a business meeting, but that's it. Honestly, if you two are happy, I'm happy. You're both official, and you know to put business first.'

Stefon accepted that, regretting the fact he'd brought it up, feeling it made him look weak.

'Speaking of business, I wanted to talk to you about your unc. I've been meaning to do it for a while.'

Natty motioned for Stefon to continue.

'I guess for starters, have you ever considered just speaking directly to him about your dad, to see what he says?'

Stefon wasn't sure what he expected from Natty, but it certainly wasn't an immediate response.

'No.'

'Just like that?' Stefon pressed.

'Just like that, cuz. I know in my gut that Mitch did it.' Stefon went to speak, but Natty held up a hand. 'I lived through it, Stef. All of that shit. I was a kid, but I remember. I remember how annoyed my dad used to get with Mitch, and I remember how Rudy was always sniffing around my uncle, even though my dad was his best friend. In all honesty, I think the only reason my uncle bumped me up the ladder in the end is so he could keep an eye on me.'

Stefon nodded, weighing up Natty's words, and the passion behind them. He'd made up his mind prior to the meeting that he would continue supporting his cousin, but he'd wanted to gauge how he responded.

Natty wasn't done.

'Look, I know it hasn't been easy. Even between us. We had a rocky start, and we're both making up for it, but I can't tell you how much it means to have you and Spence in my corner. I value you, cuz. I want us to do what we need to do, and build our thing from the ashes of my unc's organisation . . . because he's not like us. He's not a go-getter. He's happy to ignore the dudes on the street, while he moves people around like chess pieces. I know how he can sound, and I know how seductive it can be, but he'll never value you, and I think you know that. He'll only use you to fuel his agenda.'

Stefon found himself grinning. It was an impressive speech, and yet another sign of how much his cousin had grown over the years.

'You're a right fucking politician, Nat.'

Both of them laughed as the tension finally eased.

'I'm just speaking from the heart, that's all. Seriously, though . . . play it carefully. If you can find anything out, cool. If not, don't over-play your hand.'

'What if he wants intel?'

'If he does, then just feed him shit. Pretend to be frustrated with me if you need to.' Natty's grin exposed his even white teeth. 'I'm sure you have some good stuff you can use.'

CHAPTER TWENTY-FOUR

MORGAN PACED AROUND the back alley just off Roundhay Road, checking the time on his phone and shaking his head. He'd been waiting for ten minutes, growing more aggravated with every passing second. By the time a second vehicle pulled up alongside his at the end of the alley, he was seething.

'Sorry,' Otis said, rubbing his stomach. 'Stopped off to eat.'

Morgan shot him one of his patented glares. 'Clarke may allow you to get away with keeping him waiting, but I won't. Got it?'

'Chill out.' Otis's expression hardened. 'Show some respect, all right?'

'No, it's not alright. You wanted to be involved in what I'm doing, and you've made money doing so. If you want to remain involved, shape up. This is the big leagues.'

Otis's mouth twisted. He was tempted to tell Morgan to fuck off, but he was far too invested now. Morgan was right. He'd received a cut of sales from secret drug deals, and had supplemented his income by robbing other dealers in Wakefield and Halifax, using local dealers to set up meetings, and sticking them up.

Without Morgan, moving around so freely would be difficult. It was an area in which Morgan outshined Otis's other boss. Clarke was solid and dependable. He stood by those under his command, teaching them structure and other skills. Morgan was far more in tune with what people wanted, though. He was willing to go out and get it, and didn't let anyone stand in his way — even Mitch Dunn.

In a war, he had his money on Morgan finding a way to topple them all.

'You got it, Morgan. Won't happen again.'

'Good. This is important. That stuff that happened with Clarke . . . Mitch isn't gonna do anything.'

Otis's eyes widened, but inwardly he wasn't surprised. Mitch and Clarke went way back, and he was one of the only people who would stand up to the boss, never backing down from his principles. Clarke had earned his reputation as the Dunn organisation's chief hitter, and he had been there in the beginning, one of the key pillars that had helped Mitch rise.

He was old now, though. He'd been caught slipping and had been shot because of it. Otis had to think about his own future.

'Do you have a plan?'

Morgan didn't immediately respond, eyes flitting around the alley.

'Lisa.'

'What about her?' Otis asked. He'd worked with her in the past, and Lisa was as crazy as she was beautiful. He wondered if Morgan had made a deal with her, but shrugged it off. As unpredictable as Lisa was, she loved Clarke like a father. Otis was confident she would never move against him.

'We're gonna take her out.'

Otis couldn't help it. He laughed.

'Are you serious?' He started, then continued before Morgan could open his mouth. 'I know she looks like a fucking princess, but she's a monster, boss. You'll never catch her slipping.'

Morgan grinned. 'Have some faith. I can get her in place. You're gonna put the team together and remove her.'

Otis's heart was racing. If he went after Lisa and missed . . . he shuddered to think of the implications. If Lisa didn't get him, Clarke certainly would.

'Are you sure about this?'

Morgan nodded firmly.

'Yes. We can do it, as long as we work together. I'll throw in a bonus too.'

'What sort of bonus?'

'Stefon . . . Natty's cousin. He's doing a ting with Lisa.'

Otis's eyes widened. He'd tried to get with Lisa years ago, and she'd humiliated him by shutting him down. The idea that Stefon could swan back into Leeds and start something with her, irked him.

'Fuck off.'

'It's true. So, get them both in place, kill them, and whatever Stef is carrying on him, is yours. He's always wearing flashy jewellery. It'll be easy.'

Otis opened his mouth, thought about what he was trying to say, and finally spoke.

'If you take out Lisa, Clarke will kill us all.'

'He won't even know. We'll dispose of the bodies. Everyone will think the Asians did it. It's risk-free.'

Otis mulled it over. Ultimately, he knew he didn't have a choice. The fact that Morgan was confiding in him, was telling. If he even suspected he couldn't trust Otis, he would have him killed, Otis was sure of it. As skilled as he was, he couldn't take on the sort of muscle Morgan had behind him.

'Fine. I'm in,' he finally said.

———

THAT NIGHT, Mitch invited Clarke to dinner at his luxurious Shadwell safe house. A chef who owed Mitch a favour had prepared a meat-heavy meal, featuring sirloin steaks and lamb chops, served on a gleaming marble table. They'd uncorked a bottle of vintage wine and had a few drinks, their conversation meandering from the current turf wars to reminiscences about the good old days.

Around them, the safe house spoke volumes of Mitch's influence and taste. The place was well-furnished. Genuine leather armchairs, custom artwork adorning the walls—all under the watchful eye of high-definition security cameras discretely tucked into corners. A glass cabinet showcasing an impressive whiskey collection stood next to a state-of-the-art entertainment system, complete with a vinyl record player—a nod to Mitch's appreciation for the classics.

At present, Mitch was comfortably reclining in an armchair, a hand-stitched cushion supporting his back. He puffed away at a Cuban cigar, its aromatic smoke filling the air, mixing with the faint notes of a jazz record playing softly in the background. Across from him, Clarke sat on a plush Italian leather sofa, swirling the ice in his glass of single malt, equally enveloped in the ambience of muted luxury and unspoken power.

'Do you remember how it was?' Mitch pressed. 'We had people on all sides, coming for us, wanting to take what was ours. After they got Ty, people thought we were finished. We had a vision, and look how things turned out for us.'

Clarke sipped his drink. 'You built the organisation into a force, Mitch. There's no denying that. Can I ask you something, though?'

Mitch raised an eyebrow. 'You've never been shy about speaking your mind before. Why start now?'

Clarke raised the glass to eye level, swilling the burgundy liquid and watching as it sloshed up the side of the glass.

'Have you ever considered walking away?'

Mitch's eyebrows pinched together as he frowned. He observed Clarke for a moment, still concentrating deeply on his glass.

'Walking away from what?' he asked, already knowing the answer. Placing the glass down on the table in front of him, Clarke looked at Mitch and smiled.

'You know what I mean. You have all of this.' Clarke motioned with his hand around the safe house. 'Why stay in this life? We're dinosaurs, Mitch. Maybe we've had our time.'

Mitch's eyes swept around the room, taking everything in. He was facing threats and pressures he had never encountered, and the stakes were higher. That was a compliment to his adversaries rather than a slight on himself.

As his eyes fixed back on Clarke, he considered for a moment what life outside of the game would be like. Blowing out a breath, he realised it would not be the picnic Clarke's mind had envisaged. Jakkar would still be there, watching and waiting to put an end to him. Whilst he was alive, there would be no peace for Mitch.

'Do you really think Nathaniel is ready to lead?' Mitch asked.

Clarke's answer would be telling, he thought.

'I think he deserves the opportunity to try,' Clarke said, taking another sip. 'The fact is, everything Natty has been given to handle, he has. He took out Keith and Roman. The team is making more money, and he's established Little London as a lucrative stream of income, far beyond anyone's expectations. I mean, you have all the money you'll ever need, so it's not about that. Why still play the game if you don't have to?'

Mitch's eyelids flickered, but didn't shut. He tried hard to remain neutral and keep the disappointment out of his expression.

Breathing slowly, Mitch smiled, but it did not reach his eyes. Now was not the time to berate his once loyal subject. Mitch intended to extract as much information from his as possible.

'I've had all the money I could ever need for years, so that doesn't play into it, you're right. I've played the background most of my life because it was safer. Other people were warring, but after we took out those Yardie fucks, that was it for me. I concentrated on building the reputation of the organisation, ensuring everyone got a fair shake. And then, after the last lot cleared out, there I was. I established us. I'm the main guy now. The most powerful man in Leeds, and I should rule. Why would I give that up after I worked so hard to get it?'

Clarke shook his head.

'You sound different, Mitch. Honestly, you're sounding more like Ty than yourself. He was the one who wanted to rule everything, remember?'

Mitch scowled, losing his composure for the first time. 'Ty wanted to tear everything down. He had no idea how to lead; how to build relationships with other people. I carried him along, for all the good it did.'

'That's not true,' Clarke said, stunning Mitch. 'Ty was well respected and had good relationships with a lot of people and teams. Besides that, do you really think Natty would do the same as his dad, based on everything you know about him?'

Mitch stared at Clarke, incredulous. Nathaniel had turned the most loyal person in their organisation, and he was struggling to come to terms with it. Mitch lent forward, puffing on his cigar. Reaching out, he stubbed it out in the ashtray before reclining back in his seat.

'You're entitled to your opinion, however misguided it is,' he responded. When Clarke attempted to respond, Mitch raised a hand. 'I didn't invite you here to talk to you about my brother or Nathaniel. Morgan reached out to me a while ago.'

'I figured he would,' said Clarke. 'What are your thoughts on it?'

Mitch made himself another drink.

'I don't see why you can't work alongside him . . .'

'Is working alongside me what he wants? It sounded more to me like he wanted to control me. If he did, that's a problem.'

The more Mitch listened to Clarke, the more anxious he grew. It seemed Clarke had chosen his side. No matter what Mitch did, he was determined to fight against him on it.

'You're missing the point,' started Mitch, frustration bleeding into his tone. 'Morgan is a vital part of the organisation. There's no reason you can't work alongside him, as I said.'

'I'm not denying his importance, but I don't see him the way you do, and I don't want him dictating to me what I'm going to do. He's never overseen me before, and there's no reason why he should do so now.'

'Is that right?' Mitch's voice was dangerously low. Clarke either hadn't noticed, or didn't care. He leant forward, picking up his drink and sipping it serenely.

'I mean no offence, Mitch, but Morgan is a numbers man. I've worked well with Natty in the past because our roles are similar. Whether it's been Natty calling the shots and me following or vice-versa, we've always got it right. I'm sorry, but I wouldn't trust Morgan's judgement in the situations we have to deal with. Things worked well when me and Natty were working closely together. I'm not sure why you would need to change that arrangement.'

'What has happened to you?' Mitch said, eyes popping with anger over Clarke's words. 'When did you become so comfortable with disobeying orders?'

Clarke shook his head, unwilling to back down 'Mitch, you haven't given me an order. You've asked me to work alongside Morgan, but when I've seen him, he was clear that wasn't his expectation of the arrangement. I've given my blood, sweat and tears for you for as long as I can remember. I've done your bidding time and again with no complaints. All I'm asking is for you to be straight with me.' Clarke looked Mitch straight in the eye. 'What's really going on here, Mitch?'

The look between the pair lingered, Mitch's eyes narrowing. Finally, he made a show of looking at his watch.

'We'll have to cut this short, unfortunately. I have some other matters to deal with.'

Both men stood. Clarke struggled to hide his disappointment in his boss. He'd invited him to be open, to tell him what was happening, and Mitch had spurned him.

Mitch held out his hand, and Clarke shook it. Despite the gesture, something had shifted too far between the pair, and both knew it would never be the same between them again.

'We'll finish this conversation another time,' Mitch said.

'I look forward to it,' Clarke replied, his expression unreadable.

CHAPTER TWENTY-FIVE

LORRAINE AND NATTY lay together in her bed, holding one another closely. They had moved back in earlier in the day, having a celebratory dinner with Jaden.

Natty was enjoying the comfort of having her next to him again. His head felt clear, and he was anticipating resolving his problems so they could have more moments like this.

'What's your next move?' Lorraine asked.

'We still have feelers out,' Natty replied. 'Zayan and Ghazan are still on the missing list, and with the info about them being limited, it's a waiting game right now.'

'What about beyond that?'

'What do you mean?' Natty asked, looking down at her, her head resting against his chest. Despite the cooler weather, he still forewent wearing a t-shirt to bed.

'Even if you deal with these guys, that doesn't solve your larger issues with your uncle, or with this man he has a problem with, does it?'

Natty smiled. He was still getting used to talking business with Lorraine, but he enjoyed it. She had a fresh perspective and rarely held back with her opinion. Being so open had brought them closer together, and he relished it.

'You're right, but sometimes no move is the best move. You force the other sides to commit themselves, and then strike back. Stef is trying to get closer to my unc . . . that could create an opening. Forget all that for now, though. How are you doing with everything? We haven't spoken about it yet, but how do you feel about quitting your job?'

'I feel free,' Lorraine admitted. 'It was liberating, telling Angela where to go, especially in front of the rest of the staff. I hope they follow my lead and tell her about herself.'

Natty chuckled. 'I'm surprised you were so quick to leave the role, though. I mean, you worked hard to establish yourself, and you were really into your career.'

Lorraine paused, recalling Natty gifting her a MacBook to allow her to further her career. She smiled for a moment, then sighed.

'The night with Raider changed me, Nat. I felt so desolate and weak. The guilt and the loathing overwhelmed me, and I tried pushing past it . . . to look normal to the rest of the world.' Again, she hesitated, emboldened when Natty squeezed her tighter. 'The old Lorraine died that night, and it only intensified after what happened with you and Lisa.'

'Lo . . .' Natty started, but she cut him off.

'No, Nat. It's not about that. It's about feeling like a liability. I *will* stand beside you. In everything. In fact, in the near future, we can have a proper conversation about your finances, and what works and what doesn't.'

'You've spent too much time around Spence.' Natty rolled his eyes. Lorraine giggled, and the pair shared a kiss.

––––––

MORGAN WAS all smiles as Lisa and Stefon pulled up. He had requested they meet him in Armley, and sat on a step outside a terraced property on Halliday Place. As they climbed out of their car and approached, he rose to his feet, shaking hands with them.

It was the first time Stefon had seen him, and he admitted he had a presence about him, and an extremely firm handshake. He was older, and something in his eyes startled Stefon. There seemed to be a barely controlled intensity, like he had to keep a handle on himself.

'I've heard all about you, Stefon. Mitch speaks highly of you, and I've been looking forward to meeting you. You carry yourself well. Lis,' Morgan smiled at her, his eyes roving over her body, 'you look as stunning as ever.'

Stefon bristled, not liking how Morgan was looking at her, but Lisa seemed to take it in her stride, giggling in her quirky way.

'Thank you as always, Morgan.'

'What's the deal then?' Stefon said, tired of the preamble. 'I'm surprised you reached out to us. I've been back in Leeds a while, and you seem to have stayed out of the mix so far.'

'That's my role,' Morgan admitted. 'Mitch has his nephew to run the operations, along with Clarke — before his accident, anyway. I've built an empire around here and in some other areas. I generate a lot of money for the team. We can have drinks sometime and go into detail if you like. For now, I have a job for you both. Everyone's talking about the fact you're a couple. Probably be easier if you handled it together.'

'What's the job?' Lisa asked, before Stefon could question who was talking about them.

'Black Marcus is making moves.'

Lisa's face straightened, and Stefon was stunned by the shift. Gone was the jokey Lisa.

'What's *Neil* up to?' she asked. Morgan smirked. 'I thought his lot weren't active anymore?'

'They were. Just low key. My people tell me they're making inroads into Armley and Kirkstall. I spoke with Mitch about it, and he thought either you or Clarke would be best for the job.'

'I'll handle it,' Lisa said.

'Good. Pays twenty bags, plus expenses. Split it between you how you like.'

'Who do I speak to for more details, or do you have them?' Lisa asked. Stefon let her lead. This was her world. He'd killed before, but had never taken contract hits.

'Benny in Hyde Park has everything you need.'

'I'll speak to him then, Morgan.'

Morgan smiled warmly.

'Excellent. See me when you're done.'

————

THE DRIVE to Hyde park was quiet at first, but Stefon broke the silence.

'Who the hell is Black Marcus?'

'An idiot,' Lisa scoffed. 'He only started calling himself *Black Marcus* a few years ago, fashioning himself after the dead gangster from Chapeltown. Decided he was a gunman and started throwing his weight around. I took out his cousin in 2018. He faded into obscurity after that. I'm surprised he's back.'

'What about your network?' Stefon asked as he drove. 'Should him popping up have triggered something?'

'Depends on the moves he's made.' Lisa shrugged. 'Morgan has Armley and some other areas well sewn up. My people and me look for certain movements or actions, and how people position themselves. If he hasn't done anything, or hasn't spoken to the right people, it's understandable he would stay off the radar.'

Stefon was impressed by her acumen, but some things still didn't sit right with him.

'How would Morgan know about him then?'

'Good question,' Lisa admitted. 'Benny can answer that.'

'Do you know him too?' Stefon kept his voice casual as he switched lanes, but felt Lisa watching him.

'What do you mean?'

'Morgan was staring at you like you were food.'

'Men tend to stare.' Stefon could hear the humour in her tone. 'It's cute that you're jealous, though.'

'I'm not jealous,' he said hotly. 'You're not my girl. You can do what you like.'

Lisa giggled, and Stefon didn't respond, brooding and keeping his eyes ahead. The dynamics of dealing with a woman like Lisa hadn't

RICKY BLACK

grown any easier. Resolving to put it aside, he focused on the task ahead.

———

THEY REACHED HYDE PARK, with Stefon following Lisa's directions to the location. It was a small house on the corner of a street, with a faded brown door, a mostly concrete garden with a neat outer appearance.

Two men were leaning against a wall nearby, one of whom was drinking a bottle of KA Fruit Punch, and the other was telling a story that had them both laughing. They straightened as Lisa and Stefon climbed from their car, and the man with the drink nodded at them.

As they made their way inside, Stefon recognised a few more faces milled around. Three of them were gathered in the living room, crowding around two more men who were playing on the PlayStation. One of them, a skinny man with dark circles around his eyes, nodded at Stefon.

'Morgan send you?' His eyes flitted to Lisa for a moment, and she winked before nodding. 'I'm Josh. Benny's on his way, but a situation cropped up. He won't be long. You want a drink or anything?'

'Yeah, go on then,' said Stefon, immediately falling into conversation with the others. He quickly noticed that one of the men looked almost nervous. He'd met Stefon's eye, but quickly looked away, and now he was standing apart, looking fidgety. His demeanour had Stefon alert.

As he took a bottle of Red Stripe from Josh, he glanced at Lisa and could tell she'd noticed too. She was all smiles, but her eyes weren't missing a thing. After making conversation with Josh for a few minutes, Stefon feigned a yawn, stretching before speaking.

'Look, me and her have some errands to run,' he said, gesturing to Lisa. 'Tell Benny that we'll come back a bit later and have a chat.'

Josh froze. Even the men playing on the computer paused their game, glancing at Stefon.

'It's cool, man. He won't be much longer. Just wait around. He won't be happy if he has to come later.'

'He'll be fine,' Stefon said. 'We've got his number. Lisa can give him a ring.'

Josh shook his head. 'Nah, we can't do that.'

'Why not?' Stefon's grip around the bottle tightened. Josh's eyes narrowed, then he lunged for Stefon, just as two others went for Lisa. Stefon had no chance to move to her. Adjusting his body, he side-stepped Josh, then cracked him over the head with the bottle. Josh went down, and Stefon went for his gun, not a moment too soon. One of the gamers was on his feet and had his weapon out.

Stefon fired first, the bullet slamming into the man's chest, sending him toppling backwards. Stefon fired at the second gamer, but didn't stop to see if he'd hit him.

More men surged in through the front. Stefon glanced at Lisa, who had a bloodied knife in her hand, the pair that had tried to attack her bleeding out on the floor.

'C'mon,' Stefon shouted, and the pair ran out the back as the men began opening fire. Stefan screamed as a bullet clipped his shoulder. He felt Lisa slump against him, but he didn't dare stop moving. Luckily, there were no men in the back room, and the back door was open.

Turning, he fired several times, hitting the first man through the door. When he fell backwards, he blocked the way for the rest, giving Stefon the precious seconds he needed. Holding Lisa and trying to ignore the burning pain in his shoulder, Stefon rushed to the front of the house as quickly as he could. He was in luck, bundling Lisa into the passenger seat, then climbing into the driver's seat.

Chancing a look at her, his heart nearly stopped at the sight of the blood covering her front.

'They got me,' she croaked, struggling to speak.

'Shut the fuck up. You're gonna be fine,' Stefon said, pulling away as the gunfire rang all around them, shattering the back windows. He didn't stop for a second. Their lives were on the line, and they needed to get to safety.

Stefon wasn't sure if Josh and the others would come after them or not, and he didn't care. All he knew was that he needed to get Lisa out of there.

CHAPTER TWENTY-SIX

HARDING SAT AT HIS DESK, looking over everything he had gathered on Natty Deeds. Lately, he'd been painstakingly digging into his background, looking for anything he could use in order to take his investigation further. His work looking at DI Brown had hit a dead end. Brown was smarter than he seemed, and any evidence of his corruption appeared to be well hidden. He lived within his means, and any money he may have been paid had been hidden expertly.

Harding's attempts to have Natty followed had failed, and that had caused him to look further into the man's character. He knew of Natty's dad being murdered when he was younger, and his rise in the streets after this. For years he'd toiled in relative obscurity, working for Rudy Campbell, who had also been in a relationship with Natty's mum. Rudy had been murdered last year and Natty had risen in prominence after this.

That alone made Harding wonder what had gone on. Natty's promotion on the heels of Rudy's murder was suspicious on its own, and seemed indicative of the deaths that appeared to surround him. Along with Rudy, his rival Roman, and another gangster named Keith, there was another potential connection, one that Harding knew was related to DI Brown. Michael Parsons, AKA Raider, had been in a relationship with Natty's current partner, and they'd had a child together.

Raider had died some months back in what were termed to be suspicious circumstances. Beyond that, there had been little talk about the situation. No one appeared upset other than his family, who had since seemingly moved on with their lives.

Harding didn't get it. Organising the papers, he stood to stretch his legs, feeling a twinge in his lower back. His body was screaming for attention. Harding couldn't keep burning the candle at both ends, and he knew it. The case was consuming him. It felt like he had the bare bones for something he could work with, but he wasn't sure how to put the pieces together.

Natty was the one he needed to focus on, but how to get there was another story. Natty had been in the crime life for years and knew how to operate. He'd been picked up for questioning a few times, but never charged. Apparently, he had a temper and wasn't afraid to throw his weight around, but that hadn't helped them nail him.

He could certainly spot a tail, that was for sure, Harding mused. Checking his watch, he went to go and make a drink. He had meetings and briefings all afternoon. Along with a meeting with his team, he also had to give an update to his superiors.

Grabbing his drink, Harding went back to his office. Fieldwork would be the way to push his case forward. He had nothing he could use to question Natty, but maybe some of the people around him would be more receptive.

A knock on his door caught his attention, and he looked up.

'Come in,' he barked. Daniels hurried into the room, his ruddy face alight with glee.

'There's been a shooting in Hyde Park,' he said.

'Why does that make you so happy?' Harding asked, narrowing his eyes.

'It's that Dunn lot, that's why. We've got bodies on the scene, and a lot of blood and bullets.'

Harding sat up, interested now.

'What do we know?'

'Witnesses described hearing a lot of shooting and hearing cars driving off at great speed. We've secured the scene, and I was gonna get over there and find out what's what. Figured you'd want a heads up first.'

'Appreciated,' said Harding, his previous plan forgotten. 'Find out what happened, and how it connects to Natty Deeds.'

'You think this was him? His people were shot. You'll probably hear about his retaliation somewhere down the line.'

'Maybe so, but I need something viable first. See what you can find for me.'

'Got it, chief.' Daniels gave Harding a mock salute and hurried away. Harding shook his head, glancing back at his gathered paperwork. Taking a sip of his drink, he wondered what the latest crisis was.

'What have you been up to, Deeds?' he murmured out loud.

———

Natty paced the kitchen in the safe house, mind alight and breathing hard. Spence entered the kitchen, closing the door behind him, a serious look on his face.

Stefon had called a few hours ago, explaining that they'd been ambushed. Natty had acted quickly, calling in Spence, and sending men he trusted to bring them to safety, and get some medical help. Going to a hospital wasn't an option. Not only did it mean involving the police, it would also give their enemies a spotlight on where they were.

'What's going on?'

Spence wiped his eyes. He'd been on his feet for hours, and it was his first time resting. As he collapsed into a chair, Natty went to make him a drink. When he put a steaming cup of coffee in front of Spence, Spence mumbled his thanks and took a quick sip before speaking.

'Stef lost a lot of blood and took a shot to the shoulder, and another grazed his side. He'll need some rest, but he's expected to pull through.'

Natty's stomach lurched. 'What about Lisa?'

Spence sighed.

'They're still working on her. She got hit in the side, and possibly in one other place. She lost a lot of blood.'

'Fuck,' Natty snapped. 'What were they even up to? I know that they've got their little thing, but that was one of our spots, right? That Hyde Park one?'

Spence nodded.

'What the hell were they doing there without backup then? What are people saying?'

'Everyone's confused,' said Spence. 'If anyone knows precisely why they were there, they're keeping schtum on it.'

'This has my uncle's fingerprints all over it,' said Natty, growing angrier by the moment. Stefon was his family. He was also an ally, and the thought of him getting hurt on Natty's watch infuriated him.

On top of that, Lisa was fighting for her life. Despite their run-ins recently, Natty cared for her. She was part of the team, but she was also so much more than that.

Heads would roll.

'I thought it might have been a play by those Asian dudes at first, but I couldn't make it fit,' admitted Spence. 'What are we gonna do?'

Natty shook his head.

'We need to understand what happened first. Is Stefon up for talking yet?'

'I think so,' Spence said. 'Are we going?'

'Finish your drink first, mate. You look like you need it.'

————

As Spence and Natty climbed from their car a short while later, Natty's eyes shifted in all directions. He'd kept an eye on the road as they drove, ensuring that they weren't being tailed. He was armed and would remain so. If someone came for him, he planned to shoot first, and ask questions later.

Spence led the way into the safe house. Upstairs, Stefon was in bed, his arm and shoulder wrapped in bandages. He glanced up when he saw Natty and Spence, nodding at the pair.

'I've had better days,' he admitted, by way of greeting. Natty shook his head, unsmiling.

'What the fuck happened, Stef?'

Stefon sighed.

'Morgan set me up. Set us up.'

'You were dealing with Morgan?' Natty asked.

Stefon looked away.

'Guess I'd better tell the full story. Try and hold your questions until the end.'

Natty shared a look with Spence. After a moment, Stefon spoke, Natty's eyes narrowing as he listened.

'Why didn't you say anything to us? We could have provided some back up.'

'Lisa took point. She knew the players involved, and she's done work for Morgan before. There was no reason to believe anything was wrong at first.'

'What about the fucking fact we've been operating under the impression that Morgan is against us, because he's too close to my uncle?'

'We thought we had it covered,' admitted Stefon. 'Who the fuck thought we were walking into a hit squad?'

'Anyone with a bit of sense in their heads,' Natty roared, surprising both Spence and Stefon. 'We're at fucking war, Stef. Mitch killed my fucking dad, and he's been on top of this thing since the beginning. You have to use your brain and think about these situations when dealing with anyone outside of us right there.' He motioned to the three of them.

'I don't know what you want me to say,' Stefon said. Spence wisely hung back, letting the pair speak.

'Right now, I don't want you to say a damn thing. I'm gonna stop in on Lisa and see how she's doing, and then we're gonna get to Morgan and take it from there.'

'What do you want me to do?' Stefon asked. Natty didn't immediately reply.

'Fall back.'

'Fall back?' Stefon frowned. 'Why?'

'They made a move against you. You have kids you need to think about. So, rest up, take your time, and fall back.'

Stefon didn't say anything. Natty nodded at him, then he and Spence left the room. After conferring with the doctors and making sure he had what he needed, they went to see Lisa.

Unlike Stefon, she was connected to various machines and tubes, and her eyes were closed.

Natty stood over her, listening to the steady beeps of the machinery, stunned at how small Lisa seemed now. She had a giant personality, and her skills were unparalleled, but right now, she just looked like a small girl. It was hard to see her in such a fashion.

'She's gonna be fine, Nat.' Spence put his hand on Natty's shoulder. 'They both are. They're warriors.'

Natty nodded, choosing to believe Spence's words. This wasn't the time to fall apart. Not when there was still so much to do. He looked down at Lisa's pale face with pity. Reaching out, he brushed a stray her out of her face, tucking it behind her ear.

'Let's go,' he said, turning immediately and walking to the door.

They left the safe house and drove away.

———

'HE'S FINALLY HERE,' Zayan said to Ghazan, his eyes fixed on the rear-view mirror. They were parked in a back street in Seacroft, the darkness around them only disrupted by a single flickering streetlight. The erratic flickering of the light sent shards of shadow dancing across the brick walls, as if even the darkness was unsure of how to define the area. A car turned into the street, its headlights briefly blinding them before dimming.

As the car pulled up alongside them, Zayan and Ghazan climbed out, their boots crunching on the gravel. The man exited his vehicle and stepped into the patchy glow of the malfunctioning streetlight. He was a hulking figure with a brutal, hook-nosed face, wearing a black jacket that seemed stretched to its limits, well-worn jeans, and steel-toe boots that looked like they'd seen a fair share of action.

'Ahmed's men?' he rasped, his voice tinged with disdain.

'We're associates of Ahmed. We don't work for him,' Ghazan said, his voice firm. 'He said you could get us what we needed.'

The man spat on the ground, a thick wad of phlegm sizzling as it hit the gravel. Wordlessly, he motioned for them to follow him to his car boot. Scanning the surrounding area, as if expecting shadows to betray unwanted observers, he opened it.

He pulled back a ratty-looking blanket to reveal the treasure beneath: an array of firearms carefully arranged on a bed of dark cloth. Among them were sniper rifles, Uzis, and a corner stacked with body armour. But what caught Zayan's eye was a pair of Glock 19Xs—Coyote Tan editions, known for their compact frame and full-size slide, a deadly marriage of portability and power.

'We'll take two Glocks, some ammunition, and the body armour. Silencers too,' Ghazan stated, extending a thick wad of banknotes. The arms dealer counted the money with practised speed, his eyes never leaving Ghazan's face. Satisfied, he grunted and slammed the boot shut.

Without another word, the man returned to his car and peeled away, his tires screeching against the gravel like a banshee's wail.

'Piece of shit,' Zayan grumbled.

'Forget him. Our man will be waiting for us,' Ghazan said, his eyes already scanning the road ahead.

Securing their newly acquired arsenal in the car's hidden compartment, they made their way to Chapeltown. Ever since their botched assault on Natty Deeds, they had avoided the area. But tonight was different. They pulled up alongside a dark red Astra on Leopold Street, Ghazan rolling down his window just as the driver of the Astra did the same.

'Do you have what we asked for?'

'This is the first and last time I'm doing this,' the man said, wiping his sweaty palms on his jeans. 'If people find out I'm talking, I'm dead. No questions asked.'

'Ensure they don't find out then,' Ghazan said, his voice tinged with annoyance. It hadn't been easy finding people in the Hood willing to go against the Dunns. Money talked, though. Using connections Conrad the facilitator had given up before his death, they'd made contact with this jittery low-level dealer, offering him five thousand pounds for information.

'Whatever. Look, here's an address for Spence's dad. I only know it because my mum lives in the area.' The man's hand trembled as he handed over a small slip of paper, the address hastily scribbled. 'They're close, so he sees him a couple of times a week. Might be the best chance you get to make something happen.'

'Maybe you'll get a promotion when we handle him,' Ghazan said, his voice laced with cynicism.

'Look, I'm serious. Natty Deeds is official, and Spence is his boy. He'll come after you with everything he's got.'

'We can handle Natty.' Ghazan took a stack of money from Zayan and passed it to the man. Their eyes locked, and Ghazan let the moment linger, just long enough for the message to sink in. 'Make sure this information is accurate. If not, Natty Deeds will be the least of your worries. Now, leave. We're done here.'

CHAPTER TWENTY-SEVEN

'WILL SHE BE OKAY?'

The following morning, Natty and Lorraine headed back into the house, walking to the kitchen. After Jaden had gone to school, they had gone to Roundhay Park and taken a walk around the lake. On the way back, Natty mentioned what happened to Lisa and Stefon.

'She won't be on her feet straight away, but at this stage, I don't know.' Natty hadn't heard from Stefon yet, and was unsure whether he would walk away.

'What are you going to do now?' Lorraine asked. Natural daylight streamed through the windows, casting a warm glow on the marble countertops as she added water to the kettle and set it to boil.

'I need to understand what happened. It's a bold move for Mitch to make, and he'll likely be looking to finish the job,' Natty said, tension stiffening his jaw.

'Will Stef and Lisa be protected?'

Natty nodded.

'They're covered.'

Natty's phone buzzed loudly on the wooden table, making both of them jump slightly. He recognised the number and sighed.

'How are you doing?' he asked Clarke. He hadn't spoken to him in a while, but after everything that transpired with Lisa, he'd expected the call.

'We need to talk.'

'Okay. Where do you want to meet?'

'I'm outside.'

The line went dead. Natty slid to his feet and headed outside. Scanning up and down his street, he spotted a light blue Vauxhall Corsa. Despite never seeing it before, he knew it was what Clarke would be driving. Making his way over, he climbed into the passenger seat. Clarke sat in the driver's seat, glancing in his direction.

'How's Lisa?' Clarke immediately asked.

Natty sighed. There was love between Clarke and Lisa, and though he'd never said it, Clarke looked at Lisa like a daughter, and she definitely viewed him as a father figure.

'She's tough, so she's still hanging in there, but she took a few shots. Stefon got winged, and he's recovering, but he'll be okay,' Natty said, choosing his words carefully.

For the first time, Natty saw Clarke truly break down, and it was harrowing. There was no crying, but his legendary composure crumpled, and for the first time, he truly looked his age to Natty. To his credit, he took a deep breath, closed his eyes for a long second, and sought to regain himself.

'What happened?'

Natty told Clarke what Stefon had told him. Clarke listened in silence.

'Morgan . . . ' The bitterness in Clarke's tone as he said the name was something Natty had never heard before. He nodded.

'We both know who's pulling Morgan's strings. I never thought Mitch would ever put a hit out on Lisa, but then again, I didn't think he'd put one out on my dad either.'

Clarke didn't say anything, but Natty knew his words had been felt.

'Clarke, I respect you. Not just because of everything you taught me, but because you're real. You always have been. I want you on my side with this thing, and I've made no secret of that, but you have to decide what you wanna do. Either way, there's no pressure from me.'

Natty's words seemed to hang heavy in the confined space of the car. Still, Clarke didn't say anything. Sighing, Natty patted him on the shoulder.

'You know where I am if you need me.'

When Clarke didn't speak, Natty climbed from the car and headed back inside. As he walked back into the house, he couldn't shake the weight of what had just transpired. He trusted Clarke to make the right call and was prepared to give him the time to do so. But as Natty closed the door behind him, he wondered just how much time they all had left.

————

'WHERE THE HELL ARE YOU?' Morgan snapped, pressing the phone to his ear as he paced around the living room of his house. The room was a study in contrasts: lush Persian carpets paired with modern, minimalist furniture. Ostentatious yet understated, much like the man himself.

'I'm local,' Otis replied. 'We can talk now, and try to make sense of this.'

'Josh fucked up,' Morgan snarled. 'They had them there, and they had people to handle it, and they got away. You should have been there.'

'We can finish the job. Josh's people said they definitely hit Lisa.'

'It all leads back to us,' Morgan said. 'Are you a complete cretin? If Mitch doesn't already know what's going on, he will soon. Stefon was fucking there. He knows I gave them the job, and that I'm involved.'

'So, kill him.'

Otis's blasé attitude was driving Morgan up the wall. He cursed the man he'd chosen to ally with, admitting it had been a serious error in judgement. Trying to hide from Mitch would be futile. His best chance was to find a way to appease him.

'Do you know where he is?'

'No. I can find out, though. Stay low for now, and I'll get my people digging into it. Benny wants to make amends even though he wasn't there. We can use him,' Otis said. 'I'll ring around and call you back later.'

Morgan said nothing as Otis hung up. He was no closer to figuring a way out of this mess. Setting up Stefon and Lisa seemed smart at the time, but he should have taken into account something going wrong, and planned contingencies.

Trudging upstairs, Morgan stripped off in the bathroom and showered, hoping the heat would clear his mind. The more Morgan considered things, the more he realised how much Mitch was at fault. He'd returned to his house the day before yesterday after an age, but the doubt had set in. Those in the know felt he'd hidden in the shadows for too long, and it had been perceived as weakness.

Natty was the one people saw, out in the open, making things happen, ingratiating himself with the team. Mitch was old school. Morgan recognised this, but the tactics didn't always work in his favour. People had short memories, and they often remembered the last thing they saw, or the last thing someone had done for them.

In Morgan's eyes, Mitch's biggest mistake was promoting Natty and not him. He had given his nephew too much power, and it was coming back to bite him.

Towelling himself off, Morgan went to his bedroom and threw on some hastily picked clothes, unconcerned with his appearance at present.

Wiping his eyes, he headed downstairs and walked down the hall to the living room, yawning as he noticed the light was on. He was sure he'd turned it off before he went upstairs. Before he could consider it any further, he heard the click of a weapon, and froze in place.

'Hello again,' said Clarke. He was sat in Morgan's favourite armchair, dressed in all black. He looked different; vibrant, powerful, almost pulsating with an energy that Morgan had foolishly overlooked. The gun in his hand looked perfectly at home, as if it were an extension of himself.

Any scintilla of resistance immediately fell away. Morgan trembled, searching for the words he could use to save himself. He wasn't looking at the broken-down old man he felt Clarke had become. He was looking at the top shooter for the team, the man who had been putting people under the ground for decades.

'What are you doing here?' Morgan asked, his voice surprisingly steady but his mind racing.

'I came to talk to you. Did you forget that I knew where you lived?'

Morgan hadn't had a clue that Clarke knew his address. He didn't exactly broadcast it, and he certainly didn't have allies and acquaintances at his home. He'd worked hard and saved for his house, choosing not to live in the Hood. Gledhow was a nice, discreet area, and he'd had no trouble since moving in.

Until now.

'What do we have to talk about? Is it about Mitch? He said he was going to speak to you.'

Clarke slowly shook his head.

'It's not about Mitch. Though, I'll be interested to know if he was involved too.' Clarke's voice wavered for the first time.

'Involved in what?'

'In Lisa's shooting.'

Morgan hesitated. Seeing Clarke look genuinely hurt, he felt a prick of dread. He knew that Clarke had trained Lisa, but his reaction was still surprising.

'She got shot in Hyde Park, didn't she? I heard about that.'

'If you're going to pretend you had nothing to do with it, I promise that this conversation is going to get real bad, real quick,' Clarke said.

Morgan weighed his options, each worse than the last. His breathing increased.

'If I had anything to do with it,' he started, wetting his lips with his tongue, 'you know my involvement was purely operational. I follow orders, just the same as you.'

'Tell me then, what orders were you given about Lisa? Did Mitch tell you to have her killed?'

The tension was unbearable. Morgan groped for words. 'Look, I don't know anything about what happened. I gave a job to Lisa and Stefon, and some dudes in Hyde Park must have gone into business for themselves. Mitch has problems with the Asians, as we all know. I'll handle it, though, Clarke. You have my word.'

'You will?' Clarke softly asked. Morgan nodded.

'Everyone that was involved. I'll get them. I know what Lisa means to you. She shouldn't have been there.'

Clarke's eyes narrowed, and a dark, grim smile spread across his face. 'You're right. She shouldn't have been. She thinks she's so grown up, but she's just a little girl at times.' His features hardened. 'You dared to go after her, and then you lied about it, you piece of shit.'

'Clarke . . .'

'She's like a daughter to me,' Clarke's voice trembled with rage.

'I . . . just listen to me. I'll—'

Morgan's words were silenced by the two bullets that smashed into his chest. He toppled backwards, choking on blood as he struggled to speak. His eyes were wide as Clarke moved closer to him, and spoke a single sentence.

'No more words.'

With that, Clarke put the gun to Morgan's head, and pulled the trigger again.

CHAPTER TWENTY-EIGHT

NATTY AWOKE with a smile on his face, groping to his side for Lorraine, who wasn't there. With a yawn, he slid out of bed. Throwing on the clothes he'd worn the night before, Natty headed to search for coffee. On his way, he heard the shower running, highlighting where Lorraine was.

Traipsing downstairs and heading into the kitchen, he stopped short when he saw Lorraine's mum sitting at the kitchen table. She had a cup of coffee in her hand and was staring at her phone. When she noticed Natty, she gave him a warm smile.

'Hello, Natty. Sleep well?' Her eyes held a hint of mirth that made Natty feel like a naughty child for a moment.

'I did, thanks. Sorry, I didn't know you were coming, or I would have made sure I was up.'

Lorraine's mum shook her head. 'You don't have to explain, Natty. Lorraine didn't know I was coming either, but she was already awake.'

'Cool,' Natty said. 'Have you eaten?'

'I'm fine.'

Natty made himself a black coffee, deciding to forgo the sugar. He leaned against the kitchen cabinets, cup in hand, trying to ignore the feeling of awkwardness he felt around Lorraine's mum. He'd known her for years, and although he was sure she liked him, she had a probing look that made him uncomfortable. It was like she was studying him.

It was a feeling he'd never fully grown used to.

'Reading anything interesting?' he asked lamely.

'I'm glad you and Lo are back on speaking terms,' she said, ignoring his pathetic question. 'The spark is back in her eyes.'

'I just need to keep that spark there now,' he said.

'You will. I've got faith in you. Just don't hurt her. As you can imagine, she's very vulnerable right now.'

Natty frowned. Before he could ask what she meant, he heard footsteps as Lorraine padded into the room, fully dressed and radiant. She smiled at him, and he returned it, feeling his cheeks stretch. Lorraine's mum chuckled, and Natty busied himself drinking his coffee, suddenly embarrassed.

'Nat, your phone rang. Three times. I think it was Spence.'

'I'll go and see what he wants.' Taking his cup, Natty kissed Lorraine on the cheek and headed back upstairs.

Locating his phone, he saw that Lorraine was correct. He had a slew of missed calls from Spence, along with some other random notifications. Clearing those, he closed the bedroom door out of instinct, calling his friend back.

'Yes, bro,' he said when Spence answered. 'What's hap—'

'I need to see you, Nat. ASAP. Something's happened.'

Natty was instantly in business mode. 'Meet me at the main spot. I'll be there in thirty minutes.'

'Bet. Speak to you then.'

Spence hung up, and Natty stared at the phone for a moment. Spence had sounded too serious for his liking.

The bedroom door opened then, and Lorraine looked in on him.

'Is everything okay?'

'Something's happened. Spence didn't give me any details, so I'm gonna meet with him to see what's what.'

'What do you think it is?'

Natty shrugged, taking a big gulp of coffee before he spoke again. 'We've got so many plates in the air right now that it could be anything. When I find out, I'll let you know.'

'Okay,' said Lorraine, smiling. She leaned over and kissed him, wrinkling her nose. 'I hate that coffee smell.'

'Learn to love it,' Natty said. He finished the drink, and handed the cup to her. 'I'll speak to you soon, babe.'

———

CLARKE WAS PATTED down as he entered Mitch's office, the guard taking his Glock 19 and placing it on the table near the door. That was new. Normally, Mitch never felt the need to disarm him. Clarke felt like they had gone full circle. There was something strangely normal about standing in this office, waiting for Mitch to speak.

Clarke already knew what was coming. He'd known the second he pulled the trigger on Morgan. If Mitch hadn't been surrounded by guards, Clarke might've taken him out too. It was the first time Mitch felt the need for extra protection when speaking to Clarke. Normally, unless there was a meeting, it was just the two of them.

'Word is out about what happened to Morgan,' Mitch said, clearly angry with the circumstances. Even though he was back in his seat of power, he looked rattled, and older than ever.

Clarke recalled their meal, remembering his words of wisdom to his boss. *Dinosaurs*, he thought, hiding his smirk.

'I'm out of the loop. What word is that?' Clarke asked, not planning to make it easy for Mitch.

'He was shot in his house. Three times. Maybe it was a gang making a play. Maybe it was Jakkar and the Asian lot, but I suspect differently.'

Clarke's fingers clenched by his side. He quickly unclenched them, ensuring his features were schooled, giving nothing away.

'My nephew has gone too far this time.'

That surprised Clarke.

'You think Natty was behind this?'

Mitch didn't notice Clarke's tone as he went on.

'He's going to pay for flying too close to the sun. I hoped we could let bygones be bygones, but clearly not. He's forgotten who put him into play. You're going to remind him.'

Clarke frowned.

'What exactly are you saying?'

'You're going to kill Nathaniel. Take out his friend too; Spence. He's another dangerous one, and he's foolishly loyal to my nephew.'

Clarke didn't say anything. Mitch stared at him, his eyebrows slowly pulling down into a frown.

'Is there a problem with that?'

Clarke had never disobeyed an order. Whatever Mitch had asked him to do in the past, he'd done it, but this was different. Natty was innocent, and if he wasn't, Clarke wouldn't have cared. Looking into the eyes of the man he had followed for years, Clarke realised the love and respect he once had for him had gone.

'I won't do it.'

Mitch's eyes narrowed.

'What?'

'I'm not killing your nephew. I told you already, I've had enough of this shit. I'm old. Tired. Lisa could have died, and you haven't said a mumbling word about it.'

'Lisa's a soldier. Just like you. You both know the risks of the game.'

Clarke stood rigidly, his eyes hardening. He took a deep breath and reined in his rising temper.

'Even so, I'm not going after Natty. If you're smart, you'll leave it alone. This private back and forth doesn't suit anyone. You need to be working together against Jakkar.'

'It's not your job to tell me my business. It's your job to follow orders. I expect you to do that, or you'll deal with the consequences.' Mitch's eyes were blazing as he surveyed Clarke, but his words were soft.

'No,' said Clarke, his eyes flitting from Mitch to the armed guard near the door, then back to his boss—former boss. He turned and walked out, leaving his sidearm on the table.

As he left, he hoped Mitch would see it for what it was: the end of an era.

Mitch didn't say another word, and no one tried to stop Clarke as he exited the room. It was over. Whatever happened next, Mitch was on his own.

CHAPTER TWENTY-NINE

'HE'S DEAD?'

Spence nodded. He and Natty were in the living room of one of their safe houses. It had been a while since they'd been, and a thin layer of dust coated the appliances, with a musty smell in the air—like old books that hadn't been opened in years. Natty was perched on the sofa, and Spence was stood nearby, his jaw tight and hands visibly trembling.

'Shot three times in his own living room. A proper professional-looking hit, apparently,' he said.

Natty rubbed his eyes, gaining his bearings. Morgan's death was monumental, and would reignite some of the hysteria that had been present after the Dunns were attacked several weeks back.

On paper, it sounded like Zayan and Ghazan had struck again, but the more Natty considered it, the more it pointed toward another source.

'Nat? You good?' Spence was surveying him.

'Just putting things together in my head.'

'You think the Asians got him?'

'It's possible, but my money's on Clarke.'

Spence's eyes widened, before he quickly put it together.

'Lisa.'

Natty nodded.

'We both know how close they are, Spence. When I told Clarke about her, he looked broken. I think he handled it.'

Spence blew out a breath.

'What's your unc gonna think about that?'

Before Natty could respond, his phone vibrated. Checking the number on the screen, he answered.

'Yeah?'

'Nat, it's me.'

'Clarke? What's going on?'

'I need to see you. ASAP. This is no joke.'

'I'll come to you,' said Natty. 'Let me know where you are.'

Clarke gave Natty his location, then hung up.

'What's he saying?'

'I'm gonna meet him to find out,' Natty said.

'You want me to come with?'

'I can handle it, fam. Make some calls and see what you can find out. Someone will need to handle Morgan's affairs in Armley too. I don't know who my unc is working with at present, especially if Clarke has gone his own way too. Just do what you can.'

'I'll handle it, Nat. Go and speak to him.'

Natty hurried to the car and drove away. Something in Clarke's voice worried him. He didn't sound his usual serious self. For the first time, he sounded scared.

———

Natty gripped the steering wheel as he drove down Micklefield Lane in Rawdon. The engine's hum seemed louder than usual, filling the car with a constant, almost soothing drone that contrasted sharply with his racing thoughts. Sparse sunlight streamed through the windshield, yet the clouds on the horizon promised a downpour. He could already smell the distinct, earthy aroma of rain in the air. Houses lined both sides of the street, their gardens freshly watered, adding to the scent of damp soil.

As he drove, he noticed a young family enjoying their front garden, kids laughing and playing, chasing a ball back and forth. The father looked up and waved as Natty passed by. For a brief second, Natty imagined a simpler life, far removed from the dangers he navigated daily. But then he approached the meeting point, and his focus snapped back to Clarke.

'Here we go,' he muttered to himself. He could feel the tension mounting as he got closer, the morning sun doing little to warm the chill that had settled over him.

Clarke leant against his car around the corner, gun out, his face tense. When Clarke saw Natty, he shook his head.

'It's over,' he said.

'What are you talking about?'

'Your uncle. He wants you and Spence dead.'

'What?' Natty frowned. 'What pushed him?'

'He thinks you killed Morgan.'

'Why would he think that?'

'I don't know,' Clarke said. 'Maybe he just wanted the excuse. You had to know things were gonna end this way.'

'I hoped he would go quicker if I'm honest,' Natty said, his mind alight. Having his uncle directly focused on him was dangerous. He would need to speak with Spence and get him out of the spotlight.

Clarke's head tilted as he assessed Natty, clearly trying to work something out.

'The attack on Mitch outside his house . . .'

Sighing, Natty nodded, not seeing the point in denying it.

'He was in my sights, but his neighbour called out to him, threw my shot off. I had to get out of there.'

Clarke chuckled dryly. 'I should have known. I taught you. How else would you have got away?'

Despite himself, Natty laughed.

'Morgan . . . You did it?' Natty already knew, but wanted the confirmation.

'He hurt Lisa,' Clarke said simply. 'Regardless, he was too close to your uncle. If I didn't get him, you'd have had to.'

'Probably,' said Natty. 'Tell me what my uncle said.'

'He told me to kill you.'

The words hung in the air. Without thinking, Natty's hands drifted towards the gun in his waistband. Noticing, Clarke shook his head.

'I told him I wouldn't do it. Guess I've retired,' he said.

'You know he's not gonna let that lie, right?'

'Why do you think I'm here talking to you?' Clarke looked down at his gun, then back at Natty. 'You need to finish this, Nat. Before it's too late. Get your unc before he has a chance to mobilise and counter.'

'What are you gonna do? He'll come for you.'

Clarke shook his head. 'Don't worry about me. Do what you need to do. I can look after myself. I'll contact you in a bit. Keep an eye on Lisa. I need to let Paula know I won't be around for a while.'

'Is she gonna be alright with that?' Natty asked. From what he knew about Paula, he couldn't see it.

'She'll be fine,' Clarke replied. 'It's not the first time I've had to go on the lam for a while.'

Silence ensued between the pair. Natty swallowed down the lump in his throat. Clarke had looked out for him on so many occasions. Even now, Clarke continued to support him, refusing a direct order from Mitch. It was significant, and Natty worried about the consequences his actions might have.

'Thank you, Clarke. For supporting me.'

Clarke smiled. 'You're a good kid, Nat. Me and Mitch have had our time.'

Clarke got in his car and drove away. Natty watched, his heart pounding. He didn't know how he was going to do it, but he needed to get to his uncle, and quickly. He called Spence, but his friend didn't answer. Resolving to call back later, Natty climbed into his car, intending to go to Lorraine's.

————

SEVERAL HOURS LATER, Clarke's hands gripped the steering wheel as he navigated through the winding roads leading to his home. He'd already switched cars and hit up one of his bolt holes, a safe haven he'd established years ago for times like these. His senses were heightened; every rustle of leaves or distant sound of an engine made his ears prick up.

He had a war chest of cash and a hideout chosen—places where he could lie low and weather the storm. Clarke had equipped Natty with all the tools and information he could. Now it was Natty's turn to act, and Clarke had no doubt he'd pull it off.

As he turned onto his street, Clarke's eyes darted from one corner to another. He scanned the parked cars, all familiar, belonging to neighbours he'd covertly watched over the years. No suspicious vehicles idled, no men sitting, waiting for prey. His initial plan was to drive past his house and circle back, taking no chances.

But then his eyes locked onto his front door, and a jolt of realisation hit him. It wasn't just ajar—it was battered, as though someone had forced it open with violent intent. The windows, too, were shattered, their jagged edges like teeth in a menacing grin. Clarke's heart sank, and his fingers fumbled for the door handle in haste. Throwing the car door open, he bolted across the lawn, his seasoned instincts screaming that he was already too late.

'No . . .' he mumbled. *Not like this. There was no way Mitch would order this.*

The words resonated in Clarke's mind as he stormed into the living room, nearly throwing up when he saw the blood.

'Paula!'

Paula was sprawled out on Clarke's favourite armchair, a bullet hole in her head, which lolled to the side. Tears stung Clarke's eyes as he looked down at the love of his life, refusing to believe it was real.

'No . . .'

Tearing himself away, he checked every downstairs room, seeing signs of a scuffle in the kitchen. By the back door, Danny and his girlfriend lay face down in a pool of blood.

Clarke sobbed, wanting to stay with his son, but forcing himself to go upstairs.

In the girls' bedroom, they were there. A bullet to the chest apiece, their bodies so still that without the blood, you could have been fooled into thinking they were asleep.

Now, the tears fell as Clarke wept uncontrollably. Mitch had violated the rules of the game. He had gone after Clarke's civilian family, purely as a way to get back at him. As Clarke grieved, he wondered if that had always been the plan once he'd outlived his usefulness.

It didn't matter now. Nothing mattered. Mitch had taken everything from him, purely because he could.

Getting to his feet on shaky legs, Clarke called the ambulance, trying to keep the emotion out of his voice as he reported what had gone down. He gave them the address, but no name, hanging up, removing the SIM card from his phone, snapping it, and putting the pieces in his pocket. Dropping the phone on the floor, he stepped on it. Reaching out to touch the faces of the girls he loved like his own children, he shook his head and hurried from the house. It didn't matter where he went, but he couldn't be around the bodies.

Mitch would pay for what he'd taken from Clarke.

As he stepped onto the street, he vowed to exact as much pain and suffering on his old boss as humanly possible.

———

NATTY WAS AT HOME, sitting at the kitchen table, deep in thought. Lorraine was in the living room watching television. He'd spoken with Spence and warned him of the threat. They would need to discuss their next move in more detail. Having his uncle after him was terrifying. His opinion aside, Mitch hadn't earned his reputation by accident. He was a dangerous, intelligent man, and deserved his due.

After speaking with Spence, Natty informed Stefon what was going on. They'd only spoken for a few minutes. Stefon was on the mend, but there was still work to be done.

Yet another thing Natty needed to sort.

Natty wasn't sure how long he sat there, but when his phone rang, he answered instinctively.

'Who's this?'

'Natty? It's Junior, man. Clarke's guy.'

'Okay, what's happening?' Natty asked, recognising the man as one of Clarke's soldiers. They weren't hugely close, but Junior was always polite and had been on the scene a few times when Clarke was training Natty.

'Have you heard?'

'Heard what?'

'Clarke, man. He . . . his . . .'

Natty straightened in his seat, bracing himself to hear the words that the old man was dead.

'What? Just tell me, bro.'

'Mitch had his whole family hit.'

'No . . . fuck.' Natty closed his eyes, not wanting to believe the words. With a jolt, he remembered that Clarke had intended to speak to Paula before he left. 'Clarke too?'

'No one's seen him. He'll definitely know, but his phone's off. What the hell is going on?'

'My uncle has lost it,' Natty said, all business despite the situation. 'Listen, get word to everyone that you're cool with. Anyone you can think of that's loyal to Clarke. Get them to hide out. Nowhere public, and nowhere that anyone else knows. Get me?'

'I get you, but what the hell is going on?'

'I just fucking told you. My uncle is moving against me, against Clarke. Tell as many people as you can, and I'll contact you ASAP. Money, whatever else you need, I'll get you covered. Okay?'

'Okay, Natty. Speak to you soon.'

Natty got to his feet as soon as the phone call ended. He dialled Spence.

'We need to talk, fam. Meet me at the safe house as soon as you can.'

———

'You what?' Spence shook his head, the stunned expression that had been on his face the entire time Natty had been speaking, deepening.

'Mitch had them killed. I don't know who did it, but he had them all wiped out. We need to make some calls and get anyone that's on our side to mobilise. I've got some people I can reach out to who'll look after Lorraine. I can get some people to your dad's place too.

Mitch might leave them, but until he's six feet under, we need to be sure.'

Spence sighed. 'I've got some people I can reach out to as well. I'll sort my dad. He won't go with strangers, even if I vouch for them. He's stubborn. What about Clarke? Have you heard from him?'

'We'll have to wait for him to get in touch with us, fam. For now, let's focus on what's on our plate, and take it from there.'

———

HOURS LATER, Natty was on his way back to the safe house. Lorraine knew something was wrong, but after what had happened to Clarke's family, he was taking no chances. Men with no affiliation to Mitch were watching the house, at great cost.

Between them, he and Spence had made around fifty people aware of what was happening. He hadn't come up with a plan yet, and getting his uncle out into the open wasn't going to be easy, but he was heartened by the fact that they had some backing. Despite his uncle's power, there were allies and people who preferred Natty, and he found that touching, despite the circumstances.

Natty was driving down Spencer Place when he realised that the car behind him had been following at a distance for a while. He turned onto Francis Street, zooming up the road, then took a right and another left, tossing his gun into a nearby garden, then continuing down the road.

As he turned onto Cowper Street, the car that had been following accelerated to a stop in front of him, cutting him off. Natty remained in the car, hands on the steering wheel as several men climbed from theirs. He wasn't scared. He knew what they were, but not what they wanted.

'Nathaniel Dunn,' one of them said, approaching his car. 'I'm DS Daniels, and you're coming with us. We need to ask you some questions.'

CHAPTER THIRTY

DCS HARDING ASSESSED Natty Deeds as he sat in the interview chair. He was an impressive specimen, Harding had to admit. It was more than the powerful build. There was something kinglike in the way he carried himself.

Over his long career, Harding had chased a lot of criminals, and it was common to see them slowly fall to pieces when you got them in an interview room. The practised swagger and cool would slowly fall apart, leaving the real, cowardly interior for Harding and his colleagues to pull apart.

Something told him that this wouldn't hold true with Deeds. There was something in the eyes that told him this would be a tough nut to crack. Despite that, he put his game face on.

'Not many people would come with the police to the station without any real idea of what's going on. Maybe you're a smarter man than I've heard.'

'Maybe I was just bored,' Natty said, stifling a yawn.

Harding smiled. 'We could go back and forth all night, Deeds. I doubt it'll get either of us anywhere, so I'll just say what I've got to say, and we can go from there.'

'Aren't you gonna record this?' Natty motioned to the recorder in the middle of the table. There was also a video recorder in the corner of the room that was unmanned. Harding shook his head.

'No. This is just a chat. A lot of things have happened lately. A lot of bloodshed, in and around Chapeltown, wouldn't you say?'

'I tend to keep to myself,' Natty said. 'I'm shy like that.'

'I've heard differently. I believe you're actively involved in everything that's going on out there. We have reason to believe that you're a high-ranking member of the Dunn organisation. You work under your uncle, Mitch Dunn, and you were complicit in the murders of Keith and Roman several months back, as well as the murder of Detective Inspector Christopher Brown.'

Natty didn't even flinch when he heard the names. Harding was impressed by his composure, but continued.

'There's a lot more. The murder of Michael Parsons, for example. Killing him, then shacking up with the mother of his child . . . that's a bold move.'

Natty rolled his eyes, sighing.

'Did you really bring me here just to spout nonsense?'

'Maybe I was bored,' Harding fired Natty's words back at him, gratified when he chuckled. 'In all seriousness, I'm here to make you an offer. To clarify, my name is Detective Chief Superintendent Harding. I'm offering you a way out.'

'Is that so?'

'It is. As I said, there's a lot going on. Lots of bloodshed. Innocents getting caught in the crossfire, like that poor family murdered in St Martins. You probably know Paula Hart and her family better than I do, though. Right?'

'Seriously, what are we doing here? You bring me in and throw a load of bullshit at me and accuse me of things I haven't done. What is this? Your name and rank is long enough to know you don't have shit on me. If you did, I'd be chained to this desk. Because I'm not, I can get up and walk the fuck out whenever I want.' Natty rose to his feet, taking purposeful steps towards the door. Grabbing the handle, he paused as he heard the officer's voice rumble behind him.

'Your uncle will kill you.'

Natty stopped, glancing at Harding, but saying nothing.

'Work with us. Give us everything you know about him, and we'll take him out of the picture. He goes away, and you leave Leeds. Take your girl and her kid, and don't look back. Not only is it a good offer, it's also the only one you're going to get, so think hard about that.'

Natty grinned.

'I have no idea about anything you're talking about, Detective Chief Superintendent Harding. Next time you trouble me, best believe you'll be dealing with my solicitor.'

Harding smiled to himself as Natty left the room. It had been a risky move to make, but in the interim, it would show Natty that they were watching, and force him to move carefully. Standing, he stretched his arms to the ceiling, closing his eyes for a moment. Letting out a breath, he left the room after switching off the light.

———

THE WHOLE SCENARIO with Harding at the station puzzled Natty. He wasn't sure what the angle was. There was no way they'd expected Natty to snitch on his uncle. They had nothing on him other than accusations with no proof. The fact they'd mentioned Raider was puzzling, though he was pleased they were looking at him rather than Lorraine.

He planned to speak to her later, but first, he needed to speak to Spence. He didn't pick up when he called, but Natty decided to try again once he'd reached the safe house.

After getting a taxi to Cowper Street, he climbed into his car and drove away. Making his way back to the garden he dumped the gun in, he climbed out and found it after searching for a few moments.

Armed once again, he drove steadily back to the safe house, watching the roads carefully to ensure he wasn't followed. Parking around the corner, he made his way inside and fixed a drink. Standing in the kitchen, he savoured the brandy, closing his eyes.

The day felt like it had gone on forever. He hoped Clarke was okay. He would call Junior tomorrow and see if he'd heard anything else.

A social media search had shown people speaking out about the murders, calling it a home invasion. Paula had been killed, along with her three children and Rachel, the girl Danny had been dating.

Natty remembered accosting her that night at the safe house back when he'd been hunting Roman and Keith. He'd hoped she would get back on the right path. Dating Danny had been the start, but she'd never have the chance to go further, her life extinguished at a young age, and for nothing.

Danny was dead, and his promising boxing career was over.

Natty had only seen the other kids in passing, but Clarke had spoken highly of them all. He didn't care that he wasn't related by blood. He loved them the same way, and Natty knew that Clarke's example had helped him embrace the love he had for Jaden.

Natty blinked, realising he'd got too caught up in his emotions. He finished his drink, and went to pour another. He'd just grabbed the Hennessy bottle when his phone rang. Natty picked up, recognising Spence's number.

'Yo, Spence. We've go—'

Natty paused, hearing heavy breathing and scuffles. Spence shouted something, then Natty heard a gunshot.

'Spence!' he shouted. 'Spence?'

CHAPTER THIRTY-ONE

SPENCE SIGHED, glancing at the clock on the kitchen wall, the ticking hands cutting into him like blades. Wayne was busying himself with the kettle, oblivious to his son's distress.

'We need to move, pops.'

Wayne, who had just filled the kettle and clicked it on, scoffed. 'For what? This is my home, son.'

Spence's phone buzzed. He glanced at the text message, then stowed his phone. 'Natty's unc is moving against us. He wiped out the family of one of his key men. You know Clarke, right?'

Wayne nodded, finally turning from the kettle. 'Course I do. Clarke's old school. What the hell is Mitch playing at?'

'Not important right now. We have some safe houses set up. When we get there, I can tell you,' Spence said. He was losing his mind. He loved his dad, but he could be incredibly stubborn when he wanted to be. The more urgent Spence seemed, the more he dug in his heels.

'And then what?' Wayne asked. 'How are you gonna solve the problem?' He gave his son a shrewd look. 'Do you need an extra gun?'

Spence hesitated. 'Dad—'

'Don't give me that shit,' snapped Wayne. 'I was putting people down when you were still watching *SMTV Live* on Saturday mornings.

I can help you. You're my son. I'm not gonna let anything happen to you on my watch.'

A weighty silence pressed down. Before Spence could respond, there was a thump.

'You hear that?' Spence's eyes met his father's. His gut twisted as he realised he was unarmed.

'I don't like the vibe of this,' Wayne whispered, his voice tinged with a chill that made the room feel colder.

———

'We should've done this hours ago,' Ghazan grumbled, checking the ammunition in his gun.

Zayan nodded, staring intently at the house across the street. 'We go for the dad, then use him to make Spence talk.'

Ghazan cut him off, 'No time for complications. We do this now.'

Zayan sighed and reluctantly agreed. Moving like shadows, they reached the front door. Ghazan's lock-picking kit was out, and the door clicked open. Silence met them as they stepped in. No time for caution; Ghazan's finger caressed the trigger as they moved towards the kitchen.

A noise from behind caused him to whirl around, ready to shoot. Zayan cursed quietly. He'd managed to hit the coffee table, the sound magnified in the quiet.

Ghazan glared at his partner, then acted. He burst into the kitchen, firing twice, only to find the back door wide open. He rushed outside into the dark. The back garden wasn't particularly large, but had several bushes at the far end.

Figuring they were hiding there and unable to see them, Ghazan moved forward. A movement to his left startled him, and before he could move, a fist crashed against the side of his face. His grip on the gun slackened, a body taking him to the ground, nailing him with punch after punch. He heard two gunshots, the pops shattering the quiet night. Even with a silencer, Zayan's gun was still loud.

'Fucker,' the man on top of him hissed. He swung back to hit Ghazan again, but Ghazan shifted his weight and managed to overpower him. There were scuffling sounds in the garden, along with grunts, but he couldn't check what was going on.

'Spence. Stop moving. My partner won't take long with your dad,' Ghazan hissed. 'Give up, and you'll receive a quick death. Fight, and it will be the most painful experience of your life.'

'Fuck you,' Spence growled. He pushed Ghazan off and sprang to his feet. Ghazan's fist shot out, the sharp, quick hit taking Spence by surprise. Adjusting his feet, he ensured he was ready for the next hit, blocking the attempt and hitting Ghazan in the chest. They circled one another, ready to move.

Before Spence could do anything, a bullet narrowly missed him. He lunged out of the way, but taking his eye off Ghazan was a mistake. He was hit twice in the face, then kneed in the groin, sliding to the floor as Zayan stood next to Ghazan, training his gun on Spence.

'What took so long?' Ghazan asked, panting from the effort of fighting Spence.

'His father put up a good fight, but I put him down.'

Spence's blood went cold when he heard the words about his dad. He felt tears welling in his eyes, but forced them away. He was going to meet his death like a man. Ghazan noted the reaction, smirking.

'You should have listened. Give us the location of Natty Deeds, or else.'

'Fuck you,' Spence said. 'Do whatever you want to me. I'm not telling you shit.'

Zayan's grin was evident in the darkening sky.

'Fine. Let's get to work.'

Spence straightened his jaw, nostrils flaring. Natty would have to sort it. His friend had called him, but Spence lost his phone in the scuffle. He hoped Natty had heard enough to take action. If he had, he trusted his friend to do the right thing.

Steeling himself, he controlled his breathing.

A few seconds, and it would be over.

Zayan's finger tightened on the trigger.

A shot rang out, Spence realising after the longest moment of his life that he hadn't been hit. Zayan had fallen to the floor. Spence didn't hesitate now. He charged Ghazan and took him down, his hands going to the man's throat as he squeezed with all of his might.

The killer struggled, but Spence was stronger and had him pinned down. Ghazan's attempts to resist slowly slackened, before he stopped moving altogether.

When he was sure he was dead, Spence let go, standing. He looked around, expecting to see Natty.

'We cut that a bit close, didn't we?' Wayne's voice pierced through the adrenaline, holding up a smoking gun. His face was marked by a streak of blood, but he stood unbroken.

Spence hugged his dad, feeling the tears in his eyes again.

'I thought you were dead,' he mumbled, as his dad hugged him back.

'One of the bullets grazed my face. He couldn't fight for shit, whoever he was. I gave him a few slaps, but he managed to get the gun off. I went down and acted like I was dead. He probably would have checked if you hadn't been wrestling with his partner.'

Spence looked at both men.

'We need to take care of this, and quickly,' he said, slowly feeling his energy returning. 'I'd better call Natty back. He's gonna wanna know about this.'

Both men shared a nod, then trudged to the kitchen, feeling the fatigue from the fight of their lives. Spence picked up his phone, the line still active.

'Spence? Spence!'

'Nat, I'm alright,' Spence said.

'I heard gunshots, and I didn't know where you were. I'm in the car now. What happened?'

'Come to my dad's place. We're okay, but we're gonna need to clean up some messes.'

'Say no more. I'll be there in a few minutes.'

CHAPTER THIRTY-TWO

NATTY WASN'T sure what to expect when he entered Wayne's place. He hurried through to the kitchen. Spence and his dad sat at the table, both looking a little worse for wear.

Spence glanced up at Natty, grimacing over the rim of his glass. Wayne nodded to Natty, then went back to his drink, breathing heavily as he sipped the golden liquor. Noting the open back door nearby, Natty stepped outside and saw the two bodies in the garden. He walked over, recognising the men who had tried to attack him.

Sighing, Natty wasn't sure how to feel. They'd attempted to take his life, had impeded his movements, and tried to kill his best friend.

On the other hand, they were just the shooters for a much larger problem. Jakkar wasn't going away anytime soon. Natty would still need to deal with the situation, just as he would need to deal with his renegade uncle. He had little idea how to get to either person, but he would need to deal with it regardless.

'It got dicey for a while,' Spence said. Natty turned, noting his friend had come outside, still holding his drink.

'I shouldn't have left you exposed, Spence. I'm sorry,' Natty said. Spence shook his head.

'You can't be everywhere at once, bro. Can we fix this?' He gestured to Zayan and Ghazan.

'We don't have a choice. It'll cost a lot, but I'll handle it. You and your old man might wanna get some clothes together while I'm calling.'

'Less of the old, you little shit.'

Natty looked past Spence, chuckling when he saw Wayne glaring at him.

'Relax, Wayne. You know I've got respect for you. I bet you did one of these lot, didn't you?'

'Course I did. Where do you think he learnt it from?' A self-satisfied smirk unfurled across Wayne's lips, his eyes twinkling with a cocky glint.

Natty looked at Spence.

'Not from him,' Spence whispered out the corner of his mouth.

'What did you say, son?' Wayne called out. Natty chuckled. Turning to face his dad, Spence responded.

'Nothing, dad. You just chill and finish your drink.'

Natty chuckled again.

'I'll get some people round and have your house cleaned up in no time.'

'You better do,' said Wayne. 'I'm an innocent victim in all of this.'

Grabbing his phone, Natty grinned, despite the circumstances.

———

'HAVE WE FOUND HIM YET?'

Otis always believed that being given more responsibility would be a good thing, but this wasn't what he'd expected.

After Natty Deeds had killed Morgan, and Clarke had refused to handle it, Mitch had reached out to him, offering a fee of one hundred thousand pounds—along with an immediate promotion to take over as his second-in-command. Blinded by greed, Otis immediately accepted, before being hit with the kicker: Mitch wanted him to murder Clarke's family.

Otis respected Clarke. He'd given him a shot years ago when Otis was down on his luck, giving him structure and helping him train. Over time, Otis saw how others in the crew were living, and wanted that. He started spending time with Morgan, and making money on the side. By then, he was too far gone.

Knowing this, he'd made his decision. With a team of men, they'd burst into Clarke's house, and executed everyone.

It was too bad Clarke hadn't been there too.

'He definitely knows about the killings. I used good men to take out his family. Didn't use anyone that worked closely with him,' Otis said to Mitch. He was stood in Mitch's legendary office. Having never been assigned to Mitch's personal security detail, it was the first time he'd ever been. So far, he wasn't impressed.

'They'll be dealt with in time. Once we take care of the enemies in front of us. Has anyone heard from my nephew?' Mitch asked, leaning forward in his chair.

'Rumoured sightings, but he's smart. Knows how to throw people off the scent.'

'Why don't we have people watching his house?'

'We do, but we have to keep switching them up. It's hard to know who we can trust,' Otis explained.

'That brings me to my next point,' Mitch said scathingly. 'Who else could be supporting my nephew.'

Otis looked at the floor. He didn't know much about Natty Deeds' dealings, but he knew that he was incredibly popular within the organisation. He hadn't shared this with Mitch, as he didn't want to get it in the neck for pointing it out. Natty was apparently smarter than he seemed. If he was up to something, he'd approached the right people, because none were talking, meaning it was another mess for him to clean up.

'I'm assuming that Clarke's people have sided with him,' he said, looking up, meeting Mitch's eyes, and hoping his lip didn't quiver.

'I want this sorted. If you want any chance of keeping this role permanently, pick your moves carefully. I want Clarke in the ground, and I want my nephew humbled.'

'He's got a girl, doesn't he?' Otis remembered hearing talk of Natty taking up with an old flame after killing her baby father. It was a ruthless act that had impressed him, and now he wondered if he could use it to his advantage.

'So?'

'I can send some guys around to make her talk.'

'Do you know where she lives?' Mitch asked.

'I think so. I can make sure.'

'Do it then,' Mitch said. 'Get this all sorted. You've got your orders, so make it happen.'

Otis hurried from the room. Mitch glared at the door, wondering if Clarke had been right about giving it all up. It still infuriated him that his most loyal subordinate had turned against him. Clarke had been with him in the beginning, his loyalty never in question.

Mitch didn't understand it. He didn't understand what Nathaniel had that he didn't. Clarke had always been fond of him, *but was his dislike of Morgan so strong that he would go against his boss's order?*

Nothing was going Mitch's way lately. He'd made a crucial error by not organising his team. Clarke had too many loyalists, Natty was far too practised at keeping things a secret, and Morgan was too insular. His power had derived directly from Mitch, and he didn't appear to have taken the time to nail down his support and tie people in the organisation to him.

The mistakes Mitch had made were clear, and even now, the police were trying to build a case against Nathaniel. Mitch knew they wouldn't stop there. They would want Mitch too. Part of him had considered giving up the fact Natty had killed his girl's baby father, but Clarke had the details. He could reach out to the cleaners himself, but that was a difficult task at the best of times.

His cleaners were tetchy and cautious, and he had always worked through intermediaries that they trusted. Unfortunately, Clarke was the last one. Mitch would need to keep the word circulating, maybe plant some stories about Clarke being disloyal, or a thief, to ensure people didn't trust him.

'After all this time, people thinking you drew the short straw . . .

Maybe you had it easiest, Ty. Everything I've done to consolidate power for our family. It feels like the foundations are crumbling beneath my feet.' Mitch sighed, shaking his head and looking up at the sky. He had no doubt his brother was watching, sneering as things seemed to be crashing down around him.

———

Natty sipped a drink at the main safe house, going over his moves in his head. Not telling anyone other than Spence or Stefon about the safe house was a smart move. He'd dealt with the cleaners. The bodies had been removed. He hadn't asked where, and doubted they would have told him if he did.

Spence was getting his dad situated at another spot. Despite handling themselves during the conflict, they'd definitely exerted himself more than he intended.

Natty had reached out to their allies for support, but no one was willing to directly act, despite their promises of support.

Natty didn't blame them. The rulebook had been ripped up, so it made sense that people were exploring their options, as frustrating as it was. Doing dirt was one thing, but taking out someone's family was normally off-limits. They were still on board, but they were leery about giving out information at present, and wanted to move slowly.

Natty couldn't afford for that to happen.

Finishing his drink, he tidied up the safe house kitchen. After, he left the kitchen and collapsed on the sofa, just as his phone rang. His heart raced when he saw Lorraine's number.

'Hey, babe,' he said.

'Nat? Is everything okay?'

Natty almost spoke, but caught himself. What he was about to say would have been a lie. He didn't want to have to tell Lorraine what incredible danger he was in. What incredible danger she and Jaden were probably in. His natural instinct was to protect her, and that feeling was hard to shake.

'It's been better,' he said, swallowing down a lump in his throat.

Right now, it seemed insurmountable. Mitch had legions of people he could call on. Clarke would have been a great ally, but he was in the wind. Lisa was still recovering. Stefon still needed time. So did Spence.

Family came first, he mused. It was how his dad would have done it.

'What's happened?'

'Not over the phone,' said Natty, suddenly feeling the weight of everything going on. 'I'll come to the house.'

'Okay. I'll see you soon.'

———

LORRAINE WAS SAT in the living room when Natty entered, a lamp switched on, giving the room a little light. She put down the book she'd been reading, smiling at Natty as he collapsed onto the sofa next to her.

'Jaden alright?' he asked

'He's fine. How are you? Feels like days since I've seen you,' Lorraine said.

Natty sighed, trying and failing to force the smile back onto his face. By the frown on Lorraine's face, he knew it had failed.

'I'm fine,' he said, then shook his head. 'No, I'm not gonna lie to you. I'm not. Lots of shit has happened since we spoke. The men that attacked me tried to kill Spence. My mentor's family were all wiped out . . . even the kids. All of this shit . . . my unc after me . . . Some Asian man I've never even met trying to kill us all. My back is well and truly against the wall.'

'Nat—' Lorraine started, but he held up a hand.

'Please, let me finish. I'll arrange for you to have access to my accounts. I've set up a few over the last year, and there's money dotted around, and people that owe me. Spence can help with all of that. Especially with investments.'

Lorraine shook her head. 'Nat, forget that. What exactly are you planning? I don't like the sound of it.'

'My back's to the wall like I said, so I'm going to go out swinging,' Natty said slowly.

She shook her head. 'You're better than that.'

Natty laughed darkly. 'It doesn't feel that way. Mitch has more support than me, and more resources. These Asian dudes . . . they're some kinda cartel. They're deep and organised. I'm just me. My support is shaky.' He blew out a breath. 'I've just got to do what I can and hope that's enough.'

Neither spoke for a while. Natty looked straight ahead, pleased that he'd told Lorraine everything. Getting his financial affairs in order whilst trying to manoeuvre would be difficult, but he would be able to do it.

Lorraine deserved it.

'Nat, I'm pregnant.'

Natty froze, blood roaring in his ears as he comprehended the words she'd just levelled on him.

'I'm only a few months along.' Lorraine had tears in her eyes. 'I wanted to tell you when I found out. I've wanted to tell you so many times, but . . .'

'I . . .' Natty paused. Lorraine watched as his face flicked through a range of emotions. With wide eyes, Natty reached out, placing his hands on Lorraine's shoulders and pulling her close. After a moment, he released her. His eyes had softened, and Lorraine felt warm at the loving look he was giving her.

'You know, when I was younger, I never thought I would have kids. Now look at me.' Natty smiled, placing the palm of his hand on Lorraine's stomach. 'We're going to have two.'

Lorraine smiled as a single tear traced down her face.

They continued to hold one another. Natty had tears in his eyes. He had been there for Jaden since the day he was born. He was his son in all but blood. Glancing to the ceiling, he beamed as he considered what a good big brother he would be. Looking down at Lorraine, he noticed his hand still on her stomach.

'There's part of you in there, Nat,' Lorraine said with a watery smile. 'Our child is gonna need his daddy around, so you need to survive by any means necessary.'

'I will,' Natty said. 'I'll handle the situation. For now, it might be best going back to your mum's place.'

'No,' Lorraine said.

'Lo—'

'I'm staying here, Nat. I don't want my mum involved anymore. Not now that I understand the stakes. You have men guarding the house, right?'

Natty nodded.

'Good. Then trust your decision. I'll be fine. Go and handle this situation, and come back home to us.'

'Fine. I will, Lo.' Natty's eyes flickered down to her stomach for another moment. 'I'll get Tommy to keep an eye on you too, just as an extra precaution.'

————

OTIS LEFT a Dunn hangout spot with a bodyguard.

'Speak to Jimmy,' he said to the guard. 'Slap him around if he doesn't hurry up with the return. After that, we're gonna speak to that Jermaine prick. He's talking too much about Deeds, when he needs to be thinking about Mitch.'

The bodyguard nodded, adding nothing as he plodded along. Otis glanced at him. The morale in the team was at an all-time low. He needed to do something about the divide. Mitch needed more time. Once he'd hunted down all the potential loyalists siding with his nephew, they could move forward.

'Deeds has people fucking watching his girl's spot too,' he grumbled. When Mitch was in a better mood, Otis planned to hit him up for more support.

As they approached the car, Otis was so caught up in his own voice that he didn't pay attention to his surroundings. Clarke slid from a garden as if he'd materialised there, raising his gun and shooting the bodyguard, who slid to the floor, dead from the close-range headshot.

Otis froze, mouth wide open, staring at the blood pooling from the guard. He was too terrified to move, even as Clarke approached with a wild look in his eyes.

'I wasn't involved,' he stammered. 'I swear, I had nothing to do with what they did to your fam—'

The words were lost behind another bullet. Otis collapsed next to his bodyguard. Clarke looked at them with disgust, firing an unnecessary shot apiece into both, then dropping the gun and walking away from the scene.

CHAPTER THIRTY-THREE

NATTY PARKED OUTSIDE A NONDESCRIPT HOUSE, climbing from the car with a spring in his step. The thought of Lorraine, pregnant and carrying their future, filled him with a kind of energy that could either propel him forward or detonate on the spot. Taking a deep breath, he knocked on the door.

'Good to see you, Natty.' Sajid beamed at him, motioning for him to follow him inside. They headed for the cluttered sitting room they'd previously sat in. Natty hadn't paid much attention last time he'd visited, but it was an impressive, albeit messy setup, vast, open-concept room, with Kilm rugs and dark pieces of furniture. Refined Islamic calligraphy adorned the walls, framed in gold. A flat-screen TV mounted on the wall, was set to a news channel on mute.

Ornate lampshades provided warm lighting, with an aroma of incense lingering in the air. In another corner, there was a small prayer area with a beautifully embroidered prayer rug, and a shelf holding the Quran and prayer beads.

'My apologies for the mess.' Sajid brushed some papers on the sofa aside, clearing a spot so Natty could sit down. Sajid seemed as animated as ever, but Natty knew it could be a plan to get his guard down. Still, he was moving on blind faith.

From another room, he could hear an argument between a man and a woman. Natty couldn't make out what was being said, but it weirdly reassured him. Arguments happened in homes, not traps.

'Drink?' Sajid offered. Natty shook his head.

'I'm good, bro.'

Sajid shrugged, leaning against the wall.

'You've been in some shit lately, Natty. People are talking. What's the deal?'

Natty locked eyes with Sajid. 'I'm hoping to get it sorted. That's why I'm here. I need your help.'

Sajid nodded, straightening. 'What do you need?'

Natty took a moment. This was going to be a tough sell.

'How well do you know Jakkar?'

Instantly, Sajid's face tightened. He shook his head.

'Can't do it, Natty. I won't be a party to that.'

Natty tried to speak, but Sajid wouldn't be denied.

'You don't know what you're getting into. His soldiers are one thing. Jakkar is another. Going against him is suicide.' Sajid gestured around the room. 'If I help you, my whole family are at risk, Natty. I'm sorry.'

'Sajid, relax,' Natty said. 'I'm not trying to jeopardise you or anything you have going on. Do you know of Ahmed and Mustafa? Jakkar's distributors?'

Sajid slowly nodded.

'They've tried killing me several times, under orders from Jakkar. I'm willing to put all of that aside. I just want to sit down with them. Can you make that happen?'

Sajid sighed.

'I can do it, but you must keep your word, Natty. If you harm them, it won't matter where you dump the bodies. They won't send two killers next time. They'll send an army.'

'I understand,' Natty said. 'I won't dishonour your word by violating. I just want to talk.'

Sighing again, Sajid shook his head, picking up his phone from the table.

'Fine. I'll do it.'

———

AN HOUR LATER, they pulled into the warehouse on Elder Road. The space was cavernous, filled with the din of echoing voices and shuffling boxes. The air was heavy, damp—like a soaked blanket—and carried the pungent, metallic scent of rust and engine oil.

'Keep your composure, Natty,' Sajid advised as they passed through a rusting gate, its creak reverberating through the enclosed space.

Natty clenched his fists. 'I've given you my word, Saj. Let's do this.'

Inside the warehouse, Ahmed and Mustafa waited, guarded by armed men. Natty swallowed hard; this was it. The risk was monumental, but he couldn't back down now. Not with a family to think about.

Two more men approached, a third keeping his distance, holding a machine gun. Natty willed himself to stay calm as they were patted down. When that was done, they followed the distributors to an office at the back of the warehouse. They took seats on uncomfortable metal chairs.

Introductions were made. Appearance-wise, Natty wasn't impressed. Mustafa was chunky, with balding hair and a pointed nose. Ahmed had a fleshy face, dark eyes and straight black hair. Both wore black shirts, though Mustafa's was ill-fitting. Even as they sat there, he kept adjusting his jacket and grimacing.

'Sajid,' Ahmed spoke first. 'You've always represented your family well, and you're respected in our community. You made a vague request by asking to sit down with us.' His eyes bored into Sajid's. 'It's a dangerous risk.'

Sajid's eyes narrowed. He was about to speak, but Natty touched his wrist, shaking his head. He needed a result, but he wouldn't allow them to dictate the meeting.

'I can take this, Sajid.' Natty faced Ahmed. 'Zayan and Ghazan are dead.'

The reaction was immediate. Ahmed flinched, quickly schooling his expression. Sajid almost broke his neck staring at Natty. Mustafa frowned, but said nothing.

'You sent them after me,' Natty continued. 'They died. You sent a man to shoot me at a party. He failed. You backed Roman, and he died.'

'What point do you think you're making?' Mustafa asked.

'The conflict is ridiculous. At the end of the day, this game is about money. Providing for our families. Business. War isn't good for anyone. I want an end to everything, and the only way to do that is to speak to your boss.'

'Excuse me?' Ahmed's eyebrows rose.

'Jakkar. I'd like to sit down with him.'

'That won't happen.' Mustafa smirked.

Natty didn't immediately respond. He could feel the contempt radiating from the pair. Sajid was playing his role, waiting things out. He'd put his trust in Natty, and he didn't plan to let him down.

'The pair of you . . . are you businessmen?'

Ahmed and Mustafa shared a look.

'Yes,' Ahmed replied.

'I'm a businessman too, no matter what you might have heard about my reputation. I have something your boss wants. Pick the location. Pick the conditions, but all of this needs to end. The ball is in your court.'

The pair shared another long look. Natty could feel Sajid's eyes on him, but he kept his own on Mustafa and Ahmed. He wore his game face, but his stomach was churning.

If this didn't work, he had no further moves to make.

Thoughts of Lorraine, Jaden, and his unborn child bolstered him, giving him another surge of energy.

It would work. It had to work.

Finally, Ahmed cleared his throat.

'Leave a number. We'll get back to you within an hour.'

———

'I CAN'T BELIEVE YOU, NATTY.' Sajid climbed into the car, releasing a breath. 'You have the biggest balls I've ever seen. How the hell did you manage to pull this off?'

'The work isn't over yet,' Natty replied, still tense. He'd completed the first step.

Next, he would need to convince Jakkar.

————

Mitch had dismissed the guard that had given him the news. Sitting in his office, he poured the remnants of his whiskey bottle into a glass and downed the liquid, needing the buzz. Otis was dead. He'd been publicly murdered, and with the quick turnaround after Morgan's death, rumours were abound about what was going on with the organisation.

Everything was going on at once. He had no idea what Nathaniel was doing. Clarke hadn't been seen, and Jakkar was a constant, menacing presence who could strike at any time. Staring into space, Mitch contemplated the best course of action, knowing the wrong move could sink his organisation, or leave them even more vulnerable than they seemed at present.

Of his two enemies, Nathaniel was the one he needed to focus on. Despite the worry that his nephew's agenda had potentially infiltrated the team, he would still be easier to handle. He'd lost too many key personnel as of late.

Mitch continued to mull over the possibilities of how to proceed. He'd built an empire, decades ago, rising to the top of the Leeds crime pile through sheer force of will. He'd survived countless wars, overlapping men such as Teflon and Delroy Williams. Mitch felt a warmth surging throughout his veins. Throughout everything, he had not only survived, but thrived, coming out stronger.

The next sip of his whiskey tasted significantly better, and he smiled.

He would flourish. First, he would resolve his issues with his nephew, then he would turn his attention to Jakkar.

————

NATTY FOUGHT down his nerves as he approached the group of sharply dressed Asian men. The corner of Mexborough Avenue was dimly lit, only a flickering streetlight illuminating them. Stopping in front of the men, he held his hands up as they approached, one of them patting him down as the others kept a wary eye on him. When they confirmed he wasn't armed, he was led to the G-Wagon behind them and told to climb in the back.

An older man awaited. He looked deceptively normal, which was the first sign for Natty that he needed to take him seriously. Giving him a piercing stare down, the man nodded.

'You're a hard man to get hold of, Mr Dunn,' Jakkar finally said. He carefully closed an intricate pocket watch and slid it back into his waistcoat pocket, his eyes still locked onto Natty's. The subtle action felt like a message all on its own.

'You must be Jakkar,' Natty said, confirming what he already knew.

'I suggest hurrying along to the point of this meeting. You've left yourself in quite a sticky position by reaching out openly to me.'

Natty nodded, knowing that Jakkar was right. He held all the cards, and could easily have him removed at this stage with no more than a motion. The driver remained in the front, though he was facing the pair with a gun trained on Natty. Natty kept his eyes on Jakkar.

'I wanted to tell you that your quarrel is with my uncle. Not me. Not the team.'

'Your uncle played a twisted game, and he ran out of moves,' Jakkar said. 'He killed my distributors, and now you've killed more of my men, so explain to me why Mitch is my enemy, and not you.'

'Mitch killed my dad,' Natty said, pleased to see the first hints of surprise on Jakkar's face. 'They were partners, and he had him killed, too cowardly to face him down like a man and do it himself. I want him dead more than you do, but I need my team, and I need you and your people to back off them and let me handle it. That's the only way this shit ends without more tit-for-tat drama.'

Jakkar weighed up his response, though his face was impassive.

'No one does anything for free, Mr Dunn. What does helping you do for me? Drama aside, I can kill you now, then I can kill your friend Spence, your uncle, and anyone else who gets in the way.'

Natty inhaled sharply, feeling a chill run down his spine. His grip tightened around his lap, but his expression remained unflappable

'You could. At this stage, you hold all the cards. You're in the best possible position, but you're also a businessman. If you call off your men, let me risk my life to kill my uncle, then I'll replace what you lost. I'll be the sole distributor for you, and if you know anything, you know that the Dunns are the main force on the streets of Leeds. You get your return when and where you want it, and we get everything quietly back in line. That's business, Jakkar. I'll handle my uncle, because I need to.'

Jakkar showed no response to Natty's words. The seconds seemed to last hours as the look between the pair grew, along with the tension. Finally, Jakkar's eyes glinted for the first time, a subtle signal that he was intrigued.

'How will you do it?'

———

MITCH CLIMBED into the back of his vehicle. He was taking no chances, with armed men in the car, along with another following. It was a potential risk, but one he needed to take.

Putting out the word to his higher-ups, it had irked him that only half had answered the summons. It was a sign that confidence in him was at an all-time low, but he would persevere. No one had seen Nathaniel, nor any of his allies, but they couldn't stay in hiding forever.

A saving grace for Mitch was the way he'd structured his organisation. Despite the panic at the top, the streets were well-stocked with product, and sales had slipped, but not dramatically.

There was work to do, but he was ready.

When his phone rang, he glanced at the number, frowning. He definitely needed to re-solidify the structure. People calling him directly wasn't something he enjoyed.

'Yes?'

'Hello, uncle.'

Mitch almost smiled at his nephew's bravery, but the urge was quickly replaced by frustration.

'Nathaniel. How can I help?'

'I need to see you.'

Mitch's frown deepened.

'You're serious?'

'I am. You're serious too. Jakkar's a problem for both of us.'

'And?'

'And that's all I'm saying over the phone.'

Mitch paused. Digging for more information on the phone was a silly move. Nathaniel knew enough to clam up if he pushed. There was a chance he was attempting to set him up, but Mitch still held all the cards.

'I pick the spot. You'll meet my men where I say, and they'll bring you to me. Understand? Anyone attempts to follow, or ambush my men, you die. After that, I'll kill anyone who has ever smiled at you. Are we clear?' he said, his voice hard.

'I understand that making threats over the phone is short-sighted. I want to put this to bed, and I'll meet you wherever you like. Just let me know,' Nathaniel said.

Mitch hung up, feeling like his nephew had won the exchange. If he wasn't such a headache, Mitch would almost be proud of him.

'Change of plan,' he said to the driver. 'Tell the others in that car that I have a job for them.'

———

TWENTY MINUTES LATER, Natty was led from the car by Mitch's men. He'd recognised two of them, one looking like he wanted to say more while the other glared at Natty. They led him to a safe house in Wortley. Natty recalled it as being one of the spots Devon had given up, thinking how long ago that seemed. The door opened as they grew close, and a man armed with a machine gun aimed it at Natty.

Natty met his eyes. If they were going to kill him, they wouldn't do it here.

The gunman motioned for him to move, leading Natty down to the cellar. Natty resisted the urge to kick him down the stairs and take his gun. It was a foolish, suicidal move, and he needed to keep thinking clearly.

The cellar was similar to a dozen others he'd seen over the years. Natty wondered if it was a prerequisite that every spot they owned had to have one. Mitch leaned against the wall, so still he could have been asleep. He straightened when he saw Natty, his features hard to make out under the dim lightbulb above them.

'Guard the stairs,' he said to the man with the machine gun. He stepped closer to Natty, shaking his head. The dim lightbulb overhead flickered, casting a sickly pallor over Mitch's face.

'You've made a lot of mistakes, Nathaniel. I hope this trip is worth it.'

'Me too.' Natty's hands twitched. His uncle was so close. There were no others around them. He could strangle him right here, and no one would be any the wiser. As if sensing Natty's intentions, Mitch's jaw tightened, and he pulled a gun, keeping it by his side.

'Talk then.'

'I have Jakkar bang to rights,' Natty said.

'Why isn't he here then?' Mitch didn't flinch.

'He's convinced I can make a deal with you, but I'd rather we sorted things out.'

'Why?'

'Because we're family. You killed my dad, but you're still my blood. You did a lot for me.'

'I didn't kill my brother.' Mitch's eyes narrowed.

'Ordering someone to do it is the same thing,' Natty said, his eyes watering. 'You killed my dad, just like you killed Rudy when you had me do it.'

Mitch's gun hand shook.

'I suppose the circumstances of why he had to die mean nothing to you, do they?'

'Course not,' Natty said, his voice trembling with anger. 'It doesn't matter what he would or wouldn't do. He was my dad, and you took him from me. The fact is, it hurts me to say it, but that was business. I was a kid at the time, and whatever happened, happened.'

Mitch almost smiled. Nathaniel was saying all the right things, and the part of him that truly loved his nephew wanted to believe it. But, he knew Nathaniel. He knew his temperament, and there was no way he would let this go.

'What changed?' His eyes narrowed, suspicion creeping into his tone.

Natty took a deep, steadying breath.

'I'm about to be a father. My girl told me she's pregnant. I want to be a man for my child, and I want to do it without looking over my shoulder.'

'Jakkar's people will hunt you down if you kill him.' Mitch looked Natty up and down, as though measuring him for a coffin.

'I have a plan, and I have somewhere me and my girl can go. I just need shit squared away with you, and then we can go our separate ways.' Natty leaned forward, urgency in his eyes, and for the first time, allowed a sliver of vulnerability to show.

Mitch nodded, then his expression changed, a sad smile appearing on his face.

'I expected more from you, Nathaniel. Was this the play? Come here, tell me what I want to hear, and hope that I let my guard down around you?'

Natty shook his head.

'Nah, unc. I just needed to get to you.'

Mitch chuckled.

'Foolish pride. I love it. You're finished, nephew. We're family, so I'll make it quick.'

Before he could raise the weapon, shots rang out. Above, they heard people moving and shooting as more bullets sounded. Natty lunged at Mitch, wrestling the gun away from him. As he aimed it, a scuffle on the stairs startled him. He spun without thinking, firing twice and dropping the man wielding the machine gun from earlier.

Not waiting for the body to drop, he turned back to Mitch, just in time for a fist to hit him in the cheek. He stumbled back, but kept his hand on the gun. Just as he raised it, Mitch tackled him to the ground, putting all of his weight onto Natty's arm. Natty yelled out in pain.

Mitch reached for the gun as Natty forced him off. He swung it in

Natty's direction, firing a shot. Natty felt the burn of the bullet in his side, but didn't let it deter him. His considerable mass took his uncle down again, then he punched him in the face, drawing his fist back, hitting him again and again, ignoring the stabbing pain from the bullet wound.

With his uncle barely moving, Natty struggled to his feet, gritting his teeth. He grabbed the gun, aiming it at his uncle, the gunshots above finally starting to subside. Natty's eyes met Mitch's. For a brief second, he saw not a hardened criminal, but a beaten man. It lasted only a moment, but in that instant, years of family history weighed on them both.

Bloodied, Mitch shakily raised a hand.

'Please, Nat. You . . . don't . . .' Mitch's voice broke, and he raised a shaky hand, palm open as if begging for mercy.

Natty shook his head, his eyes icy cold.

'This is for my dad.' His fingers tightened around the gun's handle, the metal cold against his clammy skin. He fired four times, savouring each bullet slamming into his uncle. Breathing hard, he turned to the stairs, just as he heard someone charging down. He didn't recognise the gun-wielding Asian, but he didn't need to.

'It's done?' The man looked past Natty to his uncle's body.

'It is now,' replied Natty, wincing, his hand coming away from his bloody side. 'How did things go upstairs?'

The gunman's mouth formed a hard line.

'It went well. There was one person unaccounted for.'

Natty frowned, ignoring the stabbing pain from his side.

'What does that mean? Are they dead?'

'Someone followed us through the door. He began shooting at both sides, though he took out several of your uncle's men that had the drop on us. He exited before we could shoot back.'

'Did you get a closer look?' Natty's intrigue was growing.

'Older, dressed in all black. Whoever he was, he could definitely handle a gun.'

Natty didn't directly respond. The next time he saw Clarke, he owed him a drink. The gunman motioned to Natty's wound.

'Let's go. We'll get that seen to.'

EPILOGUE

TWO MONTHS LATER

'THAT SOUNDS like good news then, on the whole, anyway.'

Harding nodded at Detective Assistant Chief Constable Connors.

'On paper, definitely, sir. Over the past few months, there has been a marked decrease in shootings, stabbings and murders all across Leeds, especially Chapeltown and the surrounding areas.'

Connors frowned. 'I know you've covered it, but it's still surprising. I expected the streets to run wild with blood after Mitch Dunn got himself gunned down.'

Again, Harding nodded his agreement. Ever since they'd been called to the house in Wortley months ago and found multiple bodies, including that of the former Dunn organisation boss, Harding had been waiting for the other shoe to drop. The amount of bodies on the scene, along with the weaponry used, had all the hallmarks of a crew making a grab for power. As he and his team had been unable to find any dirt on Natty Deeds, they'd expected bloody retaliation, but other than a few rumours of subtle moves being made, things had been deceptively quiet.

'My team are on full alert. We'll continue to gather strings on the Dunns. By all accounts, Mitch's nephew, Natty Deeds, is the one who is now running the team. He's unproven as a boss, so it's only a matter of time before people come for the throne.'

Connors shook his head.

'Leave him alone for now.'

'Sir?' Harding was surprised by the words of the DACCC.

'We've received intelligence of something brewing in Seacroft and Gipton. Intel points towards sides mobilising against each other for a gang war. I'll have more details for your team, but this could be a big one, and I want your resources focused there.'

'What about Chapeltown, sir?'

'What about it? You said yourself, things are quiet on that front. If they heat up, then you can make the organisational moves necessary, but we need to be on top of this. Leeds as a whole is being watched, Harding. Shut this thing down, get the drugs, the cash, the guns, and show everyone that Leeds is still safe. Can you do that?'

Harding wanted to protest, but there was nothing he could say. Connors outranked him. The direction would need to change, and he would need to do as he was told. Harding's face tensed up, recalling the meeting he'd had with Nathaniel Dunn. He'd been as cocky and arrogant as the reports had suggested. Harding's nostrils flared. *He would deal with Deeds before long*, he mused.

'I can, sir,' he said.

———

SPENCE GLANCED AROUND THE ROOM, making sure everything was in place. He'd arrived half an hour ago and had organised several drinks in the middle of the long, light brown table, also checking the glasses were clean. The room had been swept for listening devices twice. The building, along with the area in general, was secure and well-protected, but it didn't stop him from checking.

He glanced at his watch just as the door opened, and Stefon sauntered into the room, followed closely by Lisa.

'Fucking hell, Spence. Did you sleep here?' Stefon chuckled, shaking his head at Spence's punctuality.

'Someone in this jumble of personalities has to be sensible, Stef. We all know that's never going to be you.'

Lisa giggled as Stefon grumbled. She was still moving slowly, even months after being shot, but was well on the way to recovery. She took a seat next to Stefon.

'Either of you heard from Natty?' Spence asked.

'Not since this morning,' Stefon said. 'You know what he's like. He'll get here.'

'His lady will make sure of that,' Lisa said with a trademark smirk.

———

'STILL DON'T SEE why I have to wear this damn thing,' Natty grumbled as he drove to the meeting, smoothing out the tailored black suit Lorraine had made him wear.

'You have a reputation to maintain,' Lorraine said from the passenger seat, the exasperation in her tone indicating it wasn't the first time they'd had this conversation.

'My *reputation* . . . I thought it was for beating people up and sleeping with lots of women?' Natty joked. When he saw the expression on Lorraine's face, he became contrite. 'Sorry, babe. I was just playing. I don't think me dressing like a discount Frank Lucas really matters. Everyone knows what I'm about.'

'Don't be silly, Natty. You look gorgeous and powerful in that suit. That's all that matters,' said Lorraine. Natty glanced over as he drove, her growing stomach making his heart swell as always.

'Are you okay?'

'I'm fine, Nat. You worry too much.'

Natty squeezed her hand. 'I just want everything to be okay.'

Leaning over, Lorraine kissed his cheek.

'It will be.'

———

AFTER PARKING NEARBY, Natty and Lorraine were shown into the backroom of the building. As they entered, Spence, Stefon and Lisa's conversation came to a stop, with all eyes turning in their direction.

'*Godfather*,' said Stefon with a smirk.

'Fuck off.'

'Sorry, sir. Do you prefer *Don Deeds?*'

'I'd prefer you to fall over and break both legs,' Natty retorted, as everyone laughed. Spence stood, moving around the table, pouring drinks as Natty helped Lorraine into her seat. When they were ready, Natty took his seat at the head of the table.

'Lisa,' he said, turning to her, 'how is Clarke doing? Any change?'

Lisa shook her head, a sad expression on her face.

'Still broken. I've tried going to cook him dinner and spend time with him, but he's hurting. I don't know what's going to happen.'

Natty sighed. 'All we can do is keep trying. Whatever he needs, let me know, and he'll have it.'

Lisa nodded, and Natty continued.

'Lo has a financial update to give. Does anyone have any other business to bring up before that?'

'There's been a spate of stabbings since last night. Rumours are there's some turf war between a few little Chapeltown dudes and some LS9 lot.'

Natty rubbed his nose, taking a sipping of his drink. He turned to Stefon.

'Can you handle it, cuz?'

Stefon nodded.

'Leave it with me, Nat. I'll take care of it.'

'Good,' said Natty. 'Spence, I mentioned this to you yesterday, but I've heard from Ahmed since. He and Mustafa have requested another sit-down.'

Spence sighed. 'I knew they would. They want us to increase the amount of product we're getting from them.'

'That won't happen for a while,' said Natty. 'Talk to them, and if they're not budging, I'll go over their heads.' He glanced at Lorraine, giving her an adoring smile. 'The floor is yours, Lo.'

Lorraine started giving her update, ignoring the vomit motions Lisa was making at the lovesick look on Natty's face. As she spoke, Natty couldn't help tuning out. Not because he wasn't interested; Lorraine had grown into her role as the accountant for the organisation far more smoothly than anyone could have anticipated. Though she hadn't been involved as long as the others, she was quickly filling the gap, and often had useful insights to give, both financial and otherwise.

Over the past couple of months, Natty and his inner circle had worked to resolve Mitch's wrongs. Lucrative deals had been made with several crews, all of whom had been impacted by Mitch's desire to eliminate Jakkar's distributors. Holding numerous sit-downs with different crews, laying out the vision and in some cases, agreeing to remain hands-off, the Dunns had used their time to regather their strength, removing the rot from inside the organisation.

Some of the more hardcore Mitch loyalists had been warned away. In two examples, this had been done permanently, with the bodies buried, never to be seen again.

As Natty watched Spence and Lorraine talking, he thought of his dad, hoping he was watching his son with pride. Natty had exceeded all expectations. He'd risen to the top of the Leeds streets, and no matter who or what stood in his way, he had no intention of giving them up again.

ALSO BY RICKY BLACK

<u>The Target Series:</u>

Origins: The Road To Power

Target

Target Part 2: The Takedown

Target Part 3: Absolute Power

The Complete Target Series Boxset

<u>The Deeds Family Series:</u>

Blood & Business

Good Deeds, Bad Deeds

Deeds to the City

Hustler's Ambition

No More Deeds

<u>Other books by Ricky Black:</u>

Homecoming

ABOUT RICKY BLACK

Ricky Black was born and raised in Chapeltown, Leeds.

In 2016, he published the first of his crime series, Target, and has published thirteen more books since.

Visit https://rickyblackbooks.com for information regarding new releases and special offers, and promotions.

Printed in Great Britain
by Amazon

44540093R00148